Love's Healing Balm

A Military Sweet Cowboy Romance in Big Sky County

Jenna Hendricks

Books by Jenna Hendricks

<u>Triple J Ranch</u> –

Book 0 - Finding Love in Montana (Join my newsletter to get this book for free)

Book 1 - Second Chance Ranch

Book 2 – Cowboy Ranch

Book 3 – Runaway Cowgirl Bride

Book 4 – Faith of a Cowboy

Book 5 – Cowboy Blessings

Book 6 – The Cowboy's Game

<u>Big Sky Christmas</u> –

Book 1 – Her Montana Christmas Cowboy

Book 2 – Her Christmas Rodeo Cowboy

Book 3 – Her Mistletoe Cowboy

Book 4 – Her Sleigh Ride Christmas Cowboy

<u>Crooked Arrow Ranch</u> –

Book 0 - Wounded Hearts Ranch (join my newsletter to get this free)

Book 1 – A Broken Heart Mended

Book 2 – Hope's Healing Love

Book 3 - Love's Healing Balm

<u>Standalone Novels</u> –

Christmas Crazy in July

See these titles and more: https://JennaHendricks.com

Other Books by J.L. Hendricks (my 1st pen name)

<u>Worlds Away Series</u>

Book 0: Worlds Revealed (join my Newsletter to get this exclusive freebie)

Book 1: Worlds Away

Book 2: Worlds Collide

Book 2.5: Worlds Explode

Book 3: Worlds Entwined

<u>A Miss Claus Shifter Christmas Romance Series</u>

Book 0: Santa Meets Mrs. Claus

Book 1: Miss Claus and the Secret Santa

Book 2: Miss Claus under the Mistletoe

Book 3: Miss Claus and the Christmas Wedding

Book 4: Miss Claus and Her Polar Opposite
<u>The FBI Dragon Chronicles</u>
Book 1: A Ritual of Fire
Book 2: A Ritual of Death
Book 3: A Ritual of Conquest
<u>New Orleans Magic Series</u>
Book 1: New Orleans Magic
Book 2: Hurricane of Magic
Book 3: Council of Magic
<u>Island of Misfits</u>
Book 0: Island of Misfits
Book 1: Coming soon
<u>Chronicles of the Fae Princess</u> –
Trilogy Published by LMBPN Publishing
See these titles and get their links at <u>https://www.jl-hendricksauthor.com/</u>

Contents

Free Short Story

Free short story when you join my newsletter
See how Jerod and Dana met and fell in love today!

https://jennahendricks.com/newsletter/

Wounded Hearts Ranch
By Jenna Hendricks
Jerod's war wounds are more than skin deep. Will he allow Dana to get close enough to heal his wounded heart?

Trust in the Lord with all thine heart; and lean not unto thine own understanding. In all thy ways acknowledge Him, and He shall direct thy paths.

Proverbs 3: 5-6 KJV

Prologue

"No." Dakota shook her head. Her long brown hair twisted around her face, covering most of it from the social worker in front of her.

"Why not? Everyone who's gone there has loved it. In fact, they have a couple of veterans who are graduating and moving back into the real world with jobs." Jacinta Jones ran a hand through her black hair. Dakota was the second patient that she had placed at the Crooked Arrow Ranch for wounded veterans. Sam Marley had been the first, and he'd done exceptionally well. In fact, he was almost ready to leave the ranch now that he had a service dog and a job. It didn't hurt that he also was seriously dating his boss and dog trainer, Nelly Wilson.

Crooked Arrow Ranch had seen some of the worst cases of PTSD there were, and they were doing exceptional work to rehabilitate the wounded veterans. Jacinta had seen how well the rehabilitated soldiers could function. She was surprised when she discovered that most of them even volunteered to help with local events. She shouldn't have been, though. It had been her experience that veterans were quite civic-minded.

"What if I went with you? Introduced you to everyone?" While Jacinta had been to the Crooked Arrow Ranch before, it had been over a year. She would enjoy visiting the friendly people of Frenchtown, Montana again. And checking in personally with Sam.

"I don't want to live in a group home. I want to go be with my family." That was the most Dakota Monahan had said in one breath since she'd arrived at the California Veterans Administration hospital six months ago.

Jacinta knew that Dakota was shy and that she was having a tough time with all of the people around her. Which was why the ranch would be the perfect solution. If she could get through to the young woman, Jacinta knew that the twenty-four-year-old would love it in Montana.

"I'm sorry, but you aren't ready to take care of yourself yet. Give the good people at the Crooked Arrow Ranch a chance. It's a small group located outside a small town. The people there are lovely." She wanted to say more, but HIPAA laws didn't allow for Jacinta to talk about the other patients there. Although, she could say what they specialized in. "This ranch has a wonderful track record with patients who suffer from depression and PTSD."

"I don't have PTSD." Dakota wrung her hands in her lap and refused to look at Jacinta. This was so confusing to her. When the Army discharged her, they told her that she had to go to the facility in Los Angeles. She didn't realize at that time that she could have said no. But now that she was out of the Army, she knew this transfer wasn't an *order* she had to blindly follow like when she was active duty. No, she was a civilian now. Granted, she was dependent on the VA to help her, but she still had choices. And heading out to some far-flung ranch in the middle of nowhere wasn't what she wanted to do. Even if it was a small home, she would still be with strangers. And who knew if they would be nice to her or not. So far, her experience in the VA hadn't gone well.

Jacinta tilted her head and watched her young charge. "Tell you what. I'll go with you, and if there are any problems at all, I'll bring you back here."

Dakota shook her head. "I want to go home."

The social worker took a seat next to Dakota and took her hands in hers. "Dakota, you know you can't. Your mother works long hours and there will be no one at home with you most of the time. You aren't ready to be alone all day long. Not yet."

Red eyes met Jacinta. "Why can't I get a care worker to come to my mom's home when she's at work?" Dakota began scratching her arm. She had at least moved away from cutting herself. But the scratching was still a sign that the medication she took wasn't working.

"Do you trust me?" Jacinta's dark eyes looked right into Dakota's brown eyes.

Normally, the young woman had flecks of gold and green in her hazel brown eyes that stood out. But today, there wasn't any sparkle or sign of contentment. No, Dakota was afraid. Jacinta could see it.

With shoulders hunched forward, Dakota turned her face away from the one woman she had felt safe with since arriving. At the beginning of her stay, the doctors wanted to keep Dakota locked up in a padded room and one even went so far as to suggest she wear a straitjacket. Another said Dakota should be kept sedated so as not to harm herself.

None of that was what Dakota needed. She knew it, but they wouldn't listen to her pleas. When she started screaming, a beautiful and tall woman with skin the color of the night entered the room and demanded to know what they were doing to make her scream so loudly. With her long hair and long flowing skirts, Jacinta had looked like an Amazonian warrior bent on destroying anyone who would hurt Dakota. In that moment, Dakota knew she had a protector.

It took some time, but eventually Jacinta had worked with the right doctor to get her medication that helped to calm her fears. The nightmares had almost gone away, and she rarely wanted to cut herself anymore. The scratching was still a problem, but at least they kept her nails so short she couldn't break skin. The only reason she continued to scratch so badly was because of the crawling sensation that wouldn't leave her alone, no matter what they tried.

In one group session, it had gotten so bad that Dakota curled up in a ball and cried while trying to get the sensation of crawling worms out of her arms. Jacinta spoke to her doctors and discovered they were over-medicating her. As they lowered her dose of anti-depressants, the crawling began to dissipate. While it still happened whenever she was overly nervous, it didn't happen enough to warrant lowering her dose anymore.

"Will you stay with me?" A tiny voice, similar to a child, barely made its way to Jacinta's ears.

"I will."

After a long moment, Dakota nodded.

Chapter 1

"Jacinta, it's so good to see you again." Jerod opened the front door to the Crooked Arrow Ranch and invited the social worker inside. He smiled at the timid young woman who clung to Jacinta.

"Jerod, thank you so much for allowing me to stay at the ranch while Dakota settles in." She grinned at the ranch owner and then looked around at the front room. It was large and had been stuffed full with three sofas and four reclining chairs.

"My wife is so excited to have more women in the house." He motioned for the two to sit down. Jerod looked expectantly at the young woman sitting overly close to the social worker.

"Where are my manners." Jacinta introduced her charge. "This is Dakota Monahan. Dakota, this is the man I was telling you about, Jerod Stevens. He runs this ranch."

Dakota turned her head up, but kept her eyes averted. Instead of saying anything, she gave him a small wave.

"It's nice to meet you, Dakota. Have you ever been on a ranch?" It was always one of the first questions Jerod asked a new resident. Since he didn't know much about a person's background before they joined the military, he wouldn't know how much training each person would need until they spoke.

If they spoke.

Dakota's mouth twisted, but she didn't say anything.

Jerod frowned, then turned his attention to Jacinta. "Does she speak?" It wasn't unheard of for patients to stop communicating when they returned home from war. However, Jerod didn't think his program would help someone who couldn't at least communicate with him and Megan, the "camp counselor" as the guys had jokingly nicknamed her.

Jacinta sighed. "She does." The woman pursed her lips and glared at Dakota. "Now, Dakota, we've talked about this. You can't keep ignoring people. You need to talk to them. Or at the very least, be polite and answer their questions."

Dakota was tired. She hadn't been able to sleep all week. Just the thought of going somewhere strange and new had terrified her. Plus, the numbness and tingling was beginning to spread to her feet. All she wanted to do was go home and sleep. Why couldn't her mom take care of her? "I'm sorry. I'm a city girl." That should be enough, right? She didn't have to give him her entire life's story.

He just needed to know that she wasn't into the whole ranch and animal thing.

"Does that mean you've never ridden a horse?" If she wasn't going to say much, the intake interview would last all day. Jerod had too many other things to take care of today for that. Maybe Megan would do better?

Dakota shook her head and her eyes widened at the thought of being near a horse. It wasn't that she was afraid, at least, not exactly. It was that she'd never been on a horse. Unless the fancy white horse she loved to ride on the carousel as a kid counted. And she doubted it would.

"Okay, then I guess you've never been around ranch animals?"

Dakota shook her head again.

"What about a farm or gardening? Do you have a green thumb?" This was the last question Jerod had time for. He needed to show these two to their room and get back outside with the guys. One of their cows was about to give birth. He had only been present for one other birthing before. He had missed most of it, and this time he wanted to be there for the whole event.

When she heard gardening, Dakota sat up and looked at Jerod for the first time. Well, looked at his face for the first time. Up until that moment, she'd stared at his muddy cowboy boots. "Yes, I love plants."

A smile spread across Jerod's face. "Great, we could really use someone who's good in the garden. My wife, Dana, started an herb garden, but we do try to grow as many vegetables as we can. And this year I was hoping to start a small orchard. Is that something you can help with?"

"Do you already have the trees you want to plant?" One thing that Dakota was good at was planting apple trees. The best time to get them in the ground was late fall. She was just in time if the ranch had containerized trees ready to go. If not, they'd have to wait for spring.

"As a matter of fact, yes." A new voice said as she entered the room.

Jerod stood up, smiling from ear to ear. "Dana, I'd like to introduce you to our newest resident, Dakota."

After the introductions were made, Dana took a seat across from Dakota and Jacinta. "I was under the impression that with our harsh winters, we had to wait for spring to plant anything."

Since Dakota was from southern California, she wasn't experienced with cold winters. "I'll check out the USDA guidelines for planting here."

"If you ladies will excuse me, I have to get outside to my cows." Jerod nodded to Dana. "My wife will show you to your rooms when you're ready, then give you a tour."

Dana stood up and kissed her husband's cheek. "Remember, if the calf is a girl, I get to name her."

He chuckled. "And if it's a bull, then Skeeter does."

Over the next twenty minutes, the women discussed planting and seasonal issues.

"How about I show you to your rooms and then we head out to see if we have a new heifer or bull calf?" Dana jumped up and was ready to go.

Dakota looked to Jacinta for direction. While she was ready for a nap, the idea of seeing a baby cow intrigued her.

Jacinta must have seen her interest since she smiled and nodded. "I think that sounds marvelous."

By the time they reached the barn, an adorable baby was in the stall with its momma cleaning it up.

Ignoring all the people in the barn, Dakota grinned and cooed over the new baby. "She's so adorable. What kind is she?"

Skeeter walked up next to Dakota. "He's," the cowboy stressed the fact it was a boy and not a girl, "a mix of an Angus cow and a Scottish Highland."

For the first time since entering the barn, Dakota shrunk back into herself and looked down at her feet.

Jacinta grinned at the newcomer. "Skeeter, so good to see you. And from the looks of things, your legs have healed up quite nicely."

"Jacinta." The cowboy tipped his hat at the social worker, then turned to look at Dakota and put his hand out. "Hi, I'm Skeeter Murphy, longtime resident of this here ranch. Nice to meet you?" He arched a brow.

When Dakota said nothing, Jacinta intervened. "This is Dakota Monahan. She's new to the ranch. I hope you'll be on your best behavior around her." Jacinta smirked but then smiled and when Skeeter feign a hurt look.

"Of course, I'll be on my best behavior." Skeeter cleared his throat. "Have you heard of this type of cow before?"

"Oh, I've heard of the Scottish cows. Is that why he's so furry?" She wanted nothing more than to climb into the stall and pet the little guy. And while she wasn't used to farm animals, she did know enough to stay out for now.

The cowboy next to her rocked back on his heels and put his thumbs in his belt loops. "Yes, ma'am. This here little guy, Don Juan, is the first of our new breed of cattle."

Dakota furrowed her brow and looked up at the handsome man standing next to her. "Don Juan is a breed of cattle?"

Skeeter chuckled. "No, that's his name. We have our first bull. And once he's old enough, he will be able to mate with the few Angus we have and help us to increase our herd of cows that we'll use for the new cow cuddling program that we're going to start."

The man seemed mighty impressed with what he just said. But Dakota didn't understand it one bit. "Did you just say, 'cow cuddling program'? Is that some sort of ranch jargon?" Who'd want to hug giant cows? That seemed very dangerous to her, and silly. Furry, baby cows sounded more like what she'd enjoy hugging.

When another man walked up on her other side, Dakota began to get a little nervous. She looked around and found Jacinta, only a few paces behind her, smiling. Once she realized her protector was close, she noticed that she'd fisted her hands at her side and stiffened her back. She released the tension in her body and looked back to the new man.

He tipped his cowboy hat and a tiny smile appeared. "Howdy, miss. My name's Mike Blankenship." He stopped to clear his throat. "I'm starting a new program to help people with various issues. Cow cuddling is exactly what it sounds like. A person can hug a cow, or just talk to it. Some people might want to pet a cow or brush them down. And the cows usually like the attention."

"Really?" Dakota scrunched her nose. The concept didn't sound the least bit appealing to her. Well, she had wanted to pet the baby. But that's a baby. Who doesn't love baby barn animals?

Mike nodded and looked back at the mother and baby. The little bull had latched onto a teat and was sucking for all its worth. He grinned.

"Mike here's the one who took over caring for the cattle on the ranch. He has several different types of cows. Some for milking, and some for beef," Jerod added when he caught the confusion on Dakota's face.

Skeeter chuckled and slapped Mike on the back. "Yeah, Mike prefers cows to humans." He winked at Dakota. "But I prefer pretty ladies to cows." He scrunched his nose. "Or the stinky men on this ranch."

Jerod's nostrils flared and he stepped between Skeeter and Dakota. "Pay no mind to Skeeter, he hasn't learned any manners yet. I think that's something we should add to our list of services here on the ranch."

Mike guffawed and nodded. "Yea, I think pretty much anyone here could teach Skeeter a thing or two."

Taking the teasing in stride, Skeeter chuckled. "Okay, okay. Don't give the new ladies a bad impression of me." He leaned closer to Jacinta and whispered loudly, "These guys are just jealous that all the ladies enjoy talking to me more than any of them."

"Skeeter, I think we should focus on the animals, not on flirting with the ladies." Jerod arched a brow and glared at the young cowboy.

Ignoring the rising tension, Mike changed the topic. "Yup. Little Don Juan is going to be a wonderful addition to the herd. Once he's old enough, we can even hire his services out to local ranches who want the beef from Scottish Highland cows."

The idea of eating one of their pets sent tingles into Dakota's hands and arms. If she wasn't careful, her feet would start feeling weird again too. She needed rest, and soon. She turned back to Jacinta. "I'm tired."

The older woman nodded. "Of course, let's get you back to the house for a short nap before supper."

Skeeter watched in wonder as the two women walked away. Once they were out of earshot, Skeeter grinned. "Looks like we have ourselves a couple of beauties now."

Dana slapped his arm. "Hey, be nice."

"I'm sorry. Dana, you're beautiful too, but you're already taken and therefore off limits. I didn't see a ring on their hands." He pointed to the women as they entered the back door to the house.

Jerod put an arm around his wife. "Skeeter, I'm only going to say this once. Don't go getting any funny ideas. Dakota is new and we need to do everything we can to make her feel safe here." He pointed his finger at the flirt's face. "If I ever hear that you've made a woman feel unsafe, you're done. Got it?"

Skeeter put his hands in the air and backed up. "Hey, now. I never make a move unless the woman shows interest."

"That may be so, but you are the biggest flirt. I mean, Don Juan? I take it you named the bull calf?" Mike shook his head, not smiling at all.

"I'm making a new rule. No dating between the residents here." Jerod looked at the men present. Mike was too shy to make a move, so he didn't have to worry about him. And Tony was already serious about someone else. He looked back at Skeeter. "In fact, no *flirting* with other residents. Got it?"

While Skeeter wasn't happy with that last order, he did understand it. "Got it." He was almost out of there anyway. Once he found a local job, he could pursue the new girl if she was interested. Until then, he'd just be her friend.

Chapter 2

"Why did you place me in an all-male ranch?" Dakota's hands flew in the air as she plopped down on her bed. "I don't think this is the right place for me."

"First off, it isn't all male. There are several women who live here, and more who stop by during the day to either work or visit their boyfriends. I think this is going to be a great place for you." Jacinta sat on the chair across from Dakota. "Just give it a chance. Meet the rest of the residents and see how it goes."

A sour look crossed Dakota's face. "That Skeeter guy is too much." She wrapped her arms around herself and shivered, even though it wasn't cold. "I don't feel comfortable around him."

"I've met him a few times. Skeeter is harmless, if not a bit exuberant. Just let him know you aren't interested, and he'll leave you alone." A grin crossed Jacinta's face.

"Who knows, maybe it's me he's interested in and not you."

Not wanting to upset her mentor, Dakota kept her eyes forward, even though her first instinct was to roll them heavenward. That boy, or cowboy, was a flirt. He was probably interested in all women. But that didn't mean he was dangerous, just annoying. Maybe if she ignored him, he'd get the hint and shove off. "What is so great about this place that it's the only one you wanted me in?"

After a short pause, Jacinta tilted her head. "Words can't really explain it, but there's a feeling here. Something that seeps into everyone's soul. I sent my worst case here and he's just about ready to leave and go off on his own. If that doesn't mean that their program is working, I don't know what will convince you."

"But what if I don't fit in with this group? Are there female patients? Or just women who work here?" Dakota hadn't met everyone, so she wasn't sure how many lived here and how many worked here, and what their gender was. She had never liked being the only woman in a group of men.

She knew that a lot of women loved being the center of attention, and even more so when it was handsome men who couldn't take their eyes off them. But that wasn't Dakota. Sure, she'd dated here and there, but men just weren't on her agenda this year. And probably not even in the next couple of years. What Dakota needed to focus on was getting better. And then using her Army College Fund to go back to school and finish her degree.

Her mom had been right, she should have finished college and let the Army pay off her debt. She could have been an officer instead of an enlisted soldier. But she hated the idea of running up super high college loans, so after only one year of attending the local community college, she enlisted. Thankfully, she had enough college credits to get her the rank of PFC when she joined. And she had done well for herself attaining the rank of Sergeant while in Iraq. If she hadn't been in that accident, she would have already been on her way to becoming a Staff Sergeant.

"You'll fit in, don't worry. I think you and Dana will get along very well. I can't tell you how excited she is to have another woman in the house. And when you meet Megan, you're going to wonder why you didn't come here sooner. There's also Nelly."

Dakota cut Jacinta off. "Isn't Nelly the dog trainer? I'm not bad enough that I need a service dog, am I?"

"Does the idea of needing a service dog disturb you?"

The idea of a service dog hadn't really crossed Dakota's mind before. She scratched her head. "I don't know. But I doubt my depression is bad enough to warrant the government spending all that money on me."

"Don't worry about the costs. If Megan and Nelly think a service dog would be beneficial, then you'll qualify with the VA, and they'll pay for it. But my guess is that you'll work with the animals here on the ranch, including Nelly's dogs, and within a few months you'll be feeling much better." Jacinta sighed. "I love being here. Riding the horses and petting the cows. It always puts me in a better frame of mind. I wish I could live here." A small smile inched up one side of her mouth. "Wait until you see Mike's dairy cows."

Dakota shook her head. "I'm not sure I buy into this whole 'cow cuddling' thing. Seems pretty far-fetched, if you ask me."

With a quick nod, Jacinta stood. "Alright. Why don't you take a nap, and after supper we can talk about all the programs they have here and see what interests you the most. I think tomorrow you'll have an intake meeting with Megan to decide how best to proceed with your counseling and therapy. But for tonight, just relax and take the time to meet everyone. It really is a great place to be. You'll see."

The older woman left Dakota to her nap and went to her own room to unpack. She wouldn't be staying long, but she hated rummaging through a suitcase looking for what she wanted, so she preferred to unpack her clothes. Even if she was only staying for a few days.

While Dakota was tired, she was also restless. It took her longer than normal to fall asleep. And when she finally did nod off, the dreams started, and her period of rest came to a quick end.

It was always the same. Either she'd be at base camp playing cards with her friends, or she'd be washing her truck. Then they'd get a call to head out and pick up soldiers. She never knew what she might find on the road. Roadside bombs were a serious issue, so she kept her eyes out for anything amiss.

But because she was so worried about packages left on the road or people milling about where they shouldn't be, she missed an obvious sign that something else was amiss. When her Humvee hit a pothole as big as Disneyland, the front tire blew, and she lost control. The next thing she knew, she was upside down next to a ravine. Her truck had flipped over, and the front bumper hung precariously over the edge.

All Dakota could make out was the loud sounds of people yelling and the hissing from her motor before everything went sideways. It wasn't a roadside bomb or even a suicide bomber that was about to take her out—it was a Jeep headed her way. One with a machine gun attached to a pole and a man standing up firing it.

Since she hadn't picked up her soldiers yet, it was just her and her escort in the truck, which was probably a good thing. If she'd had soldiers in the back, they probably would have gone over the side of the cliff. Although that sort of death might be preferable to the one heading her way.

"Dakota, come on. We gotta get out of here." Stanley, the soldier assigned to ride with her and protect her, was trying to get her out of her seatbelt, but it was stuck.

"I can't get out. You go and save yourself." Maybe if Stanley got away, he could get help and Dakota wouldn't have to worry about the men coming to kill her, or worse.

"I'm not leaving you here. Now get that seatbelt off and get out of this truck." The demanding sound of Stanley's voice surprised Dakota. He was normally always cracking jokes and so easy-going.

Since arriving on her second tour of duty in Iraq, Dakota hadn't seen any direct fighting. Sure, they had the occasional missile fire into their base, but it rarely did anything more than fizzle out. A latrine caught fire once, but that was the worst of it. The toilet paper on fire actually made most soldiers laugh. It really was a sight to behold. One she wished she could see again, although the smell she could do without.

"How'd they know I'd blow a tire?" She scrambled to try and get her seatbelt undone in time to get away.

"My guess is that they put a strip of nails across the road and just waited for us to hit it." Stanley took out a knife and cut the seatbelt just in time to get them both out of the truck before the Jeep arrived.

With bullets spraying everything in sight, Dakota and Stanley ducked on the back side of the truck, praying that God would stop the Jeep. Or better yet, cause the Jeep to go over the cliff before the terrorists could get to where Dakota and Stanley were hiding. The only option they had was to try and climb down the treacherous cliff on the other side of the truck. But it wouldn't hide them from the terrorists. As soon as the Jeep stopped, the terrorists would be able to see where Dakota and Stanley were. Since there wasn't anything along the cliffside to hide them, they'd be sitting ducks, just waiting to get picked off.

This was the part of the dream that never varied. Probably because it was based on the truth of what happened that day. Dakota carried a 9-millimeter Sig Sauer M17. She carried only two seventeen round magazines. Since she had Stanley, who had the Army's M16 rifle, she didn't need anything more. It was Stanley's job to fight and hers to drive. Too bad that wasn't how it always ended. Way too many noncombatant soldiers saw actual combat.

In reality, Dakota had been injured, but both she and Stanley had been rescued in the nick of time. In the nightmare however, Stanley always died while she was captured and tortured.

Dakota rolled around in her bed in Montana, sweating and calling out for help. Thankfully, Jacinta had been in the room next to her and was able to run in the room before the entire house heard her screaming for help.

"Dakota, wake up." Jacinta pushed on the young woman's shoulders. "It's only a dream. You're safe now. You're stateside and everything is fine."

Blinking and still flailing around on the bed with her heart pounding, Dakota punched Jacinta. "No, don't touch me."

"Dakota Monahan! Don't you dare hit me again." This time, Jacinta's voice got through to the girl.

"Jacinta? Where? What?" Wide eyes took in her surroundings, and she finally started to relax. "Did I hit you?"

"Yes, you did. You haven't had nightmares like this in a while. What's going on?" Jacinta sat on the edge of the double bed and waited for Dakota to settle down.

As she lay there, Dakota ran a hand over her face and worked to calm her heavy breathing. "I'm safe. I'm no longer in Iraq. I'm in..." She looked around the room and it hit her. "I'm in Montana." Dakota took a deep breath and slowly exhaled. "I'm safe."

"Yes, you are."

Her mouth was dry, and she began to shiver. The adrenaline was beginning to wear off and Dakota's breath hitched. "Water."

"Here." Jacinta handed her the bottle that sat on her nightstand. "What happened? Was it the same as before?"

As Dakota drank her water, she envisioned herself at the beach. One of the tools she had in her arsenal for defeating the anxiety was picturing herself somewhere serene. It wasn't the same as doing yoga or meditating, but it worked for her.

The lapping of the soft waves while her toes dug into the moist sand always tamed her beating heart. She'd hear the screeching of the seagulls and feel the wetness from the foamy water as it sprayed her face. Then she would sigh, and the tension would leave her shoulders. She'd imagine the last of the sun's rays warming her cheeks, and she'd close her eyes as all worries left her body. She would even pray while she imagined herself on the beach and ask God to give her peace.

This was the best form of treatment she'd found, other than actually being alone on the beach at sunset and praying. If she could have afforded a place on the beach, she would have bought herself a little bungalow and lived happily ever after all alone. It was still the dream, but one she doubted she'd be able to afford all by herself.

"I think the stress of being somewhere new and meeting so many strange people did it." Dakota put her water bottle back on the dresser and got out of bed.

"Do you think you might have worried yourself into a panic attack?" That was one thing Dakota liked most about Jacinta—she didn't pull any punches.

At first, Jacinta's straightforward style of communication bothered Dakota. But after a little while, it was like a breath of fresh air. With Jacinta, Dakota knew exactly where she stood. There were no games with the social worker. And while it could be a bit rough at times, it turned out to be exactly what Dakota needed.

She shrugged. "Maybe? I don't know."

"How about we go and check on Don Juan before dinner? It won't be ready for about an hour." Jacinta made her way to the bedroom door and waited for Dakota to get up and follow her.

"Don Juan." Dakota chuckled as she followed Jacinta. "I can't wait to hear what the other animal's names are."

Chapter 3

"Skeeter, have you thought anymore about where you want to move when you're released?" For the past two weeks, Jerod and Skeeter had been discussing his options. The young man was ready to move on. His leg had healed as much as it was going to from the shrapnel, and he had also shown he knew how to deal with his PTSD in a healthy manner.

"I love ranch life. This is what I want to do." Skeeter used his pitchfork to move some of the dirty hay around in the horse stall. Then he straightened up. "Well, not *this*, exactly." He chuckled when he pointed to some horse droppings. "Isn't there any way for me to stay here and work?"

If it were up to Jerod, none of the guys would leave. "I wish I could afford to hire you, but I can't at the moment. It's time to open up a couple of beds and bring in some new residents." Jerod leaned against the door of the stall where Skeeter was working.

"I've asked several ranchers and even a couple of farmers, but no one is hiring right now. They already have their harvest help." Skeeter loaded up the shovel and dumped the dirty hay into the wheelbarrow sitting outside the stall. This was the worst part of the job, but even it wasn't so bad. Skeeter could handle mucking out stalls if it meant he could stay close to his friends.

"I know of a few ranches in Wyoming and South Dakota that are hiring. You could apply there."

Skeeter shook his head. "I don't want to leave French-town. I have my doctors all set here, and my friends." He shrugged, then mumbled, "Plus, I like the local church."

Jerod chortled. "Yeah, I get it. I love this area, too. The people are good and they support us. It's not always like that." He ran a hand over the stubble on his chin. "Look, I can give you a few more weeks. But by November, I really do need the space. I've got two new residents coming at the beginning of November. With Sam moving out, that just leaves you."

With the pitchfork in hand and fresh straw in the stall, Skeeter moved the horse back inside, then stopped next to Jerod. "I know I should have moved on a while ago. I get that, I do. But I can't imagine being anywhere else. The Hendersons were going to hire me, but then...well, the fire."

It had only been a few weeks since the wildfire had raged through the Henderson's land and destroyed everything, they had worked so hard for. While they did have good insurance, the family wasn't sure if they wanted to rebuild or move away.

"Have you spoken with Nelly? Now that her house is ready for her to move into, maybe you can share the barn apartment with Sam and work her land in exchange for room and board. Just until you find something local." It wasn't the best option, but Jerod did want the young man to stay if it kept him in church.

Ever since the fire a few weeks back, something had changed in Skeeter. He was still a flirt, and very immature, but there was something going on in the cowboy's heart. He had grown much closer to God, and that spiritual growth had helped to mature him, if only a little bit.

It was no longer difficult to get Skeeter to do the worst of the ranch chores. In fact, the man was mucking out stalls without Jerod having to browbeat him into it.

As Skeeter made his way down the horse stalls, cleaning and freshening up the hay, he heard a melodious voice call out, "Don Juan? Don Juan, where are you baby?"

Skeeter's head popped up when he realized it was the pretty new girl's voice. Dakota was back from her nap and looking for their newest addition to the family. He smiled from ear to ear when he realized how he was going to finagle time with the pretty lady before he was forced out of the ranch.

Once Jerod had left the barn, Skeeter put away the equipment he'd been working with and washed his hands. While he didn't care if they were dirty from the old leather gloves he wore, he doubted the smell would go unnoticed by Dakota and Jacinta. After he ran a wet hand through his unruly hair, he put his hat back on and went searching for the pair of newcomers.

"Hiya, Dakota and Jacinta." Skeeter waved and smiled his greeting to the two ladies. "You looking for our baby bull?"

When Dakota turned to look at him, Skeeter could have sworn she was scowling, but her face quickly went neutral, and she nodded.

"Momma and baby are out in the pasture behind the barn. We try to get them outside as quickly as we can so they can get moving around and socialize with the herd, what there is of it." The cowboy motioned for them to follow him.

"They have a herd of cattle here?" Dakota whispered to Jacinta as they followed Skeeter.

The woman grinned. "Well, I wouldn't call it a herd. They have about twenty head of cattle, maybe more if they've started breeding them. It's more a way of teaching the residents how to care for the cows. They learn how to do the daily care and feeding. And, as you know, Mike has a few dairy cows that he cares for. I think they sell a few every year as well as butcher some for their own meat."

"I guess there's more to do on a ranch than I realized." As they walked toward the door in the back of the barn, Dakota looked around and noticed Mike in a back section with five cows. From the equipment she saw, it looked like he was milking them. "I thought it was standard to milk cows in the morning?"

Jacinta turned just in time to see Mike pulling on an udder before she walked outside. "Actually, you have to milk cows twice a day."

"Huh." Dakota stopped in the doorway and watched the man working. She wondered if that was something she could try as part of her chores.

Skeeter turned back to the women. "You coming?"

Thankfully, the previously flirtatious cowboy was now all business. "I believe Don Juan is just over there." He pointed to a small section of land enclosed with wood fencing. "We're keeping him and his momma close, but still letting them roam a bit to feed."

"Is it normal to keep the newborns close by?" Dakota walked toward the enclosure and stopped at the fence to look around for a tiny bull. Well, 'tiny' was relative. The baby probably weighed close to one hundred pounds already. That would be too heavy for Dakota to pick up and cuddle with. "Are there any puppies or kittens around?" All of a sudden, she felt the need to hug a pet.

After scratching his ear, Skeeter turned to look at her. "Ah, no. We do have a few barn cats, but they're mousers. And the dogs we have here are working dogs."

"So, no actual pets on the ranch?" The level of endorphins was beginning to diminish as Dakota realized that there wouldn't be any cuddling for her. Unless she wanted to cuddle with some cows. Which she didn't.

"Why do we need pets when we have all of these animals?" Skeeter stretched his arms out wide and turned in a circle. "We have several types of cattle, horses, a couple of goats, working dogs, service dogs, mousers, and I think there might even be a lizard or two. Not to mention all of the natural wildlife in the area."

Dakota shivered. "I've heard about bears, no thank you."

Skeeter grinned. "Did you hear about the one inside Nelly's ranch house?"

The eyes of both women bugged out.

"What? Do bears actually go inside houses?" If this was what life was like on a ranch, Dakota was going to leave no matter what Jacinta said.

Feeling a bit bad for scaring the women, Skeeter held up a hand. "I didn't mean for it to sound so bad. When Nelly first came to town, her ranch had been sitting vacant for years. And, well, some not so nice people squatted. We aren't sure how it happened, but they trapped a black bear inside and killed it."

"Oh, no." Jacinta put a hand over her heart.

"That's just wrong." Fear turned to indignation, then anger. Dakota never wanted to hear about mistreatment of animals. She may not want to get anywhere near a bear outside of a zoo, but she couldn't stand the idea of anyone killing one for fun.

"The worst part was they didn't even do it for food." Disgust dripped off Skeeter's words. "I mean, I could understand killing a wild animal if you needed the meat, or even the pelts to protect you in winter, but to do what they did?" He shook his head. "You don't have to worry about bears coming inside of our ranch. There are too many of us here. Bears are usually smarter than that."

It was time Jacinta changed the subject. She could see Dakota pulling away from them. The young woman barely spoke to the other residents back at the VA Hospital, so to see her speaking so much here, already, was a miracle. And Jacinta wasn't one to let miracles go unused. "So, Skeeter, tell Dakota what a normal day on the ranch is like."

It was obvious Skeeter was in his element when his dark brown eyes sparkled. "I love it here. The only downside is getting used to getting up so early." He grinned. His face was covered in a five o'clock shadow and it made him look rugged, handsome even.

"How early?" Dakota bit her lower lip, praying it wasn't as early as she'd heard.

"We're always up before the rooster crows. Oh, yeah. We have chickens and a rooster, too. Fresh eggs are the best part of the morning." Skeeter went on to inform them what they did on the ranch. "And everyone has to volunteer at least thirty hours a month for community service. But that's always fun. Most of the time we help out at the Christmas tree farm or with the town's various fairs and parades."

That didn't sound so bad. Dakota had always enjoyed helping out with her local church events. And a real Christmas tree farm? That sounded like something out of a romance novel. "With it being fall now, how soon before we can start helping with the tree farm?"

Skeeter chuckled and stuck his thumb through his belt loop. "That's the best part. The farm is open year-round with different events. The fall harvest festival will be starting soon, and I know that Daniel, the foreman, is looking to have us over to help get the place ready."

With all evidence of her shyness gone, Dakota asked to be included in that group. She even began to feel the bubble of excitement rise throughout her entire being. She had always wanted to go to one of those real Christmas tree farms and cut down a fresh tree. But, living in California, she only got trees from the local Home Depot. They were nice trees, but she'd heard that if you cut one down yourself, they lasted much longer.

Just as Dakota was starting to think that life on a ranch would be good, she heard a crashing sound followed by the screeching of an angry mother cow. "What's going on?"

"Stay here, don't get any closer." Skeeter ran off toward the momma cow and her baby bull.

Only a few seconds later, Mike rushed out of the back of the barn, cursing when he saw the mess in front of them.

Chapter 4

"How in the world?" Skeeter ran a hand down his face and looked at the fence line that had been mown down by Custard, the crazy Jersey bull that he'd once tried to hug on a dare.

Custard thought of himself as the man, or rather, the bull, of the ranch. He was the alpha bull, and he wasn't going to allow any other bull to take his place. It didn't matter that Don Juan was only one day old.

Mike laughed, hard. "Well, I guess we know who's gonna end up ruling the roost soon."

"What do ya mean?" Skeeter took his cowboy hat off and scratched his head. Custard was a bull who mated with the Jersey cows. Don Juan would only breed with Angus or Scottish Highland cows. There wouldn't be any need for Custard to feel threatened.

With a loud snort, Mike walked back to the barn to gather the supplies he'd need to get Custard in a pasture far away from here. "Custard knows that Don Juan is a...well...Don Juan. Doesn't matter that the bull was just born, when he gets a little older, he'll be young and studly. All the girl cows are going to be mooing over him. I mean, come on, with his name?" Mike chuckled.

"Wait, you mean to tell me that just because I named the bull calf after one of the most notorious ladies' men ever, Custard already thinks he's gonna take away the attention of the ladies?" Skeeter waved his hand in a dismissive gesture. "Go on with yourself."

"I never said bulls were smart. But they are jealous and territorial creatures. Why do you think most big ranches don't have more than a couple on hand?" Mike quirked a brow at the younger cowboy.

With a shrug, Skeeter followed Mike back to the barn to get the supplies and tools for fixing the fence. For it being such a small ranch, they sure did their fair share of fixing fences. "I think we need to put blinders on Custard."

Mike ignored the silly notion and got to work getting Custard as far away from Don Juan as he could. It wasn't like they had hundreds of acres of land and could easily take one bull to the back forty so he'd never have to see his competition again. "Do you think we should sell Custard and just pay for a breeder each year?"

Skeeter stopped and stared at Mike. "Why are you asking me? You're the one who spends all of his time with the cows, not me." He started fixing the gaping hole in the fence left by Custard's show of dominance and testosterone.

"Ah, Skeeter? Is it safe for us to be around Don Juan?" Jacinta called out.

He'd forgotten about the two women who had come to see the calf. Skeeter looked around to see if there were any other holes in the fences. "I'd stay close to the barn and avoid any broken fences. Mike should have Custard back in another pasture shortly, but he's one onery bull. Don't go near him, ever, and you should be fine."

Under her breath, Dakota asked Jacinta, "I thought they were going to start a cow cuddling program here? I wouldn't want to be within two miles of Custard, never mind getting close enough to pet him."

"I don't think they intended anyone to hug a bull." Jacinta pointed to the small pasture where a few Angus cows roamed. "I think those cows might be the sort to hug. Or they will be once they're bred with Don Juan."

Dakota nodded, even though she really didn't understand the whole concept. Would breeding a cow make it more docile? Or did Jacinta mean the baby calves that came from the Angus cows that were bred with Don Juan would be the ones they were going to cuddle with? Either way, she was going to steer clear of the bulls.

Once the fence was fixed, Skeeter walked over to where Jacinta and Dakota stood watching Don Juan with his mother. While his momma ate the remnants of green grass, the little bull calf was drinking heartily.

"By tomorrow, he'll be eating grass, too." Skeeter pointed to the baby and watched as both bovines ate away.

A ringing noise hit Dakota's ears, and she looked around to find the source. "What's that sound?"

"Dinner bell," Mike said when he walked past them toward the house.

Dakota chuckled. "Really? You guys use a dinner bell, like in the old movies?"

"How else are we gonna know when dinner's ready?" Skeeter turned from the cattle and waved Dakota and Jacinta in with him.

The table was full of fresh vegetables and roasted meat. The meat smelled heavenly. Skeeter licked his lips and took his normal seat. All he wanted to do was fill his plate sky-high and dig in, but he knew the drill.

Jerod sat at the head of the table and Dana was at the foot.

"Let's welcome our guest and new resident to the Crooked Arrow properly by allowing them to serve themselves first." Jerod motioned for Jacinta and Dakota to start.

Dana handed the bowl of green beans to Dakota while Jacinta pulled a slice of juicy roast onto her plate.

Once everyone had served themselves, they all sat there waiting. Jerod cleared his throat and then bowed his head. Everyone followed suit and when he was finished with his prayer, Skeeter smiled and began eating.

Conversation flowed freely amongst all those at the table. The only one missing was Sam Marley.

"So, Dakota. Why don't you share a little bit about yourself?" Megan, the counselor for the ranch residents, suggested.

With a mouth full of the best roast beef Dakota had ever tasted, she looked around at all of the eyes staring at her. "Mmm." She shook her head and pointed to her mouth.

"Well, since you've got a full mouth, how about I start?" Skeeter put his fork down on his plate and began telling everyone a little bit about his background. Even though everyone else there knew his story, he knew it was important for the new arrivals to have this time to meet everyone in a group environment. And it was also important for the residents to learn more about the newbie.

"I'm an Army veteran. I was injured in Afghanistan when a roadside bomb went off. I took shrapnel to my legs. This place," he gestured around with his hand, "really helped me to recover. When I first arrived, I had to use crutches for quite some time. But now I'm about ready to leave thanks to the great care, and delicious food, I received here." He winked at Dana.

"Please," Dana waved a hand to dismiss his praise. "You got better because of the ranch, not my cooking."

"Oh, I don't know, hunny. I think good cooking can go a long way to healing a body." Jerod, Dana's husband, rubbed his taught belly before taking a large bite of the roast. He partially closed his eyes and looked like he was in heaven.

Skeeter shook his head. "They're newlyweds, so watch out. I can't tell you how many times I've caught them kissing around the ranch." He stuck his tongue out and shivered, just like a kid when he caught his parents kissing.

Most of the table laughed and kept eating.

Jacinta pointed her fork at Skeeter. "Hey now, there's nothing wrong with a newlywed couple kissing. In fact, it's a good thing."

With his hands raised in surrender, Skeeter grabbed another slice of the roast.

Dakota had already finished her bite of food, but she wasn't comfortable talking about herself in a group. In fact, group settings always made her feel awkward. If it were up to her, she would have taken her tray up to her room and eaten by herself.

"Go on, you can tell them." Jacinta urged Dakota.

Instead of looking around at the people eating dinner with her, Dakota kept her eyes on the plates in front of her. "Well, I'm also Army. I was injured in Iraq. Spent some time in LA and now I'm here." She prayed that was enough. The last thing Dakota wanted to do was tell more about herself.

The stress of it all had her stomach in knots. Her appetite was all but gone now and she'd only taken a few bites of her meal. Most of the food still covered her plate. But there was no way she was going to be able to eat any more. She'd learned from experience that if she ate now, she'd be sick in the bathroom for the next few hours.

Instead of eating, she pushed the food around on her plate, to make it look like she was trying. Jacinta always knew what Dakota was up to. But she rarely made her eat. At least not since the older woman had walked in on Dakota retching over the toilet after dinner.

That had been so embarrassing. Jacinta had spoken with Dakota's doctors, and they ran some tests. After a few weeks, the psychologist had said it was her nerves. When Dakota became too agitated or anxious, then her stomach did somersaults and caused her to vomit. The doctor said it was best not to eat when she got that way. But they did have her drink protein shakes. A lot.

Still, Dakota had lost almost twenty pounds while in that facility. Which was partly why Jacinta had pushed so hard to get her moved to the Crooked Arrow Ranch. With a smaller group of veterans living with her and the ability to learn a new trade, everyone agreed that the environment of a small ranch would be healthier.

So, here she was, having a group dinner, and her stomach was a mess. If she wasn't careful, she'd end up losing more weight and getting put in an institution and then they'd force feed her through a tube.

With that awful thought in mind, Dakota took another bite and grimaced when it hit her stomach like rock.

Dakota was up early the next morning. She wasn't exactly bright-eyed and bushy-tailed, but she dressed to work. When the delicious scent of strong coffee caught her attention, she followed the invisible trail to what promised to be heavenly.

She stopped short when she noticed Jacinta was already in the room and in front of the blender. "Jacinta? You're up early."

The woman turned around with a smile and nodded. Jacinta turned on the blender and the loud noise filled the kitchen.

Knowing she couldn't really yell her question while the blender was going, Dakota made a beeline to the coffee pot. It was one of those larger, industrial kinds. There was even a K-cup machine next to it. It made sense. They probably made one large pot of coffee in the morning, then during the day as people needed it, they could get...well, just about anything. Dakota looked at the basket next to the one-cup coffee machine and noted they not only had coffee, but also a nice selection of tea and hot chocolate.

When she caught sight of a clear jar containing mini-marshmallows, Dakota couldn't help the grin that overtook her. She couldn't remember the last time she'd had hot cocoa with real marshmallows. The VA hospital had those packets that also included freeze-dried mini marshmallows, but they were nothing like the real thing. Maybe she'd mix a cup of coffee with the hot cocoa. Then top it off with mini marshmallows. It wasn't the foam or whipped cream a good coffee shop would add, but it would be a nice change of pace.

The blender stopped crushing ice and the room grew quiet. "Ah, I'd hold off on that if I were you." Jacinta took the glass jar off the blender and poured a chocolate concoction into a large, insulated mug. "Here, start with this. I even added some coffee for a bit of a kick."

"Thanks. But I ate pretty well last night." Under her breath, Dakota mumbled, "For being in a new place."

Jacinta's shoulders slumped. "Dakota, I saw how little you ate. Please, for me?"

Dakota scrunched her nose and took the offered protein drink. She hated these. The doctor told her they were delicious since they had a chocolate flavoring, but Dakota had never felt like she was drinking a milkshake. But the added coffee might cover the chalky taste. Especially if Jacinta added the coffee that scented the very air she was breathing. She was going to have to get a mug of that coffee, too.

After taking a sip, Dakota's brows furrowed. She looked inside the mug, then took another, longer drink. "This isn't the same thing they served me back in LA. What is it?"

Boots sounded on the kitchen floor and a feminine voice answered, "It's my own concoction. Jacinta told me you might need protein shake supplements. Do you like it?"

"Dana, this is great." Dakota took another long drink and sighed. "If the VA had this recipe, I think a lot more people would gladly drink it."

"Well, it's not exactly institutional ingredients." Dana smiled at Dakota. "I add coffee beans and a scoop of protein powder that I get from Costco. And I use real cocoa, not the fake stuff that most hospitals use. Then I add some Stevia in the Raw for a little added sweetness and top it off with real whipping cream."

"That's not exactly dietetic." With a happy tummy, Dakota finished off the mug. "I'd happily drink that every day."

"I think that can be arranged." A sparkle shone in Dana's eyes as she topped off her mug of coffee. "Have you tried this coffee yet?"

"Dana also works part-time in the local coffee shop where the owner roasts her own beans. This is always the highlight of my trip here." Jacinta closed her eyes and savored the flavors of the coffee.

Everyone's heads turned when they heard someone clearing their voice.

Chapter 5

It was too early. That's all there was to it. While Skeeter loved ranch life, he never liked getting up while it was still dark. Even in the height of summer, there was barely any light when they rose. Now that it was fall, the sun wasn't shining as long as it once did. And when Skeeter looked out his window that morning, he could have sworn the moon was still shining brightly. He had to do a double take to make sure someone hadn't messed with his alarm, since they were always up before the rooster crowed at sunrise.

In the beginning, Sam Marley would complain that they had done several hours of work before the rooster did his job. Skeeter and Sam had arrived at Christmas time, so there was that. Most days in the middle of winter they didn't see sunlight until after nine in the morning. Of course, Skeeter didn't arrive until after the first Christmas at Crooked Arrow. But still, he'd been here for the past two Christmases, and he knew firsthand how long they worked before the sun rose or the rooster crowed.

This morning, however, there seemed to be a cloud hanging over the kitchen. When he stopped around the corner from the kitchen, he tried to stifle his yawn. Then he heard the women's voices talking about Dakota and needing to drink protein shakes. The little lady was a bit on the skinny side. Was she trying to rebuild muscle? He knew some guys who drank protein shakes to add muscle, but none of those guys had lost a lot of weight first. Or was she just naturally skinny?

Since meeting Dakota the previous day, he hadn't really thought much about her weight, until now. While he'd noted she was rail-thin, he didn't care. She was too pretty to worry about her weight. But now? It sounded as though she might have an eating disorder. Or was it that most food just didn't taste good to her?

Skeeter remembered dinner the night before and realized that she hadn't eaten much. Her plate wasn't even half empty when she got up from the table. He hoped she wasn't the sort to starve herself. He had seen some women back in high school who did that. It wasn't pretty what happened to their bodies when it went too far.

He felt his stomach drop as he remembered his buddy's sister. She had been a little chunky when she started high school. After a few months of the other students teasing her and bullying her over her weight, she went on a diet. At first, no one thought anything of her weight loss. But when it continued, quickly, her family did worry.

Skeeter prayed right then and there that what happened to his friend's sister wouldn't happen to Dakota. Before that year of high school was over, they were attending her funeral. Skeeter refused to attend another funeral for a girl who literally starved herself to death.

But he had stood there too long and heard too much. He knew he shouldn't have been eavesdropping. He rubbed the back of his neck as he thought about what to do. If he stood there much longer, someone would catch him. It was the time that everyone came through for their morning coffee. And if he walked into the room while they were still discussing Dakota's health problems? That would just be awkward.

For just a moment he considered turning around and hightailing it back to his room. But he needed his coffee to get going. So, with a deep breath, he decided to be a man and entered the room.

"Oh, Dana, is this Saturday pancake day at the coffee shop?" Jacinta bounced on the balls of her feet like a kid in a candy shop.

"Actually, it's omelet Saturday. Next weekend is pancake day. And we're even going to offer crepes with fresh strawberries and cream." Dana's proclamation wasn't news to Skeeter, but it seemed to be to the two other women in the room.

"Strawberry crepes? Really?" Dakota's eyes widened and she licked her lips. "Will there be a Nutella option, too?"

"Nutella? On crepes?" Skeeter scoffed and scrunched his nose.

"You haven't crepes until you've tried Nutella, banana, and strawberry with fresh whipped cream." Dakota sighed and looked off into the distance. "I haven't had those since I was in high school."

Dana exchanged a glance with Jacinta. "I think that can be arranged."

Skeeter knew Dana would do it, too. It sounded very fattening, just the sort of thing that a skinny woman with an eating disorder needed. "I guess I could give it a try. I'm always game to try anything once."

"Oh, yeah?" Mike chuckled when he entered the kitchen. "Does that mean you're finally going to try my goat's milk?"

Skeeter help up a hand. "Now wait a minute. I've tried goat milk before. There's no way you're gonna get me to drink any more, ever."

"That sounds like a challenge to me." Tony walked into the room and went straight to the coffee machine. "I think I know just how to do it." He grinned and looked over the brim of his mug at Skeeter.

Skeeter's nostrils flared. "Don't you dare." He pointed a finger at Tony.

"I never said it would be me." Tony's lighthearted reply sent shivers down Skeeter's spine.

"What's going on? I don't get it?" Dakota looked from one man to the other.

Dana sidled up next to her. "You gotta watch out around here. The boys like to play practical jokes on each other. Nothing harmful, mind you, but some of them can be rather annoying."

"Yeah, like the time someone," Tony glared at Mike, "put glowing eyes outside of all our bedroom windows."

Mike held up his hand. "Hey now, it wasn't me who did it." He turned to look at Skeeter. "Most of the juvenile pranks are Skeeter."

"That wasn't me and you know it. I had one of those toilet paper rolls outside my window, too. If memory serves, you were the only one who didn't have those creepy eyes staring into your room." Skeeter arched a brow and returned Mike's glare.

"Yeah, because you set me up to take the fall." Mike's voice was starting to rise and the tension in the room was as thick as pea soup.

"Alright now. Quiet down." Jerod's loud voice boomed through the room, and everyone quieted down. "We've got a new resident, who is a lady." He eyed the men in the room. "I don't want to see any pranks pulled on her, got it?" He looked directly at Skeeter, then to Mike.

"Ugh." Dakota shook her foot out in front of her and scowled down at her left leg.

"Is it tingling again?" Jacinta took Dakota by the arm and led her to the table. "Take a seat."

"Yeah, but I don't know how much weight I can put on my foot this time. It really hurts." She inched down into the chair, holding her leg out.

"Skeeter, go get Megan," Jerod ordered as he went to stand in front of Dakota.

Skeeter nodded and left the room.

All thoughts of practical jokes flew out the window, and everyone in the room looked to Dakota. Her cheeks flared red, and she looked down at her foot.

"Dakota, how often does this happen?" Jerod, while not a doctor, did need to understand the needs of all of his residents.

"Not too often," she replied.

"More often lately than before." Jacinta took the seat on the other side of Dakota. She was about to say more, then realized the kitchen had filled with most of the ranch residents. "Do you think we could take her somewhere more private?"

Jerod's head popped up and he looked around. He scowled. "Why don't you all get to work?"

The men scattered without their coffee.

"I'll put your coffee in the large thermos and bring it out to the barn along with all the fixings." Dana moved to get the large, insulated thermos and began pouring what was left in the coffee maker.

It wasn't even five minutes later that Skeeter came back into the kitchen with Megan trailing him. He looked to where Dakota sat and bit the inside of his cheek to keep from saying anything. It was most likely her poor nutrition that was causing the issue. But he knew it wasn't his place to say anything.

"Dakota, what's going on?" Megan moved Jerod away and pulled a chair to sit in front of Dakota.

While Megan wasn't a medical doctor, she was a psychologist who had experience with the various ailments of the returning veterans. She would triage a situation before calling in the local doctor or ordering an ambulance to take a patient to the hospital, if needed.

"Sometimes my feet get a numbness and tingling feeling, like they're going to sleep," Dakota said.

"How long has this been going on?" With the girl's foot in her hands, Megan began taking her boots off.

"Oh, this is normal. It's a side effect of the medication I'm on. Or, at least, that's what the doctors said." Dakota grimaced and put a hand out toward her sore foot.

"Does that hurt?" Megan asked.

Dakota nodded.

"What medication are you on that would cause this type of side effect?" Megan slowly lowered the foot in question to the floor.

"It's my anti-anxiety medication." Dakota named the generic drug and Megan pursed her lips.

"I'm very familiar with that one, and this is not a normal side effect. In fact, I've never seen this in any of my patients who take that drug." She paused and thought for a moment. "How long have you been on it?"

They spoke about her history for a few minutes and the different meds she had tried over the past year.

Skeeter knew he should have left the room as soon as he brought Megan to Dakota, but he couldn't. So he stood in the back corner listening and watching quietly. If there was anything he could do to help, he wanted to be there for her. Yes, the girl was pretty, but it was more than that. He wasn't sure if this was his way of trying to make up for not helping his friend's sister. Skeeter knew that he could never make up for the loss of the teenager, but maybe, just maybe, he could help prevent another person from dying.

After a few minutes of Megan questioning Dakota, and examining her foot, Megan stood. "Dakota, I'd like for you to get a second opinion. I have a friend at the VA hospital in Fort Harrison. Do you mind if I call him and speak to him about your symptoms? I'd like for you to see him if he thinks he can help."

"Will he be able to get me off this medication?" Dakota asked.

"I can't make any promises. The first step is to ensure that you have a correct diagnosis. Then we can look at your meds." Megan pulled her cell phone out, then put it back in her pocket. It was too early to call a doctor. "I'll give him a call after nine. He should be in the office today."

Skeeter looked at his wrist and noted the time. The little hand had just touched the seven. He didn't know if he could wait another two hours to hear if Megan's doctor friend could help.

Jerod looked around the kitchen. He scowled when he noticed Skeeter standing in the back corner. "What are you still doing here? Shouldn't you be out helping with the morning chores?"

"Sorry, I thought I'd stick close in case you needed anything." Skeeter wasn't about to admit his real reason, but that was close enough it wasn't a lie.

"Help Dana get the coffee outside to the barn." Jerod kissed the top of his wife's head and headed to his office.

A niggling feeling overtook Skeeter as he helped to carry the coffee and the supplies to the barn. That poor girl needed a friend who could understand her. And Skeeter was going to be that friend. Not because she was pretty, but because he knew it was the right thing to do.

Chapter 6

Megan's doctor friend had made time on his schedule Monday afternoon. Until then, Dakota would just have to deal with the horrible side effects of the medication she took. Jerod told her to take it easy and rest for the day. But rest was the last thing Dakota wanted, even if it was what she needed.

If she didn't get a good night's sleep, Dakota could be a bit listless all day, and since she'd had nightmares last night, it was one of her bad days. But sitting around with nothing to do but worry about what the doctor might say wasn't a good thing. After spending an hour watching TV, her eyes were crossing, and her mind had gone numb with all of the stupid drama. She had never been one for soap operas or daytime talk shows. Not that there was anything bad about them, they just weren't for her. That was the kind of thing her grandma watched.

Dakota's generation was more into reality shows. But that was primetime viewing. Watching TV during the day wasn't something she ever really had time for. And if she did, then she usually watched Netflix. The site had most of the older seasons of her favorite reality shows, and she'd binge those when she was sick.

The only problem with that was the ranch didn't have a smart TV. They did have Wi-Fi, but she didn't have a tablet and the screen on her phone was a bit small for watching *The Bachelor*. Although, those shows about bidding for storage lockers might work on a small screen. Dakota opened her Netflix app on her phone and began searching for something that might be entertaining.

As she searched, she heard voices in the hallway outside the living room.

"We should invite her. It might be fun." The voice sounded familiar to Dakota, but she didn't know these guys well enough yet to easily identify their voices. Especially through the wall.

"I don't know. Jerod said to let her rest today. Her foot is hurting her. I don't want to be responsible for her having to leave after only two days on the ranch." The other voice, she thought it might be Mike, seemed hesitant.

Dakota made the decision for them when she stood up and walked out into the hallway. "Hey, guys."

Mike jumped when he heard her voice behind him.

Skeeter waved. "Hiya. Are you tired of laying around yet?"

She bristled at the insinuation that she wasn't pulling her weight. But to be fair, she wasn't. Not yet at least. "Actually, I am. I was hoping to find something to do that wouldn't hurt my foot more. What can I do?"

"I'm glad you asked." Skeeter leaned against the wall and grinned.

The man seemed to smile a lot. How was it that someone in his shoes could be so happy? Her first instinct was to frown. It hadn't always been that way. She used to smile all the time. Something as simple as the sun shining could make her smile. Or something as complex as a rainbow could cause her to get downright giddy. She'd even tried on multiple occasions to find the end of a rainbow.

Now, she didn't believe the hype about their being a pot of gold at the end, but she was curious if she could find a way to bend the light waves enough for her to see either the beginning or the end. Instead, she'd just see the rainbow either move with her, or disappear altogether.

Dakota raised a brow and waited.

Skeeter continued to stand there, watching her and smiling.

It didn't take long for Dakota get tired of his game, so she turned her eyes to Mike. "Would you mind telling me what this is all about?"

"Ah." A nervous chuckle escaped the man. "I...well...Skeeter thought you might like to come and help me churn butter."

That sounded good to Dakota. In fact, she realized that if she was there long enough, she could find out how to milk a cow. She nodded. "I think that sounds like fun. Let's go." Under her breath she added, "Anything's better than sitting around twiddling my thumbs."

It was only an hour later, and Dakota was wishing she stayed in the living room with nothing to do. It would have been better than the foot pain, followed by the back pain, and the fresh, warm milk that had squirted all over her jeans. Thankfully, she was wearing her boots, so at least her feet were dry.

"How do you make this look so easy, but it really isn't?" Dakota took the offered towel and tried to dry some of the milk off her pants.

Mike tried to cover his laughing but couldn't. "It's easy, if you're paying attention to what you're doing instead of rubbernecking to see what's happening in the barn."

When Dakota had first began pulling on the teats of the cow, she'd thought it was gross. But she hadn't wanted to throw in the towel so soon. She'd decided that she was going to prove her worth and milk all the cows. It was only five, that shouldn't have been too difficult, right?

Instead of taking only twenty minutes like she thought, it was more like thirty minutes—per cow. Mike must have spent most of his days in the barn between milking them twice a day and making butter and who knew what else.

After only two cows, her back hurt and she was bored. It wasn't fun. And to make matters worse, several of the guys were in a different part of the barn and, from the sounds of it, having fun. Laughter assaulted her ears and she wanted to see what was so funny.

So, when she took her eyes off of what she was doing and turned her head as far as it would go—and no, she couldn't turn it around like Linda Blair in the *Exorcist*——her hand moved. Yup, she squirted warm milk out from the cow directly onto her leg.

Skeeter and Tony came over as her loud shriek pierced the calmness of the ranch.

"What happened?" Skeeter cried out.

"Are you alright?" Tony asked.

Both men stood in the way of her retreat back to the house. Dakota was starting to think that she might not be built for ranch life. Her arms flailed out to the side, and she blew a raspberry with her lips. "I need a shower."

Tony covered his mouth but didn't say a thing.

"Don't worry about it. You aren't the first one to squirt milk on yourself. At least you didn't squirt it on an un-suspecting innocent bystander." Skeeter glared at Mike.

"Hey, you weren't so innocent. And I didn't do it on purpose. If anything, it was your fault." Mike crossed his arms over his chest and returned Skeeter's glare.

"I was on crutches man, how was I supposed to know that it would scare a cow?" Skeeter slapped one leg.

Dakota raised a hand. "Um, if you guys will move, I'd like to head back inside now."

"Sorry." Tony moved to the side while Skeeter stayed put. When Tony realized Skeeter wasn't moving, but still glaring at Mike, he shoved the young cowboy out of Dakota's way.

She turned a thankful glace his way as she walked past Tony and toward the house and a hot shower.

Chapter 7

Saturday morning brought sunshine and simple happiness to the ranch. It was only omelet Saturday, but still, the residents of the Crooked Arrow Ranch enjoyed their Saturday morning breakfasts at the Frenchtown Roasting Company. In fact, most of the town and the surrounding ranchers and farmers came in on Saturdays for the weekly special. There was always a line out the door, but when Lottie did her famous pancakes, the line was so long it could wrap around town.

When the weather was nice, Lottie and her crew put picnic tables and small bistro tables out front so more people could sit down and enjoy breakfast with friends and family. While it wasn't a party or a carnival, it did feel like it at times.

As the men and women of the Crooked Arrow prepared to leave to go into town, Skeeter spotted Dakota looking around. "Hey, you looking for me?" He grinned.

While he wasn't exactly flirting, he thought he was being funny.

Dakota didn't. She frowned. "Have you seen Dana?"

"Oh, you don't know, do you?"

She shook her head.

Jerod stepped up and answered Dakota's question. "My wife works part-time at the coffee shop. Every Saturday it's all hands-on deck for the breakfast rush. She'll work all day today. And we'll barbecue something simple on the grill tonight."

It was just one more thing her stupid brain had forgotten. Why did she always forget? Dakota wondered if she shouldn't start taking notes on her phone's note app. Maybe then she could start to remember the simple stuff.

"Is that why everyone goes to the coffee shop for breakfast every Saturday? Because none of you can cook?" A tiny glimpse of a smile appeared on her face for a moment, but it disappeared just as quickly.

Another rancher walked up, this one with a beautiful boxer dog. "Nah, most of us can at least make oatmeal or eggs, but this is a chance for us all to have fun for a little bit. Once we're done, we either head over to the Christmas Tree Farm, or stay in town for a little bit visiting." Sam Marley motioned for Dakota to walk in front of them.

Dakota looked down and noticed the service dog vest. "How often do you let Rogue play?" While she had met them both during the previous day, she hadn't really had a chance to speak to Sam, or spend any time with his service dog, Rogue. She loved dogs and had hoped to be able to spend some time when Rogue wasn't on the clock.

"Most of the time when he's here on the ranch, his vest is off. But if we go anywhere, I try to keep his vest on, that way he learns the difference between working and relaxing." Sam bent down and patted his partner's head. "If it were up to me, he'd never have to wear the vest. I'd love it if he could enjoy the attentions of the kids in town. I think he would, too."

"So, you can't let anyone touch him when his vest is on?" She tilted her head and narrowed her eyes.

"I can, but it's best if he gets used to working with me first. I've only had him for a few months. It's still new for us both. Once he's accustomed to being my partner, and can instinctively know when I need him, then I'll sometimes take his vest off when we're in town." Sam gave a few instructions to Rogue in German, who sat on his haunches and looked up at his human partner, tongue lolling to the side.

"He's so cute. I've always liked dogs." Dakota inched closer but kept her hands to herself. While she didn't know much about service dogs, the one thing she did know was to not touch the dogs while they wore their work vests.

Sam looked around. "You can pet him, if you want. Just don't do it in town. I don't want anyone to think it's alright. At least, not yet. And this way, Rogue will have a chance to learn your scent."

For the first time since Dakota arrived, she grinned from ear to ear. Well, maybe the second time. That baby bull did give her some happiness. She leaned down and put her hand in front of the dog.

Rogue sniffed it, and then licked her.

She giggled and put her hand on his head, giving him a good scratch behind his ears. "Good dog."

"*Braver hund*," Sam instructed.

"Pardon?" Dakota stood up, smile gone, as she looked to Sam for clarification.

"It means 'good dog' in German. I try to only speak the German commands and phrases when he's working. It's just one more indicator to him that he's on the clock, so to speak."

"Oh. *Braver hound*." Dakota looked to Sam to ensure she'd said it correctly.

"You got the first word right. But the second one is pronounced 'hoont'. The d at the end has more of a 'T' sound."

Once the rest of the residents walked into the front room where Sam was giving Dakota a German lesson, Jerod led them outside to the ranch van.

Tony and Sam, along with their service dogs, got into a truck, while everyone else hopped into the van. Dakota sat in the back, watching and listening as everyone chatted about what they wanted to do for the day. When Megan brought up the fall festival, Dakota's ears perked up.

Since she was out in the boondocks, she figured she might as well get the entire experience. The fall festivals back in Southern California were fun, but nothing like what she'd seen on movies. Dakota was fairly certain most of what she saw on the screen was exaggerated, but surely there would be at least a corn maze and pumpkin carving. Shoot, even California's festivals had apple bobbing at parties when she was a kid.

"When does the harvest festival begin?" Dakota had to practically yell her question since everyone was so loud.

"Huh?" Skeeter, who had been sitting in the seat in front of her, turned around and asked her to repeat her question.

"Is the fall festival beginning soon?"

"It's gonna start in less than two weeks. Cody Makinaw, the guy who owns the place, is already starting to decorate. A few of us will go out next week and help hang banners and the like. You should come with. It's a lot of fun."

Megan turned around. "And I'm dating the foreman of the ranch, Daniel Caruthers. He and Cody are best friends. This is going to be their second year putting on the festival. I'm really excited to see what they have planned this year."

"Yeah, they've only being doing festivals for just about a year now. Well, outside of Christmas. Two years ago they almost went under," Dixon added.

Eyes wide, Dakota wanted to ask the history of the farm, but thought better of it. It wasn't any of her business. But knowing that they turned around their farm made her want to see it even more. She was excited and planned on asking Jerod if she could be one of those who went to help.

Then she remembered her doctor appointment for Monday. She said a quick prayer that it would all go well and that she'd be able to help at the tree farm when everyone else went over.

The moment Dakota stepped onto Main Street; she knew she was in a dream. When she and Jacinta arrived a couple of days ago, they drove straight to the ranch and bypassed the small, picturesque village of Frenchtown. As she looked around, mouth agape, she wished they would have stopped in town first.

It was exactly like something out of a Hallmark movie, only smaller. Sure, cars and trucks lined the streets, but they also had a few hitching posts outside some of the buildings. And they weren't all empty posts, either. It seemed some of the locals enjoyed riding their horses into town for breakfast.

While some of the buildings were more modern—and by modern Dakota assumed they'd been built within the last fifty years—others looked to be real western stores. There was an old-fashioned general store, which was one of the shops with a hitching post outside. The sidewalk wasn't made of wood, like in old westerns, but it was still like something she'd seen out of a recent movie.

"Hey, does the Hallmark Channel do any of their filming here?" Dakota asked Megan as they walked slowly toward the long line outside of what she assumed was the coffee shop.

Megan chuckled. "I wish. No, I think they film all their movies up in Canada. But I see where you're going. This would be a great town to film in. And with all of the local cowboys and the various festivals, a romance book could easily take place here."

"Is it always so packed in town?" The line outside of the coffee shop went down the sidewalk and past two storefronts. Dakota hoped it wouldn't take an hour to get seated. "Have they thought about utilizing a paging system so we don't all have to stand in line for so long?"

"Hm, I don't know. I suppose we could ask Dana about that." Megan led Dakota to the back of the line where a small group of the men from the ranch stood. "Where are Sam and Tony? I would have thought they'd get here before us."

"They were, but when I walked up to join them, they said they needed to take the dogs for a walk." Skeeter chuckled and pointed toward the small grassy area only a block away.

"And that is why I don't have a dog." Dakota grinned and shook her head. "Too much work."

"Oh, I don't know. I think the benefits far outweigh the work." Nelly Wilson, the local dog trainer, said when she walked up to them with two dogs wearing service vests.

"Nelly." Megan hugged her friend and pulled back. She nodded to the two dogs sitting quietly at Nelly's feet. "I see you brought your new dogs with you. Care to introduce us?"

"Sure, but who's your new friend?" Nelly nodded toward Dakota.

"Oh, where are my manners?" Megan put a hand to her chest and sighed. "I'm sorry about that. This is Dakota, she just arrived at the ranch a few days ago." She turned to Dakota. "And this is Nelly. The wonderful service dog trainer. Next week you'll see her around a lot at the ranch. She comes out several times a week with her dogs to train with our veterans."

Dakota shyly smiled and took Nelly's outstretched hand. "Nice to meet you."

"You as well." Nelly looked down at her dogs. "And these are my two newest additions—Bam Bam and Pebbles."

"Ah," Dakota started to ask where she got the names, then remembered something from her childhood. "Are those the kids from the *Flintstones*?"

"Yup, they are. I loved watching the *Flintstones* and *Jetsons* when I was kid. I know, those cartoons are sooo old. But so good." With a glint in her eye, Nelly turned her head and spotted her boyfriend.

Dakota noticed the way Nelly stood taller when she looked at the men down the street coming towards them. The dog trainer was probably happy to see the dogs she'd placed with two of the ranch residents.

But when Sam came up and pulled Nelly into a tight hug, Dakota felt her cheeks heat up. She'd heard something about Sam dating a woman, but she didn't realize that it was Nelly. They were cute together.

Then another memory popped up. "Are you the one Sam is working with part-time?"

The couple pulled apart after Sam gave her a quick kiss on her forehead.

"Yes, and he's going to move in soon." Redness covered Nelly's face when she realized what she'd said. "I mean." She cleared her throat.

Skeeter laughed. "Yes, do tell, Nelly. When is Sam moving in with you?"

"It's not like that, and you know it." Nelly glared at Skeeter. "When are you going to grow up and stop acting like a teenage boy?"

"This is growing up for Skeeter. Just a couple of weeks ago we were all complaining about him acting like a ten-year-old." Sam laughed and patted his friend's shoulder.

"Hey now. I resemble those comments." The man in question grinned and took the ribbing as intended, just fun.

It had been a long time since Dakota had seen people so relaxed and carefree. Living in a VA hospital, even though it was group home sort of living, she didn't see a lot of happy faces. This was nice. Maybe Jacinta was on to something with sending her here. If she could learn to relax, maybe she could get past her depression and get off the meds that were causing her issues. The side effects of such strong medication weren't fun.

But she realized that they must have been working. She hadn't felt this free since, well, since she first went to Iraq. Ever since her first day in the sandpit—as those who'd been there for a while called the desert of Iraq—she'd felt off.

It only got worse over time. Dakota had lost friends her first week there. Then, when the terrorists began sending short range missiles into her base camp, she thought for sure she was a goner. Thankfully, they were more annoying than anything else. But the sounds of the missiles firing into her camp always made her jump. No one ever knew if it would be an annoying shot or a kill shot.

One night, a group of special forces guys were so annoyed, they started shooting down the projectiles before they even crossed the fence. While it was good the Army guys were showing their superiority, it was still nerve-wracking to hear the firefight. Then, two nights later, one of the Ranger groups set up a trap. That stopped the terrorists from firing into the base camp anymore. Which was good. But Dakota still walked around fearful of any loud noise for a couple of weeks. Eventually, she settled in.

And wouldn't you know it? The moment she thought she was going to be alright; a convoy was attacked and two more of her friends were sent home in caskets. The idea of death didn't bother Dakota as much as how she might die. She knew exactly where she was going when she died, so she never worried about that. Instead, she feared the *how* and the *who*. Too many stories about what the insurgents did to women had her up late at night, unable to sleep. Eventually, the Army Chaplain had a talk with her about why she feared death. And he ended up showing her passages about how God would take care of her and how He wouldn't put her in a situation she couldn't handle. All she could do was pray and trust that God would take care of her. Yes, evil surrounded them. But so did good. And it was up to them to ensure that the innocent people in the villages got a chance at life, and a chance to hear the Good News about Jesus.

After that, she settled down and didn't fear nearly as much. The sounds of distant gunfire and the occasional rocket into their camp set her teeth on edge, but she'd recite some of the versus she learned, and all would calm again.

As Dakota looked at all the strange, new faces in town, she remembered John 16:33—*These things I have spoken unto you, that in me ye might have peace. In the world ye shall have tribulation: but be of good cheer, I have overcome the world.*

Even though crowds still bothered her, Dakota knew she was right where God wanted her to be. The people of Frenchtown, Montana were nice and they cared about their neighbors. At least, that's what Jacinta had promised her. She'd have to give them a chance before she made up her mind. Everyone deserved that, didn't they?

Around her, Dakota knew that her new roommates were laughing and joking. But she had been stuck in her own head, reliving memories, or maybe nightmares, from her time in the Army. She needed to get her head back to the here and now. It wasn't until she heard Jacinta's voice that Dakota shook herself and focused on those around her.

"Sam, I know you aren't actually moving in with Nelly. So, tell me, what's going on?" The lady who had placed Sam at the ranch arched a brow and put both of her hands on her hips.

He put his hands in the air, surrendering to the truth. "Okay, okay. I'm actually moving into the barn apartment when Nelly moves into the house. Now that it's all cleaned up and ready for her, she's going to move inside."

"And deal with the ghosts all by herself?" Skeeter looked appalled by the thought. "Don't you think you should be the one to live in the haunted house? And not your girlfriend?"

"Hold up." Nelly put a hand up to stop Skeeter from saying any more. "The house isn't haunted. It was just a literal dump. But now that it's all been gutted and redone, it's really beautiful. Y'all should come by and see it once I get some furniture in there."

The idea of a haunted house intrigued Dakota. "Wait, why is Skeeter saying it's haunted? Did someone die there?" Not that a death was anything to be excited about, but if the original owner had died, say over a hundred years ago, she could enjoy a good haunting.

Nelly smiled and shook her head. "I guess you haven't heard?"

"Are you talking about the bear?" Dakota had heard something, but she didn't think she knew the entire story.

"Well, when I first moved here the main house was trashed. And I mean it was *trashed*. Emphasis on the trash part. It looked as though an entire town had used it as their city dump for years. There were all sorts of dead animals. But one in particular had the town going crazy with gossip. A full-grown black bear was found upstairs. Someone had used it for target practice." Nelly shivered and stuck her tongue out as though she had smelled a skunk.

"Didn't you know that before you bought the place?" Jacinta asked.

"Pft," Nelly scoffed. "You'd think that my realtor would have told me about it, but no. He didn't. Instead, he showed me pictures that must have been from before the previous owners died. Like, years before they died."

Skeeter interrupted. "Tell her about the barn."

"Wait," Dakota put her hands up. "Do I really want to know?" A shiver went down her spine as she thought about the scary and disgusting possibilities.

When Nelly's posture relaxed and she smiled, Dakota felt safer about the answer.

"Actually, Jerod had gone to the trouble of making sure the barn was in great shape and locked up good and tight for me. And all right before his wedding, too." A distant look crossed Nelly's eyes as she seemed to be thinking about those days.

"That's when we first met," Sam added. "The first day she was in town."

"Was it love at first sight?" While Dakota wasn't normally the fairy tale type, she did sense that the couple in question were deeply in love. It would be nice to know if that sort of love really existed.

Skeeter guffawed. "Not at all. It was more like hate at first sight."

Jacinta raised a brow. "Now now, Skeeter. Don't be so harsh."

The cowboy waved his hands in front of him. "Okay, so maybe not hate, exactly. Probably more like oil and water. But now," Skeeter looked at the couple who were making googly eyes at each other. "Get a room." He practically choked when he stuck a finger down his throat.

Dakota laughed, not at the cute couple, but at Skeeter. Sometimes the guy could be funny. She'd give him that much. But not an inch more. "So, what changed? You obviously mix well now."

"Time. That was all we needed to get to know each other better. Sam helped me with the cleanup and renovations, and we ended up spending a lot of quality time together. Once we were more comfortable with each other," Nelly shrugged.

"We began to gel," Sam said.

"And now you're finishing each other's thoughts." Dakota liked them together as a couple. It gave her hope that one day she might find her special someone. She knew it wouldn't be here, but the idea of meeting a cute cowboy who could curl her toes made her heart race and hope stir in her belly. Hope that one day soon, she'd have someone like Sam in her life. A man who looked at her as though she were the sun, moon, and stars all wrapped up in one pretty package. Jacinta had said that Sam was an old curmudgeon, but Dakota didn't see that.

No, she saw a man in love. A man who was happy, but, more importantly, content with his life. And now he was getting ready to move in with the woman he loved? Wait, that wasn't exactly it. She wracked her brain, trying to think of what they had said when she was off in another world. Something about the barn?

"That barn apartment!" She snapped her fingers. That was what they'd said.

"Yes? What about it." Nelly asked.

Dakota felt heat burning its way up her neck and into her cheeks. "Ah...I mean...You said you lived in the barn apartment when you first got here? Tell me more." She wasn't certain that she'd covered up her goof but prayed no one realized what she'd done.

Sam smiled. "Yes, the barn apartment is tiny, but livable. When Nelly moves into the house next weekend, I'll move out to the barn. It has a serviceable bed, kitchenette, and tiny washroom. It's all I'll need, since most of my time will be spent working with Nelly and the dogs. I'm going to be her new assistant and learn how to train service dogs."

"Really?" Dakota's brows rose. She was intrigued with the idea. "Do you have to go to college to learn how to do that?"

"No, not exactly. While there are training courses out there, it's more of a trade and therefore someone needs to apprentice with an experienced trainer. Then there are all sorts of tests and certifications to get." Nelly went on to explain in detail what Sam would do.

The idea of working with the dogs sounded fun, but maybe not the sort of thing she'd do for a living. "You come out to the ranch with your dogs a few times a week. What's that all about?"

"Well, while I can train my dogs to do most anything, it really helps if they spend some time working with veterans who have various disabilities. That way, I can train the dogs to handle different situations. Most of the guys at the ranch won't need a service dog, but I've found that they see improvement when they spend time working with the dogs, and the dogs learn more about different disabilities. It's a win-win for us all."

They continued to talk about the dogs and the various programs until they were next to be seated. Dakota enjoyed hearing about the dogs, how they were trained, and what they could do for their partners. She especially loved that the dogs weren't pets, but true partners. Not only did the veteran have to take care of the dog, but the dog also took great care of his or her vet. It was like a symbiotic relationship, except that the dog didn't inhabit the soldier's body.

Okay, so it wasn't a symbiotic relationship, but it was an intriguing partnership. One Dakota looked forward to seeing up close this week.

Chapter 8

It turned out she didn't need to wait for Monday to see how the dogs interacted with their partners.

Sunday morning brought sunshine but lower temperatures. Fall was in the air and everyone on the ranch was excited for cooler temps. Even the dogs seemed to have a little spring in their step.

Though Dakota seemed to be walking a bit slower, Skeeter had a giant grin on his face. His first instinct was to help her, but he remembered what Jerod has said just the night before about not flirting, so he stayed back. But not too far. All Skeeter could think about was his high school buddy's little sister, Cindy. This time, Skeeter wasn't going to let anything deter him from keeping an eye out.

Dakota may not want him flirting with her, and Skeeter understood that. He would respect her wishes. But one thing he learned in the Army was that everyone needed a battle buddy when they were in the thick of it. And Dakota was in the thick of something. Until Skeeter was ordered to leave, he was going to be the rock she needed.

He watched as the young woman winced whenever she took a step. All he wanted to do was take her pain away. When Tony's canine partner, Buffy, noticed Dakota, she led Tony closer to her. Buffy preferred women over men, except for Tony. So, it was natural that the dog would want to help Dakota out. The dogs seemed to have a sixth sense when it came to wounded veterans, and they always wanted to help.

Buffy nudged Dakota's right side, while staying on Tony's on left side. Tony couldn't hear on his left, and that was the side Buffy instinctively chose to be on. The three of them walked out to the van and Tony helped Dakota get inside.

When Tony and Buffy took the spot next to Dakota in the back, Skeeter felt the green-eyed monster of jealousy rear its ugly head. But he tamped down on the urge to pull Tony out of his seat. The man was dating Hope—Dana's cousin—and Skeeter knew that the man was head over heels for the pretty rancher. Besides, Skeeter knew if Dakota were to choose one of them, it would be him. He was the better looking out of the two.

Not that Skeeter was the least bit vain.

Instead of sharing the seat with Dakota, Skeeter sat directly in front of her. That way he'd be there to help her get out of the van and probably get a chance to sit with her in church.

In the back seat, Tony and Dakota were talking and joking. She sounded like she was more comfortable with Tony then she was with him. Which only served to inflame his jealousy even more. Although, he'd never admit to being jealous of anyone else. That would mean he thought there was a chance that another man might be a better fit for Dakota, which just wasn't true.

So, when they parked, he made sure to wait outside the van to help Dakota out. The only problem? Tony got out first, then practically pushed Skeeter back a few paces so he could help Dakota.

"Thanks, Tony." Dakota grinned at the cowboy, but, just as she was about to put her foot on the ground, she wobbled, then fell out of the van into Tony's arms.

"Whoa, are you alright?" Concern was etched on Tony's face.

All thoughts of jealousy fled as Skeeter realized that Dakota might actually be injured. She had put her head on Tony's chest, and her body was shaking.

"Dakota?" Skeeter put a calming hand on her back. "Can I help?" Since Tony had already asked how she was, Skeeter wasn't really sure what to do or say. If she needed him, he could be there for her. Even if he wasn't the one who got the chance to hold her in his arms, he'd move mountains to ensure her safety.

Skeeter heard her take a deep breath. "I'm fine. Just lost my balance, that's all."

Strong arms moved Skeeter to the side, and he noticed Jerod clearing a path for Megan.

"Dakota? Are you feeling woozy or nauseous?" Megan's soft voice was so low that Skeeter could barely hear her.

"My head's spinning. But my stomach's fine. I feel weird. What's going on?" Dakota's muffled words bounced off Tony's chest.

"I think you might be experiencing vertigo. If you can move, we should go sit down." Megan looked around. "Skeeter, can you get Dakota a bottle of water?"

"Sure thing." He ran to do as Megan requested. When he got back with a bottle of cold water, they were sitting in one of the comfy chairs in the corner of the church entrance. "Here ya go." He handed the bottle to Megan.

Church was about to start, but Skeeter didn't want to leave Dakota. If he was serious about being there for her, he needed to stay and help. Even if Megan had him running all over for stuff. Plus, he knew he wouldn't be able to concentrate on the sermon if he couldn't at least see for himself that Dakota was alright. So, he took a seat in one of the padded folding chairs to the side.

It didn't take long for Dakota to look up. Her eyes were glassy, and she had beads of perspiration all over her face.

"I'm sorry to cause such a ruckus. I don't even know what happened." The bottle in Dakota's hand was about half empty. But she still took small sips on it as they listened to the choir singing a special.

The soft melody of the worship song filled Skeeter with hope. Hope that Dakota would be fine. And hope that she wouldn't push him away. He knew God could work miracles still. Look at Sam. That man had done a complete about-face and was even ready to be discharged from the ranch. If God could heal that man, then God could heal Dakota.

Depression was something Skeeter understood. He'd seen many friends and family deal with the disease. Thankfully, he'd not really had any problems with depression. He'd been in a funk after the explosion, but no one had ever diagnosed him with depression. PTSD? Sure. Anyone who'd almost lost both legs to a roadside bomb would have PTSD. But his time at Crooked Arrow had helped him to grow closer to God and, in turn, not only did his body heal, but his soul, too.

God deserved all the credit even though He used the doctors in the Army, and then the VA, to help him keep his legs. There was one point where he thought he might lose one, or both. But he fought tooth and nail to save his legs. It was amazing what a stubborn streak and lots of prayer could do for a body. Skeeter had learned not to underestimate the power of God.

So, he prayed.

Skeeter prayed for Dakota's healing. And he prayed that the doctors would diagnose her correctly. And he prayed that Dakota would be happy with her life. It was amazing how much a body could heal if the soul was satisfied. He was a prime example, but so were Sam and Tony, as well as all the others at the ranch.

Medical stuff may not be Skeeter's strong suite, but he could pray. So, he did.

When the message was over, no one would have ever known that Dakota had been so ill. The sparkle was back in her eyes, and she stood up without help. She even made it back to the van on her own. While most of the guys left the church to head to Main Street and the different places that served a Sunday lunch, Skeeter stayed with Dakota.

"So, do you feel like headin' over to the diner for lunch?" Skeeter was hungry, but when wasn't he? If Dakota would go with him to have lunch, he'd get another opportunity to get to know her better.

"Sure, that sounds good. In fact," she put a hand over her stomach, "I think my belly is trying to tell me that I need food. I didn't eat much this morning and now I'm starved."

"Great. Do you want to walk? Or ride the van?" Jerod was going to take the van to a more central location on Main Street where they would all meet up later in the afternoon before heading on home.

"Let's walk. I don't get to do much of that anymore." She didn't elaborate on that, and Skeeter prayed that she'd tell him why over lunch.

Chapter 9

When Dakota agreed to grab lunch at the diner with Skeeter, she wasn't sure what to expect. But it certainly wasn't a giant table full of locals planning the harvest festival. She doubted it was what Skeeter had expected, either. She got the feeling that he had wanted to eat lunch with her and her alone.

But when the group of a dozen locals invited them to join, she couldn't say no. Dakota had to know if reality was like TV. Did small towns really go all out for fall harvest festivals like they did in sappy romcoms? This was her chance to find out, and she wasn't going to miss it.

A part of her hoped it would turn out to be just like the fall romance she'd recently watched on *GAC Family*, and another part of her really doubted it would even come close. If small town festivals really did go all out like in the shows, then wouldn't more city folks head out here for the various festivals? Or wouldn't smaller cities in Southern California do this kind of stuff?

What if they did and she'd just never known? That thought caught her off guard as the waitress came to take their drink orders. Everyone at the table had greeted her nicely, but then two women began bickering about the size of booths and she ended up tuning them out. Really, who cared if the booth was ten by ten or eleven by eleven? Did it really make a difference?

"Oh, I'll take an iced tea, please." Dakota smiled up into the face of a teenager chewing gum. She wore one of those old fifty's poodle skirts, had on a white buttoned-up blouse and did her hair as though she was Sandy from *Grease*. But the look worked on the young lady, and Dakota felt as though reality just might measure up.

After the pleasant surprise of a twenty-first century teenager dressed like she belonged at a sock-hop, Dakota decided to tune back into the conversation, or argument, at her table.

"I'm telling you, the extra foot on each wall will make a big difference. We can display more on the walls and have a bit more product inside the booth," a dark-haired woman who looked to be in her sixties argued.

The other woman tried to say it didn't matter, but she couldn't come up with a valid excuse.

"Excuse me, ladies. But does it really matter? I mean, do you have the space to accommodate the larger booth sizes?" She hadn't meant to interrupt, but the words came flooding out once Dakota decided that she'd be a part of the planning. Since she had to do so many hours of community service, this seemed like the right thing to do.

"Why, yes it does." The woman who looked like she was in her seventies and dyed her hair pink glared at her.

Dakota held up a hand. "I'm sorry, but I'm trying to learn about what it is you're doing. If the sellers want a little more space, wouldn't you think it would be a good thing?"

The first woman, whom Dakota still didn't know, grinned triumphantly. "See, Gladys, I told you it made sense."

Gladys turned steely gray eyes on the woman she was arguing with. "Maybell, that's because you don't realize that we've already built the booths at the ten-by-ten size. If we go larger, we'll have to make all new ones. And who has time for that?"

Skeeter laughed. "Why didn't you say so to start with?"

Gladys turned her gray eyes on to Skeeter and pursed her lips. She didn't say anything, just glared.

Maybell laughed. "He got you good there."

Not wanting this to go on even longer than it had, Dakota held up a hand. "Ladies, I think we've realized that the booths need to stay the same. No need to argue. If you really want larger booths, maybe you can get the high school woodshop teacher to work with his best students to make new ones for next year?"

Both Gladys and Maybell stared at Dakota.

"What did you say your name was again?" Gladys asked.

"Dakota Monahan."

"Well, Dakota. You're going to be on my team now."
Gladys smirked when she noticed Maybell was none too
happy about her snatching up the new girl with great
ideas. "And you, too Skeeter. I'll need a big, strong man
to help with set-up." The older lady winked at Skeeter.

Dakota did everything she could to keep from laughing. Skeeter, the town flirt, now had women old enough
to be his grandmother flirting with him. Somehow, she
doubted this would make Skeeter happy.

But when she turned to look at the man, he was grinning from ear to ear. "Now, Miss Gladys, you know I'm
always open to helping wherever I can."

OH, he was good.

Gladys tittered and waved a hand in front of her face.
Dakota was surprised the older woman hadn't brought
out a fan or handkerchief to fan her heated face with.

"Okay, now that that's out of the way, can we move
on? I need to know what I just signed up for." No matter
what, Dakota would do it, but she really did want to
know what she'd agreed to. The only thing she didn't
want to have to do was be in a dunk tank. Especially
since fall was upon them and it would be cold once the
festival started.

When Monday morning rolled around, Dakota was nervous. She was on her way to seeing Dr. Smythe. He was
the specialist that Megan had referred her to. She hoped

she would be learning that she had a different issue than depression. Since she'd arrived at the ranch, Dakota didn't think anyone would describe her as depressed. In fact, she'd spoken more in the last week then she had in the previous three months combined. Even Jacinta had commented on her word count just the night before.

However, today was a different story. Dakota didn't think she'd said more than three sentences since getting up and here she was stepping out of the truck and about to head into the VA hospital.

Dakota's right foot was almost numb, but her left leg wouldn't stop bobbing up and down. She couldn't stop herself. This man might have a better diagnosis for her. One that might help her recover faster. Sure, being at the ranch the past few days had made a big improvement, but she still had some issues that didn't fit with depression.

If she were being completely honest with herself, she'd realize that her problem with a diagnosis of depression was more about her pride than anything else. Depression had a very negative connotation in the Army. If anyone was thought to be clinically depressed, they were looked down on. In fact, she'd seen several people taken away with straightjackets who had been depressed, and some of the onlookers made disparaging remarks.

Clinical depression was different from a situational response, or even seasonal depression. Those types could be treated and may never come back. But someone who had been diagnosed with clinical depression was always looked down on.

She would never look down on anyone who had an illness or disease.

If this doctor wasn't nice to her, she'd go off on him. And that was probably what had her so nervous. She'd seen what can happen when someone diagnosed with depression goes off on a doctor. She had zero desire to be locked away in a padded room.

If he was ambivalent, she could deal with that. Maybe she'd even pay to go see a civilian doctor. These extra symptoms were getting worse, and she needed answers. No one else was going to advocate more for her than herself. Sure, Jacinta had done so much for her. Getting her to the ranch was huge. And Dakota already knew it was a good place to be.

But the details of her medical treatment? She'd have to be the one to stand up for herself and demand better treatment. Maybe she was depressed, and maybe it was something else. Until she got more tests, she wouldn't know. And neither would the doctors.

All the Army docs wanted to do was give her Ibuprofen or anti-depressants and call it a day. One would think that, in this day and age, the military doctors would be better. However, she did recognize that things today were much better for her than they were for those who served before her. She'd heard the horror stories from some of the old-timers at the Los Angeles VA hospital.

As her stress levels increased, she began to chew on her fingernails.

"Stop that." Megan pulled her hand away from her mouth. "Don't worry so much. Even if Dr. Smythe can't figure it out, he'll send you to someone who can."

Dakota scoffed at the thought that a VA doctor would care enough to work hard to find the real reason for her issues. But she sensed that Megan knew what she was talking about.

"Why don't we pray? You're a Christian, right?" Megan asked.

"Yeah. That would actually be nice. Thank you." The stress and worry surrounding Dakota began to lesson, as they started praying. And by the time they were done praying, it felt as though a ton of bricks had been taken off her shoulders. "That was exactly what I needed. Thank you for the reminder that God is in control. Not me, and not the doctors."

"Listen, you're here for a reason. It might be to find the right doctors, and it might be for something else. But whatever the reason, God's timing is perfect. Just keep that in mind."

Before Megan could say anything else, a nurse appeared. "Dakota Monahan?"

She stood. "That's me."

"Follow me." The nurse led her back and did the normal intake routine. But she started asking questions that no one had asked before. "Have you been exposed to any chemical agents while in service? Or even outside of service?"

"Well, I served in Iraq, so most likely yes." While Dakota hadn't been told she was exposed to anything specific, she'd heard enough rumors to know that chemical weapons were in play at times. And the temporary bases weren't the best at disposing of their environmental waste.

The nurse didn't say anything, but she wrote it down. "Do you have a family history of neurological disorders?"

"What are those?"

"Anyone in your family been diagnosed with Alzheimer's, Dementia, Parkinson's, ALS, or have strokes?" The nurse waited while Dakota thought about it.

She shook her head. "No, everyone I can think of on both sides of my family are pretty healthy." She held a hand up. "Wait, my great-grandmother on my mom's side had a heart attack when I was really little. But I think everyone else died from natural causes. Even crazy old Uncle Bob who was schizophrenic died of old age."

The nurse looked up at Dakota. "You had an uncle diagnosed with schizophrenia?"

"Well, he was a great-uncle and from what my grandma said, he did some pretty crazy drugs in his youth. I think he was even at Woodstock. Oh, the stories I could tell." Dakota thought about the time she visited him with her grandma, and he was wearing a hat made from aluminum foil because "the aliens were watching him." As a kid, that was funny. But now, she saw it for what it was, and it wasn't so funny anymore.

"Anything more on either side of your family tree?"

No one had really discussed any family history of disease, except for the two instanced Dakota had already mentioned. "None that I know of."

"Okay, the doctor will be with your shortly." When the nurse left her alone in the small exam room, Dakota began thinking about her family members. There was a distant cousin who died in a car crash, but that was it. And what was with the questions about neurological disorders?

Not sure what to think, Dakota stood up and began looking at the frames on the wall. Most were pictures. But one was of a certificate. Dr. Smythe was a neurologist who had graduated with honors from the University of Michigan. The more she thought about it, the more sense the questions made. They were probably standard questions any neurology doctor or nurse would ask.

Before she could sit back down, the door opened and in walked a nice-looking man wearing a white coat. He was probably in his fifties, maybe sixties. When he looked up from his chart, he smiled. It was the kind of smile that would make anyone feel welcome and relaxed. Dakota got a good vibe from him. She only prayed her senses were working properly.

Chapter 10

"Why is it that when you want to hear from a doctor you don't, but when you don't want them to call you, they bug you non-stop?" Skeeter paced the floor of the barn while Mike milked his cows on Monday night.

"Dude, it hasn't even been a day. She still has tests to do. It's going to take a while before she knows anything." Mike pulled on a teat with one hand and the liquid made a swooshing sound against the metal pail. Then he pulled on another. He went back and forth in time.

Eventually, Skeeter stopped his pacing and sat down on a stool, listening as the sounds of the barn quieted his soul. The horses whinnied to one another in a way that always made Skeeter think they were trying to whisper to each other. Then their tails would woosh the flies away. Outside, he could hear a few cows close by waiting for their turn to get milked. One was a little louder than the other. She probably was trying to force her way to the front of the line.

Mike had said that if the cows didn't get milked on schedule, it could hurt. Skeeter had made a joke about it hurting like when he had to pee really bad but there were women were around so he couldn't just go behind a tree. He thought it might compare, but Mike ignored him, and Sam slapped him upside the back of his head.

He probably deserved it. He always tried to push Sam's buttons to see how far he could go before Sam turned his anger on Skeeter. It was a game to him.

However, lately, he hadn't felt like being such a jerk. Jerod had said it was time for him to grow up and be a man. Until the fire, he hadn't agreed. Skeeter wasn't ready to completely hang up his fun, but maybe his idea of fun was beginning to change.

Yesterday with Dakota had been fun. He'd never enjoyed planning the events at the tree farm before. Sure, he loved to be out and about at the farm mingling with the guests, especially the pretty ones. However, he didn't think he would be flirting with all the pretty girls next week when it started.

"Do you think she'll be up for heading over to the tree farm tomorrow to get started with the set-up?" Okay, so yes. He was looking forward to spending more time with one girl in particular. But he was also looking forward to working at the tree farm. The guys who ran it were a hoot, especially Joseph Makinaw. That old man had the best stories to tell. And it never got old seeing him leave the house without his teeth in and scaring a kid or two.

He only hoped he would be as spry as Joseph when gets to his seventies.

"I don't see why not. Unless they performed some sort of surgery on her, she should be just fine." Mike didn't look away from his duty, he just kept pulling down until the cow went dry.

Once the cow was finished, Mike took her by her harness and led her out to pasture before picking out the cow that Skeeter had heard making a lot of noise. As Mike led her into the barn, she didn't stop telling him off in her own language. Typical female. She was unhappy so everyone else had to know it.

In fact, she didn't stop giving Mike what-for until he was at least one-third of the way done with her.

"Is she pregnant or something?" Skeeter motioned to the cow.

Mike stopped what he was doing and looked at the Jersey milker. They did have a Jersey bull, and while Mike had wanted a few more heads so he could make cheeses to sell at the fairs next year, he didn't think the current cow had been pastured with Custard. At least, not yet. "Why do you say that?"

"Because she's so loud. It's almost like she's screaming to the world that she's preggers and not happy about it." Skeeter slapped his thigh and laughed at his own joke.

Mike shrugged and went back to work.

"Well, if you're not gonna chat, I think I'll head inside and see if there's anything going on." With his chores done for the day, Skeeter really didn't have anything to do until dinner was ready or Dakota came home so he could find out how the appointment went.

When he walked into the kitchen to see what they were having for dinner, Dana gang pressed him into service.

"Here, I need you to skin these potatoes." Dana handed him a peeler and a five-pound bag of spuds.

"What? Why me?" It wasn't his turn to help in the kitchen. And that was one chore he always hated doing. In fact, the last time he had KP he traded with Tony and took mucking out stalls for a week instead of the kitchen chores.

"Because I need help and you're here." She put down her spatula and turned around. With the hot stove to her back, she gave Skeeter the look that said, 'either do what I say, or go to bed without dinner.' Or at least, that's what it meant on his mother when he was growing up.

"Fine, fine, no need to glare at me." Skeeter did as he was told. It turned out to be a good assignment since Dakota didn't show up until they were all seated at the table and ready to eat. The potato peeling kept his thoughts off her for a while.

But when he looked around and noticed that their potatoes still had their skins on them, he narrowed his eyes and stared at Dana. She must have read his mind because she shrugged and passed a plate to Jacinta.

It was just as Mike had told him. No news yet.

"I still have a few more tests to do. Next week I'll have to go into Missoula and get an MRI. Today I did some X-rays and blood work. Lots of blood work." Dakota made a disgusted face and looked to her arm. "I swear, the VA employs vampires who just love to take extra vials from patients for their own nefarious deeds. They might as well have taken a whole pint out of me. I counted the vials—fourteen! Who takes fourteen vials of blood?"

Blood didn't bother Skeeter. But it appeared that it did bother Arthur Landbury. The man was leaving the ranch after the fall festival for a job with North Western Energy. Even though the man only had one good eye, he could still work with power equipment. Skeeter didn't understand it all, but Arthur was an electrical engineer and really good at his job.

The man was quiet, but it looked as though he might be ready to make some noise if they didn't stop talking about blood.

A few months ago, Skeeter might have pushed the issue. But now? He didn't want to cause a scene at the dinner table. Besides, tonight's dinner of porkchops, roasted potatoes, and baked asparagus was too good to mess up. The homemade bread alone was worth ensuring that nothing ruined dinner.

"So, did the doctor give you any indication of what it might be?" Since he was going to change the subject from blood to anything else, Skeeter figured he might as well see if he could get some answers to his own questions about Dakota.

"No, not really. They asked me a ton of questions and told me the tests they were going to run, but other than that, I didn't get anything else out of them." Dakota slumped over her plate and moved the food around.

"Do you want a protein shake?" Jacinta, who was scheduled to leave in the morning, asked.

Dakota shook her head. "No, I'll eat." And she did. During the course of the dinner, once the topic moved away from her and onto the upcoming festival, she seemed to regain her appetite. Her plate was almost clean, and she even ate two slices of bread.

After dinner, they all went into the large living room where they had coffee and tea.

"What time are we heading over to the tree farm tomorrow?" Dakota was sitting with Jacinta, but she looked to Skeeter when she asked her question.

"After morning chores are done, so probably around nine. Will that work for you? Do you have any doctor appointments tomorrow?" Skeeter remembered everything she had said at dinner, but he wasn't sure if Dakota mentioned all of her appointments or just a couple.

"Nope." She shook her head. "No more doctors until next week. Thank goodness." Dakota sighed and sat back in her seat before taking a sip of hot tea. "Mmm, this is good."

"Thank you, it's one of my favorites. Peppermint." Dana smiled over the rim of her teacup.

Skeeter watched the women sip their hot tea and thought more evenings like this might be nice.

The next morning, Dakota wasn't sure what to think when Jacinta left. The woman had helped her so much. Dakota would never be able to thank her enough for all of the guidance she'd given.

At first, when she arrived at the Crooked Arrow, Dakota wasn't sure this was the right place for her. But now? So much had changed in only a few days. Somehow Jacinta knew exactly where Dakota needed to be. As she watched everyone saying their goodbyes to Jacinta, Dakota wondered if God hadn't had a hand in bringing her here.

Chapter 11

It was just as she thought it would be, and yet it wasn't.

"No corn maze?" Disappointment tinged Dakota's words. One of the fall harvest events she had been most looking forward to was the corn maze.

When she arrived at the tree farm, Cody and Daniel were waiting to greet them. The work crew consisted of Megan, Skeeter, Mike, Dixon, and Dakota. The rest of the ranch residents were back at the ranch working.

"Don't worry," Jerod had said. "We will all take turns working the fair once it starts. Until then, you five will be on set-up duty and the rest of us will continue with our ranch chores here."

Dakota thought Jerod sounded like he wasn't too happy with staying behind, but maybe that was her own opinion. If she'd had to stay at the ranch and miss all that the Christmas Tree Farm had to offer, she would have been bummed. Instead, she put on a smile and told Jerod she'd see him later.

But after the disappointment of not seeing a corn field, maybe Jerod had the right idea.

"Why isn't there a corn field? Do you at least have a pumpkin patch?" Dakota really hoped she didn't sound condescending or even ungrateful. The place was amazing. She knew that when Christmas and snow arrived, it would truly be a winter wonderland.

Cody only laughed and shook his head. "This is only our second year for the fall festival. Traditionally, this has only been a Christmas tree farm. But we had to diversify." He looked to a beautiful woman with dirty blond hair and smiled.

She walked up next to Cody and kissed his cheek. "Good morning, handsome."

Cody wrapped an arm around her waist. "Sadie, we have a new helper from the Crooked Arrow." He motioned to Dakota. "This is Dakota. She's new to Montana. Dakota, this is my wife, Sadie, the savior of our farm. If she hadn't come to us two years ago, I would have lost our family farm by now."

"Oh, stop. No, you wouldn't have." Sadie shook her head as pink began to show on her cheeks. "He would have figured it out. Maybe not as fast, but he would have."

"Well, however it happened, I'm really excited about a good, old-fashioned fall harvest festival. I've never been to one on a real farm before." Dakota felt like she was a kid experiencing a festival for the first time. She even had butterflies in her stomach.

"Dakota asked about a corn maze. Was that on the plans for next year? Or the one after that?" Cody tugged his wife closer to him.

It was obvious to anyone with eyes that the couple were still newlyweds, and very happy to boot.

"I was thinking two more years, but if you think a corn maze would go over well, I don't see why we can try it next year." Sadie took a notebook out of her bag and made some notes. "We do have a maze this year, it's just made from a lot of haybales. That should still be fun, don't you think?" She directed her question to Dakota.

Dakota bit her lower lip and nodded. "I think any sort of maze will be a blast. I'm from Southern California and we always had mazes made from hay. They were short and easy to figure out, but that was only because of space. Everyone still loved it."

A slow grin passed over Daniel's face. "I think you'll find that our maze isn't small, and it's going to take you a while to figure out." A look passed between Daniel and Skeeter.

Dakota wondered what that was all about.

"Come on, Skeeter, let's set up the maze." Daniel motioned for Skeeter to follow him.

The man hesitated, looked at Dakota, then grinned. "Just wait and see what we have planned. Daniel and I have been working on this for a few weeks now."

"Why don't the rest of us get started with decorating the booths and the food court area." Sadie led the rest to the space they had roped off.

When the day was over, Dakota asked herself for the millionth time why she thought helping to set up for a fall harvest festival on a real, honest to goodness farm would be a good idea. There wasn't a single muscle or tendon in her entire body that didn't ache.

She didn't feel this badly after her first day in Iraq, or even after her last day. Although, to be fair, her last day in country did end with her on some pretty good pain killers. She had, after all, been in a Humvee accident. This day, while difficult, didn't require pain pills. No, this day called for an Epsom salt bath before dinner.

The next day on the farm was a lot more fun. It was more like what she had hoped for. When they arrived at the farm, Daniel approached Dakota. "Hey there, wanna give our maze a try? See if you can make it through?"

Skeeter stood behind her and his chuckle made her turn around.

"What? Do you have monsters and vampires coming out to scare people?" While it was a fall harvest festival, it wasn't exactly a Halloween fair. Or at least, Dakota didn't think it was.

"Not vampires." The cheeky grin Skeeter gave her made Dakota wonder what would be coming out at her in the maze.

"Actually, until the weekend, we don't have any workers in the maze. Today, I just need you to try it and see how easy it is to figure out." Daniel frowned at Skeeter.

"Did he just give something away? Will you have workers jumping out at people?" The idea kinda intrigued Dakota, but she wasn't sure how she felt about it. At least, not yet.

"I guess you'll just have to try it out this weekend." Skeeter headed toward the beginning of the maze.

Dakota couldn't believe how long it took her to find the end. She kept getting lost and then wound up at dead-ends. But some of those dead-ends had little stands in them. If this was Hollywood, she was sure there'd be talking heads or something sitting in those spots. Now, with the exit in sight, she grinned and headed that way.

"Ah!" She screamed when a hand grabbed her from the side. A side she thought was fully covered by hay bales. "What? Who?" She put a hand to her heart and looked around. The hand had snaked out and grabbed her arm, then disappeared. "Who's there?"

There weren't many workers on the farm yet, so it had to be someone she knew. The only problem was she didn't see where the hand could have come from. Dakota put her hand on the hay bales and moved it around, looking for a weak spot, or a hole. But there was nothing except a seven-foot-tall wall of hay. In fact, the entire maze was at least seven feet tall.

It wasn't until she looked up did she find out what it was. On an elaborate contraption hanging over the side of the hay was a scary hand. She reached up and grabbed it. Then she laughed when she felt the fake latex fingers and cringed. It was cold and clammy. "Oooh, gross."

"What?"

Dakota jumped when she heard the deep, gravelly voice behind her. Hand to her chest again, she turned around to see Skeeter dressed up in tattered overalls and holding a chainsaw. When she looked closer, she noticed that the chain was missing. "Oh my gosh. Is that what I think it is?"

Skeeter sneered and showed off blackened teeth. "If you think it's the object of your demise, then yes. Yes, it is."

She laughed and checked out Skeeter's entire costume. "This is fantastic! Will you do this all day long?" While she loved it, she wasn't too sure most young kids would.

"No, it's only for Friday and Saturday nights. We're going for an older audience on the weekends. There will be fair rides each night, and even a concert over Halloween weekend." Cody had walked up and was checking out Skeeter's costume. "I really like what you've done. Great job."

"Thanks, boss." The young cowboy stood taller and grinned, again showing off the blackened teeth.

"Oh." Cody leaned back. "That's fantastic."

Dakota tilted her head. "Will there be enough people who will want a haunted maze? I mean, no offense, but this is a small town."

Cody and Skeeter exchanged smiles.

"People come from all over to experience the festivals and fairs we put on here. And since we're so close to a couple of the larger cities in Montana, the teens and college kids come. I think we're the only one in Montana doing something like this. At least for the fall and Halloween season. There are other harvest fairs, and some farms do a few things, but nothing on this scale." Skeeter turned off the chainsaw and set it down.

"Plus," Cody added, "we are allowing people to pick out their Christmas trees early. They can pick out their tree and, with a small down payment, we'll mark it as sold."

"While I love the idea, what happens when someone comes through who wants a sold tree? Where I'm from, quite a few people would think nothing of taking a sold sign off and putting their own on it." Dakota would never do that, but she had known a few people who wouldn't even blink at the dishonesty.

"Each of our trees are numbered and listed in a log. Once someone puts their tag on a tree, we mark our logbook. When they come to pick up their tree, we double check it's the correct one." Cody seemed to be pleased with his procedure.

Dakota thought it was great. "I can't wait to see what happens when the fair opens. I noticed there's multiple pumpkin carving tables and lots of booths for people to sell their crafts and other homemade goods. Where will the carnival be set up?"

Skeeter took her shoulders and moved her so that she could see a large open space. "The carnival will set up here and basically stay until New Year's Day. We'll have some downtime in between holidays, but the carnival will operate every weekend from now until the end of the year. Locals as well as others will come just for the rides and fair food even if there isn't a big festival."

"That's really cool. Every day I find more reasons to be happy I'm here." Dakota smiled from ear to ear and rubbed her hands together. It was like she had turned back the hands of time and was getting a chance to be a kid all over again. This time, instead of having to make do with city fairs, she was going to be spending most of her time at a real, downhome country event. Or 'events', as it really was.

"Come on, I'll show you a few other things we have going on here." Skeeter put his hand out for Dakota, and she took it.

They spent the next hour walking around the grounds, checking out the Christmas trees and the different spots where the fair would be set up, as well as where some of the other events would go.

"This is where we'll set up a stage right before the concert." Skeeter pointed to a spot next the barn. Then he led her inside the barn. "And here we'll have a petting zoo for little kids. And just outside in the small corral, we'll have a few goats for kids of all ages to pet and feed."

They walked around and Dakota noted the variety of animals they had. "Will you guys do that thing I've seen on TV for kids at rodeos?"

"What thing?" Skeeter asked.

"You know, where the kids ride sheep."

"Oh." Skeeter laughed and shook his head. "Have you ever seen mutton busting in person?"

"Mutton busting? Is that what it's called?" She scrunched her nose. "Makes it sound like they're preparing for bull riding when they grow up."

"Some will ride bulls. Other will ride busting broncs. And some will become team roping stars." Skeeter leaned up against the rails of the corral and put his thumbs through his belt loops. "But we won't have mutton busting, not now anyway. A rodeo will come through in the spring, and that's where the kids will get their chance at being a rodeo star."

"Have you ever done any of it?" While Dakota didn't know much about Skeeter, she knew he was a cowboy. Or at least, he looked like a cowboy. For all she knew, he was a city slicker like her who'd come to the ranch and only recently learned how to be a cowboy.

He flashed his pearly whites. "Maybe." Then he flicked the brim of his cowboy hat and walked away.

"Hm." Skeeter was starting to grow on her.

Chapter 12

"**I** can't believe the transformation." Dakota looked around the tree farm, or rather, the fall harvest farm, with wide eyes. The past few days had been tough, but also great. She had worked so hard that she slept like a baby. If she could sleep this well all the time, maybe she wouldn't be depressed. Part of her problem had been lack of sleep. But now? Sleep was good.

Dakota couldn't help but grin when she thought about the different places around the farm. This upcoming weekend would be a soft opening, as Cody called it. They didn't have the official opening for another week, but all locals knew about it and would show up. It would give the farm a chance to iron out any kinks they might have before the masses showed up, whatever that meant.

This was Montana, not California. Dakota couldn't imagine the place being crowded. At least not by California standards. But when she looked around and saw all of the supplies stored in the booths and around the farm, an inkling of doubt crept in. Could that many people really show up to a remote Montana farm to celebrate the fall harvest?

While she wouldn't have traveled from California to attend this specific event, she would have been willing driven a few hours to get to something like it.

"Pretty cool, huh?" Dana grinned and put her hands on her hips. She surveyed the area around them and watched as people from not only Frenchtown but also the surrounding areas worked hard to finish the set-up for the festival. That night would be the first of the Harvest Festival After Dark, the time they'd designed to appeal to older teens and adults. While they didn't sell alcohol on the premises, they would have plenty of food and other drinks on hand, as well as more of a Halloween vibe.

Skeeter walked up already in costume and holding his chainsaw, sans dangerous blade and chain. In place of the metal blade that would normally be used was a plastic piece that only looked like a real blade. "I wish I could use the blood packs on the teens when I get them in the maze."

With a hand over her mouth to cover her laugh, Dakota shook her head. "Sometimes I wonder about you, Skeeter."

Innocent eyes looked back her, but the rest of the crazy cowboy looked like a real Montana Chainsaw Killer. "Who? Me? I'm fine. I worry about you."

Dana chuckled. "Skeeter, I think everyone worries about you. But I guess if you were all grown up, then we wouldn't have the perfect person for scaring the teens when they get here."

"I think I should be offended by that comment, but I'm not." When Skeeter grinned, his blackened teeth sent shivers down Dakota's spine.

"You know, I think I prefer a daytime hay maze." Dakota gulped and turned her gaze back to the craft booths. "Do they really sell enough to make this worthwhile?"

Dana nodded. "Oh, yes. Most will make enough over the rest of the year to help them have a great Christmas and even have enough to supplement their income next year." She looked around and lowered her voice. "Plus, it keeps the older residents busy and gives them joy."

Dakota thought about that for a moment. "It's important to stay busy and have a purpose no matter your age."

"True," Dana agreed.

"My purpose is to make everyone happy." When Skeeter smiled again, his blackened teeth on full display, the girls couldn't help but laugh along with him. Or was it at him?

"Well, I think you're on your way to accomplishing your goal." It was strange, Dakota didn't think she would fit in here at first. But now, she couldn't imagine being anywhere else. This crazy group of wounded vets were turning out to be the healing balm her soul needed.

Maybe God really was in control.

Later that night, everyone was in place and waiting for the festival to open. Dakota couldn't stop biting her nails.

"Stop that." Dana pulled Dakota's hand away from her face. "Are you nervous?"

Dakota wiped her hands on her jeans and grimaced. "I haven't been around crowds since coming here, so I'm not sure what to expect."

Dana tilted her head. "Weren't there a lot of patients at the Los Angeles VA Hospital where you stayed?"

Dakota nodded. "But it was different. They weren't rowdy or..." Her hands flew in the air, and she sighed. "I've heard that people with PTSD can, um, have trouble with large crowds that are loud and boisterous."

"Oh." Dana rubbed a hand over her face. "Do you suffer from PTSD?"

With a quick shake of her head, Dakota said, "no, not that I know of. May main issue is depression, or so the doctors say. But I hear that sometimes a person doesn't really know it's a problem until it is."

"Ah, yes." Dana nodded her head. She'd seen it before. "Well, why don't you stick close to me and if you don't like what's going on, I can take you back to the ranch."

"Thanks." Dakota screwed up her lips and prayed that God would give her strength. She didn't want to be a chicken. Scratch that thought. Dakota knew that people with PTSD weren't chickens, but she felt like she would be if she couldn't handle the night. There was something about being weak and showing it that really bothered her.

Dakota was a strong woman, wasn't she? Why was she letting this bother her? Crowds had never been an issue for her before her accident. But now? Well, she wasn't certain how she was going to feel. Everything she'd heard was that most people didn't realize they suffered from PTSD until a trigger hit them. Would it be the same for her?

When six o'clock came and went, Dakota still wasn't certain how she felt. So, to ensure she didn't have any problems, she stayed close to Dana and the food booths. Most of the crafters stayed home that night, only a few who sold cool jewelry that teen girls would like showed up. And they were busy. Busier than Dakota thought possible.

"What's going on here? Are all the girls here shopping while the guys go through the haunted maze?" When Dakota was younger, she would have gone through the maze, not shopped.

Dana chuckled. "The girls love the earrings that Mrs. Baxter makes. She comes from one town over and only sells them here. I tried to tell her she should open an online store, but she scoffed at the idea of online shopping. She said that nothing sells a pair of earrings or a necklace like trying them on."

"I can't blame her. I usually don't like what I buy online and nine times out of ten return it." Dakota looked out at the booths and wondered if she should go and look at what the local women had made.

Dakota asked, "have you looked over the booths yet?" Without looking at Dana, Dakota began walking toward the jewelry section.

One vendor made personalized leather bracelets, but not the simple ones where she tapped a thing on the band to put the name on it. Instead, she used multiple strands of leather that had already been dyed different colors. Then she added beads that the customer chose. And if someone wanted it, she could also use the alphabet beads to put a name on the bracelet.

"Oh, I love Mrs. Thunderhawk. She makes the best bracelets. And have you seen her necklaces?" Dana headed right for the elderly Native American woman who had long, gray hair pulled back into a thick braid hanging all the way down her back.

"Dana, so good to see you. Who's your friend?" The older Native American woman clasped her hands in front of her and gave a closed-mouth smile to the ladies.

Dana put her hand out and motioned to Dakota. "Dakota, this is Mrs. Thunderhawk. She used to teach home economics at the high school. Her sweet potato pie is to die for."

While sweet potatoes weren't really Dakota's thing, she did know how to be polite. "Nice to meet you, Mrs. Thunderhawk. Will your sweet potato pie be a part of the town's Thanksgiving meal?" One of the things that had warmed Dakota to the tiny hamlet of Frenchtown was the many stories about the upcoming Thanksgiving meal the entire town shared together. Everyone who came brought something they were famous for.

"I bring three pies every year." The older woman nodded, then motioned to her table full of beautiful jewelry. "I also make all of this jewelry myself. No hired labor or massive machines. It's all handmade with love."

"And if you're lucky, she'll even put a Salish blessing on it." Dana winked at Mrs. Thunderhawk.

Before the Indian woman could respond, Skeeter walked up, hamming it up with his fake chainsaw and moaning.

Dakota rolled her eyes and squeezed her lips together. The last thing she wanted was to let Skeeter know he was funny. She didn't know how, but this silly cowboy was starting to get under her skin. She'd always thought he was cute, but at first she felt awkward around him. And maybe even a little uncomfortable with his flirting.

But his childish antics were fun. He wasn't really boyfriend material, but he was cute and enjoyable to be around. Maybe he could be a great friend? Dakota wasn't really sure what she wanted from him, but he did make her laugh. And that was a very good thing.

Chapter 13

Boy howdy did Dakota look sweet in her tight jeans, button up shirt, and borrowed cowgirl boots. Skeeter knew she didn't have her own boots and that Dana had loaned her a pair until she could get some. The woman was starting to look like a real cowgirl. Now all she needed was a hat. Shoot, even a straw hat would be nice on Dakota.

Skeeter had to rein in his thoughts. Jerod had made it very clear that he wasn't to flirt with her or ask her out, especially if he wanted to stay at the ranch until he found a job. Now more than ever he wanted to stick close to Frenchtown. So, he decided to do what any self-respecting goofball would.

Make the girl laugh.

"Ahhh, fresh meat." Skeeter held up his makeshift chainsaw and widened his eyes while showing off his menacing blackened teeth. Slowly, ever so slowly, so as not to spook them too much, he inched closer to Dakota and Dana revving the tiny engine on his chainsaw. It sounded more like a toy than an actual machine. Taking off the chain and replacing the metal blade really changed the sound.

But it worked.

Both girls started squealing, and old Mrs. Thunderhawk grinned. It took a lot to get the old lady to smile, so Skeeter felt as though he had done his job for the night.

"You know, it's not nice to scare the spirits around all hallow's eve." The old woman arched a brow and took a step back from the group. "I think you should move along."

Behind Skeeter, a group of teenaged girls watched the antics with wide eyes. A couple of them covered their mouths, pointed at Skeeter, and giggled. He could feel their penetrating gazes, and without warning, he turned around and growled loudly.

The crowd of teenagers squealed and ran away screaming. Skeeter couldn't help himself—he gave chase.

"You know, this reminds me of one of the local amusement parks back home at Halloween. Such good times." Dakota sighed and looked off into the distance, remembering a time when being chased by men in costumes was the most exciting thing she'd ever experienced.

For Skeeter's part, this was the most fun he could remember having in forever. All night long, teenagers, both boys and girls, sought him out. It seemed the local high schoolers enjoyed a good Halloween fright. It was still several weeks away from Halloween, but if the soft opening was anything to go by, the Harvest Festival After Dark was going to be a success.

Skeeter hoped he would be around next year to participate.

As midnight drew closer, Skeeter found himself in the maze chasing kids the wrong way and laughing when they bumped into each other. One even knocked over the display of heads at a dead-end trying to escape him.

All in all, the night was a true success. When the place finally closed, Skeeter found himself counting down the time until the festival opened again. "That was such a blast! Don't you think?"

Dakota had been helping Dana with crowd control and taking tickets for the maze once they'd finished looking over the different booths. She had seen first-hand how much fun Skeeter'd had. "I don't think anyone had as much fun as you did."

"I think one of the football players even peed his pants!" Dana laughed so hard, she had to bend over to catch her breath.

"Yeah, that was great, wasn't it? But he didn't pee his pants. He dropped his soda on the front of his jeans. And his friends decided to tease him the rest of the night." With a huge cheese-eating grin displaying his scary teeth, Skeeter slapped his thigh and chuckled.

"Once word gets out about how great tonight went, I think we're going to be inundated the rest of the month with high schoolers and probably college kids. This is looking to be so much bigger than I thought it would be."

Dakota couldn't believe she'd never been to something this exciting before. She took a drink of her bottled water and followed Skeeter and Dana back to the ranch van.

"Hey, are you guys as wired as I am? I don't think I'll be able to sleep the rest of the night." Skeeter bounced on the balls of his feet and looked around for something to do. "Let's go get some coffee, or ice cream. Or both?"

Dakota shook her head and laughed. "I am about ready to pass out. And we get to do this all over again tomorrow. I need my beauty sleep."

Under his voice, Skeeter responded, "Not from where I'm standing."

Dakota turned toward him. "Hm? Sorry, I didn't catch that."

He waved a hand. "Oh, it was nothing. What time does your shift start tomorrow?"

"I think I'm expected to be here again by four o'clock. What about you?" Dakota asked.

"Same." Skeeter looked to Dana. "What about you? And the rest of the gang?"

Dana hadn't been paying them much attention. She had hoped to let Skeeter get some time with Dakota since the two of them seemed to be getting along so well. "Me? Oh, I'm coming back with Jerod at ten when it opens back up."

"We won't be working together tomorrow?" Dakota furrowed her brows, and Skeeter thought she looked sad about not spending more time with Dana.

He hadn't realized how close the two women had become in such a short time. But that was probably good. Dakota was the only female resident at the ranch. She would need other women. While Megan was great, she was the camp counselor. A friendship with Megan wasn't really in the cards for Dakota.

"Don't worry, you won't be alone." Dana grinned and looked between Dakota and Skeeter.

Unsure of what she meant, Skeeter arched a brow and was about to ask. But Mike and Jerod showed up in the van to get them before he could.

"So, how did tonight go?" Jerod had parked the van next to the exit gate and got out to greet his wife. He kissed her cheek, then smiled at the rest.

"Really great. I think Nelly should bring some of her dogs out here for training." The look Dana gave Skeeter sent chills down his spine. "I'd love to see how they react to Skeeter and the other ghouls."

He held a hand up. "Ah, I for one, think that's a bad idea. Maybe during the day would work better."

"What's the matter? Afraid Spike or one of the others might try to take a bite out of you?" Jerod joked.

"Hey, don't joke about that." Skeeter shivered. "Those dogs are serious."

"Wait, I thought service dogs weren't aggressive?" Dakota furrowed her brows and looked around at everyone.

Mike said, "They aren't aggressive. Jerod was just teasing Skeeter. He's not the biggest fan of the dogs."

"Right, and they don't seem to really care for him, either." Jerod laughed and patted Skeeter on the back. "Don't worry, they wouldn't really attack you."

"Unless they felt threatened." Dana grinned from ear to ear. Apparently, she wanted in on the ribbing as well.

"Dogs are the best." Dakota tilted her head. "Let me guess, you're more of cat person?"

"More like a barn cat person." Mike laughed and moved to give Skeeter room on the bench seat.

Skeeter slid in and glared at Mike. "You know I don't care for the mousers either." He made a disgusted face, almost like he was envisioning the cats going after the mice.

"Oh, I don't know. I think mousers are cute." A slow smile spread across Dakota's face. "I mean, come one. They work hard. And their work feeds them, too."

"Gross. Not you, too." With one hand on his stomach, and the other covering his mouth, Skeeter looked more like he was going to be sick then he did a scary, crazy chainsaw killer.

Everyone teased Skeeter the rest of the way home. But he didn't mind. As long as Dakota was smiling at him, they could tease him all he wanted.

Chapter 14

Sunday morning dawned bright for everyone at the Crooked Arrow Ranch. The soft opening at the Harvest Festival After Dark, in addition to the regular daytime Harvest Festival, had everyone in great spirits, if not a little tired. The festival would be closed on Monday, but the ranch was going to be busy with catch-up work.

Church was first up, and all the residents were looking forward to the assistant pastor preaching today.

"You know, Pastor Mason hasn't had a chance to preach on a Sunday morning in quite some time. I can't wait to see how he does." Jerod popped a piece of bacon in his mouth while the rest of the men at the table nodded and gobbled up their breakfast.

"Who's Pastor Mason?" Dakota looked around. The weekend before, when she had attended the Baptist church in town for the first time, it was an elderly man who had kind eyes and a knowing look whenever he glanced her way.

"He's the youth minister. He also preaches for our Senior Pastor whenever he's gone. This week he's speaking at a conference in Kalispell." After putting his fork down, Skeeter went on to tell Dakota about the youth minister and how he also coached baseball at the local high school.

"Wow, sounds like this guy's pretty busy." Back home, Dakota went to one of those mega churches where they had multiple pastors who each focused on one thing. Sure, any of the pastors would step in and preach the Sunday sermon if the head pastor was gone, but he didn't take too much time away. He was a self-proclaimed homebody.

So, when Dakota sat down in a middle pew and looked around, she wasn't too surprised to see a youngish man stepping up to the podium. The youth minister looked to be in his late twenties or early thirties. He had a nice smile and was good looking. Although, she really shouldn't have noticed that since she also noticed he wore a wedding ring.

The young pastor was tall and had curly brown hair that touched the top of his collar. He looked like the quintessential cowboy in his blue jeans, blue and black checkered button up shirt, and brown cowboy boots. If they weren't inside the church, he'd probably be wearing a Stetson and look like he belonged in some sort of country-western magazine.

When Pastor Mason stepped up to the podium, she was ready to focus on the message God had given him. She always found something interesting in the sermon, something she could apply to her life. But, for some reason, this sermon hit her hard.

"Open your Bibles to Philippians chapter four." Pastor Mason cleared his throat and took a drink of water as everyone found the book and chapter. "It's strange, but God gave me this sermon a few weeks ago. Normally, pastors keep a sermon stashed away for when they're called up to preach at the last minute. I thought this would be that sermon. I knew that Pastor John would be away this week, and I had something else planned. But God told me to use this one." He smiled at the congregation who looked on as he told his story.

"You see, God knows exactly what you need to hear, and when you need to hear. As a pastor, I may not always know in advance what I'm supposed to say, but God never lets me down. He always guides me and gives me exactly what I need to do His work." The pastor paused for a moment to let his words sink in. "Today, this message is one God told me to deliver at the last minute. So, pay close attention. God might have intended this message for you."

When the pastor looked directly at Dakota, she felt a tingle of excitement slowly creep up her spine and she wondered if God changed the course of today for her. But why would he? She was no one. Just a wounded veteran who no longer knew where she belonged. Or even what was wrong with her.

As the pastor began reading from Philippians, a curious thing happened to Dakota. Her heart began to open to the Word of God, and she slowly began to let go of all of her worries and fears.

"Rejoice in the Lord always; and again I say, Rejoice. Let your moderation be known unto all men. The Lord is at hand. Be careful for nothing; but in every thing by prayer and supplication with thanksgiving let your requests be made known unto God. And the peace of God, which passeth all understanding, shall keep your hearts and minds through Christ Jesus." – Philippians 4:4-7 KJV

The pastor made it sound so simple. But Dakota never thought peace was a simple thing. Rejoicing? Sure, she could almost always find something to rejoice about. But the peace that passed all understanding eluded her. No matter how much she prayed and asked God for that peace, it never came. No matter how many hours she spent each week reading her Bible, it still didn't come. So how could she get this peace if prayer and reading didn't bring it about?

This was one sermon that had Dakota rooted to her spot and kept her attention. One would think that was an easy thing, but it wasn't. Too many times as she sat in church other things would cross her mind and she'd start to think about something she had forgotten to do, or something that happened in the past—good or bad. She'd listen to a preacher's message, but she often had a difficult time staying focused.

Not today.

Today, every bit of her focus was on the preacher and his message, so much so that she didn't even notice when Skeeter kept looking at her. He sat next to her and occasionally smiled at her, but Dakota never gave him a thought.

"People, praying alone is good, but it isn't always enough. When you need something and God hasn't provided it, go to him humbly and make your request known. But don't just ask for something. You also need to be thankful for what you have." Pastor Mason looked around the room. "Most of us just ask for stuff. Like little kids, we are almost always fixated on what we want. But what does God want for us? Or from us?"

Sitting there, Dakota wanted to raise her hand and ask that very question. But she knew the pastor would get around to finishing the thought.

The youth pastor moved away from the stand, holding his Bible, and walked to the side of the pulpit. When he looked out at the congregation, Dakota noticed that everyone was focused on him.

"When was the last time you thanked God for what you have? Are you even thankful for the life you have now? For the home you have, or the family? Or—and here's a big one—are you thankful for your current job, or are you unhappy and grumble to God about it whenever you pray?"

A few of the people chuckled, and Dakota noticed one person two rows in front of her looking down. Did he feel as guilty as she did? Most of her prayers lately had been about what she wanted and complaining about not getting it. Occasionally, she'd thank God for something. When she first got home from Iraq, she did thank God for bringing her back alive. But that thought didn't last long. As more and more issues began to surface, she complained more and thanked God less.

By the end of the sermon, Dakota was bound and determined to thank God for everything she had, even the little things. Thinking back to the Los Angeles VA hospital, she was lucky. Or was she blessed? Was luck tied to blessings? She'd never thought that before, but what if they were the same thing? The idea that luck came from God had her reeling for a moment, then she pulled her thoughts back to the subject at hand.

God had blessed her by sending her to the Crooked Arrow Ranch. It sure didn't seem like it at first, but she'd not had anywhere this much fun since she her first day in Iraq. Though life wasn't just about having fun, it was needed at times.

When she got home that afternoon, some of the first things she gave thanks for were all the new friends she had made. These were godly people who understood her and understood what she'd gone through in a way no one else could. Not even her own family got it. Forget about her high school or college friends. They'd never understand what it was like to be driving in the deserts of Iraq and fear an ambush or IED around every corner.

Dakota also gave thanks that she had all her limbs. And that she was in better shape than most of the guys who came to the ranch for help. Not that it was a contest or anything. But God had spared her from a lot. When she thought back to what might have happened, she shivered. The horror stories about women soldiers who'd been kidnapped and tortured gave her nightmares.

She really did have a lot to be thankful for.

Chapter 15

Skeeter watched Dakota as she did her chores. Somehow, they'd both been assigned to work in the barn on Monday. While they weren't doing chores side by side, they were close enough that he could watch her. And not in one of those creepy ways like on horror movies. No, he was keeping an eye on Dakota so that he could make sure she was alright.

After church on Sunday, Skeeter noted that Dakota had been more quiet than usual. Not that she was the sort to talk a mile a minute, like him. But she had been opening up the past few days. It was almost as though she was going back into herself. But she did smile.

When Dakota smiled, the sun shone, and the birds chirped. Yeah, Skeeter was a sap. What could he say, he was the kind of guy who loved to watch romance movies with chicks. Mostly because they enjoyed them so much and he'd get a chance to spend more time with women he was interested in. And they always went so mushy when he said he liked to watch chick flicks.

Nine times out of ten, he'd also get a whopper of a goodnight kiss after one of those movies. So, it was worth it in the end. Eventually, he began picking up on the lingo that women seemed to love and used it to his advantage. Hey, don't mock him. In this day and age, men need as much help as possible to impress a lady. And nothing's wrong with hoping to get a kiss out of it in the end. He was a gentleman, and never forced the kisses. Usually, they went in first. Who was he to say no to a pretty gal?

His momma raised him right. He opened doors for them, put his hand on the small of their backs, and never said no to a goodnight kiss. Plus, he'd call them within two days, instead of the normal five days most guys thought was appropriate. And if he really liked a girl, he'd send her flowers and call her the day after a date. Though that was rare.

While he wasn't ready to settle down, he did enjoy spending time with the ladies. He was clear about the fact that nothing could get serious. Which was why he usually enjoyed dating the women who came to town to visit the area. There was one local girl he liked a lot, but her daddy wasn't too keen on him, so it didn't last long. Which was alright with Skeeter. Especially now that Dakota was here.

Although, she was off limits. But that wouldn't last long. As soon as he got a job in the area, he'd ask her out. Until then, he'd focus on being friends and helping her adjust. Which was why he was keeping a close eye on her that day.

Every time he was about to worry about her, she smiled. And not the obligatory kind that never reached the eyes. No, her smiles were full of joy and sunshine. And considering that it was an overcast day, her radiant smiles were more than welcome for his parched eyes.

The lunch bell rang, and Skeeter put his rake to the side. "So, how's it going with the horses?"

Dakota had been assigned the task of bathing them all and ensuring their tails and manes were glistening. "At first, I wasn't sure what I was doing. And when Star rolled all over the ground after I had just finished washing and brushing him, I about had a heart attack."

Skeeter chuckled. "Didn't anyone tell you about horses and how they love to roll around after they get bathed?"

She pursed her lips and glared at him.

"Ah, I take it that's a no?" He grinned, knowing full well that no one had explained it. Washing horses with no real direction, other than what soap to use, was just part of the welcome all new residents received.

Without a backward glance, Dakota headed for the house and lunch.

"Wait up. What happened with Star? Did you have to wash him again?" Skeeter knew the answer, but he didn't want her to know he'd been watching her all morning.

She continued to ignore him, and he just laughed. Dakota was fun to tease. While he hoped they would eventually be an item, he was going to enjoy the time they had as friends. Once the kissing started, he wouldn't do anything to ruin it or get her mad at him. The last thing he wanted was for her to cut him off from her lips.

A sharp pang hit him in his gut as he thought about those luscious lips. The way she smelled after a shower and put on her frou-frou soaps and lotions was enough to drive any man insane. Maybe it was a good thing dating wasn't allowed between the residents. He'd never get anything done if he could spend his days kissing her, holding her hands, or staring into her beautiful brown eyes and counting the green specks. He'd bet the number would change with her moods. That was something he really wanted to see.

Shoot, he just wanted to get to know everything about her. "Hey, what's your favorite food?" The question came from nowhere. He hadn't consciously thought to ask her.

Dakota stopped at the threshold to the back door of the ranch house and turned around. When she put her hands on her hips and narrowed her eyes, Skeeter wondered if he'd done something wrong.

"Why do you want to know?"

Uh-oh. He'd been caught without an answer. He stumbled over his words and then a thought hit him. "Because, with the fair here, we have a ton of options. I was just wondering if there was something at the fall festival that might catch your eye." He paused and waited, but she continued to glare at him. Then he pointed to his chest. "Me? I love the fried pickles and the chicken tenders. The sauce is out of this world."

Dakota took a deep breath and let it out slowly. "I only like fried pickle chips when they have the spicy ranch dip."

He had her, and he knew it. But she had him too, with the talk about dipping fried pickle chips into the southwest ranch dressing. It was enough to make his mouth water. "Oh, that's the best, isn't it? I know just the booth to go to. Tomorrow, when we're back there, I'll show you the best one."

She snorted and turned around to enter the house. By the time they made it to the dining room, they were the last ones to sit.

True to his word, when they arrived Tuesday afternoon at the tree farm, now dubbed the Fall Festival Farm, Skeeter walked Dakota over to the Hidden Valley Fried Pickle booth. The owners used actual Hidden Valley Ranch dressing. They had both plain and southwest types. But the only kind that did it for Skeeter was the Southwest Chipotle with the savory tastes of the chipotle chili and added southwest flavors. His mouth wouldn't stop watering until he put the first fried pickle chip into his mouth.

"Mm, this is the best. How do they do it?" Dakota moaned around a mouthful of pickle and dip.

Skeeter shook his head. "I don't know, but I've tried the stuff in the grocery store, and it just isn't the same.

I even tried the Hidden Valley Ranch brand. Still not right."

"That's because we have a secret ingredient." The cashier winked at Skeeter. She was pretty, and had the type of long, silky hair that he loved. But, somehow, he was more interested in the food than the girl. Which would have him questioning his manhood later that night. He'd figure out why the pretty cashier didn't catch his attention, but it would be a little while.

"Okay," Dakota licked the sauce from her fingers and looked at Skeeter once she'd finished her boat of fried pickles. "What's on the agenda for us tonight?"

"We're both going to work the maze and the surrounding area. I got you a costume." The evil glint of his eyes had Dakota worried about what she'd gotten herself into.

"Please, no. I'm not like you. I don't do well with that sort of thing. I mean, I like to see it, sure. But I can't be outgoing like you." The fear in her eyes was real and Skeeter worried he might have gone too far.

"Hey, it's alright. You're just going to be like my sidekick. That's all. You don't have to say anything if you don't want to. Just act afraid." He had planned to make her essentially the quintessential young woman who always died in the slasher movies—the kind who wants to run into a dark cemetery while being chased by the bad guy, or the one who runs toward the killer's house instead of a car where she can drive away.

Skeeter never thought it would be an issue for her. Sure, she'd been kinda shy at first, but he thought that was because she had moved into a house full of soldiers she didn't know. He never thought she might be shy with everyone.

She rubbed her hands in front of her. "Look, I want to help. Maybe I can take tickets like over the weekend? Or I can put my hand through a hay wall? Something where people won't really see me?"

Using the end of the dull, plastic blade of the chainsaw, Skeeter scratched under his chin. "Well, I suppose you could find corners to hide behind and then jump out once someone passes you. They wouldn't exactly see you, but they'd hear you scream. You just can't touch anyone. But if you jump right behind them and scream, that should work."

While he knew it would work, Skeeter had hoped she'd be by his side all night and they could work together scaring kids. That was the best part, making the kids run with fear. They knew it wasn't real, but it was enough to get their adrenaline going and their fight or flight response would almost always be to run. He thought it was funny.

It felt like one giant prank all night long.

She bit her lower lip. "I, ah, I suppose I could try it. I don't need a costume for that, right?"

He narrowed his eyes. "Is it talking to strangers or wearing a costume that bothers you?"

Dakota answered without any hesitation. "Both."

"Okay, how about no costume. And you let me chase your around a little bit? Then I can veer off when I see a couple of kids who are itching for a good scaring? That could be a lot of fun. You won't have to say anything, except maybe scream a little. Most eyes will be on me, not you." It was a compromise, but one that would still keep her close and give them a chance to bond over the hilarity of the kids' fear.

Dakota sucked her lips in, and Skeeter could see the wheels churning behind her eyes. She was really considering this. He crossed his fingers and hoped she'd say yes.

"You know, next year they should seriously consider doing a maze or haunted house where they play out some of the scenes from the Book of Revelation. I think that might be scarier." And with that, Dakota followed Skeeter to where he'd change his outfit. She waited outside while he prepared for being the Chainsaw Killer.

Chapter 16

Dakota stood next to the changing room in the barn. It was actually a tack room, but it was the only small space that had a locking door. While she waited, she shook her head. The idea that Dakota Monahan was going to take part in a fright fest, working to help scare kids, had her smiling and thinking back to her teen years again. Running around the theme parks with her friends back in high school, praying they'd be the ones a ghoul or monster would try to scare, had been one of the highlights of her youth. It was one of those things she'd never change, not in a million years. Was it the same for the kids in Montana? Was getting the snot scared out of you at Halloween a universal teenaged thing?

When Skeeter walked out all hunched over and licking his black lips, she shivered. This was going to be fun. He was the perfect choice for this role. Kids had gravitated to him all weekend, and they loved it.

Tonight, families were here and, while Skeeter had to tone it down a little bit, especially when little kids were around, she knew he'd still go after the teenagers with everything he had. However, when Sadie walked up, she didn't look too happy.

"I thought we were keeping the fright part of the festival to the weekends only?" Sadie walked around Skeeter and inspected his costume.

"Oh, we are. Tonight, I'll focus more on chasing Dakota around and pretending like she's the one I'm after." He grinned and those blackened teeth gave both women the creeps. "But if teenagers are around..." He shrugged.

Sadie chuckled and shook her head. "Alright, but play it cool when the little kids are present. We don't want to give them nightmares. Then their parents won't bring them back."

Standing at attention, Skeeter put a hand to his temple and saluted. "Aye, aye, Capitan."

The wife of the farm owner turned to Dakota. "Is there any way you can get this goofball to stay in line?"

Dakota laughed. "I haven't known him long, but something tells me he's gonna do what he wants, which is going to be to have fun scaring all the teens, and probably some adults as well."

Sadie stepped closer to Skeeter, but then stopped when he brought up his improvised chainsaw. She put a finger in his face. "No scaring little kids. Got it?"

"Got it. I don't want to give them nightmares. No worries."

"Alright." Sadie looked to the roof above them. "I'm probably going to regret this, but go ahead. Have fun, but not too much fun." She arched a brow at Skeeter, then turned to Dakota. "And you, I think you've got one of the best, and hardest, jobs of all. Enjoy."

Dakota was unsure what Sadie had meant about the best job, but she agreed it was most definitely the hardest. Dealing with Skeeter and making sure he didn't go overboard? That was next to impossible.

When Dakota left the barn, Skeeter held back a few seconds, giving her time to get out in the open. Then Skeeter walked out, growling and pulling the cord on his make-shift chainsaw. He caught all the attention around him. Dakota looked back when she heard some squeals and almost laughed as a couple of young teenagers, probably not even in high school yet, saw him, screamed, and ran for their lives.

On a Friday or Saturday, she knew that Skeeter would have given chase, but tonight, he was only supposed to chase her. He acted as though he was going to follow the girls, then caught sight of Dakota and changed direction, heading straight for her with the look of a crazed chainsaw killer on his scary face.

When he was only a few paces away, he revved his chainsaw and pointed to Dakota.

She screamed and turned to run. Memories of her teen years flooded her, and she pretended like she was there with Bethany and Michelle, her two best friends from high school. Dakota ran, zigzagging through the crowds in an effort to keep away from the smaller kids.

Skeeter was hot on her trail, but never got too close to her.

After a few minutes, she found herself on the midway where it was mostly high schoolers in their cliques, and she ran around and through them. Most of the kids moved out of the way, laughing or screaming as they watched the show.

After a few minutes, Dakota realized that Skeeter wasn't behind her any longer. She turned to see what had happened but couldn't find him. When she back-tracked, she realized that a small group of young girls, maybe sixteen or seventeen years old, had blocked him and looked to be flirting with him. He was doing a good job of keeping a respectful distance, but he didn't try to get away.

She wasn't sure why, but it irked her that he'd taken his attention from her and put it on those girls. They were way too young for him to be flirting with. Dakota pursed her lips and watched as one red-headed teen cupped one of her hands under the edge of her hair and pushed it up a few times while looking him up and down. She was too far away to hear them, but Dakota could tell the girl was saying something to Skeeter.

His head jerked back, and he looked around. When he made eye contact with Dakota, he pointed his finger at her and narrowed his eyes. "You. Will. Be. Next." His gravelly voice sent shivers down her spine.

Chainsaw Killer Skeeter got away from the girls and headed toward her. He kept revving his chainsaw and glaring at her. Then he yelled and started to run at her.

Dakota turned around and tried to hightail it out of there. Her first instinct was to get away from the scary murderer. But she also wanted him away from those flirty girls. She tried to tell herself it was just to protect him. They were underage, and he wasn't. But deep down she knew why it bugged her. The little green-eyed monster was starting to rear its ugly head.

That was one monster she wanted absolutely nothing to do with.

Chapter 17

By the time Friday came around again, Dakota and Skeeter had perfected their act. And Skeeter was in deep water. The more time he spent with Dakota, even if it was all an act, the more he liked her. She had a slow start, but, within a couple of days, she was like an old pro. She knew exactly who to run toward, and then Skeeter would veer off and scare a few kids only to find himself hot on her trail again.

The kids loved it. Each night more and more people showed up, some more than once.

When midnight came around, Cody and Sadie were waiting for them back at the tack room.

"You know, if you find a job in this area, you're gonna have to make sure your employment contract has a clause that allows you to come work for us during the month of October. I don't think I've ever seen a non-Christmas season week do so well here." Cody chuckled and patted Skeeter on the back.

"And I think that we need to expand this idea next year. Skeeter, you'll have to be the trainer for our ghosts and ghouls program." Sadie smiled warmly at the pair. "And Dakota, I hope you stay in the area as well. I'd love to have your help through the entire season."

"Oh, I don't know about that." Dakota shrunk back into herself and looked down at her feet.

The young woman had done so well, but Skeeter noted that any time he gave her a compliment, she withdrew. He'd heard of people who didn't take compliments well, but this was just crazy.

"Well, be sure to do your best tomorrow night." Sadie winked at Skeeter.

He was about to ask what she meant, when he realized what she was talking about. Sadie was the best marketing manager he'd seen, not that he'd seen many. But, she also had an 'in' with the media. To be honest, he was surprised she hadn't brought the press out sooner.

Then it hit him—Dakota. There was no way Dakota would do well if she knew the press was coming. He'd have to keep this from her and then try to steer her away when the cameras were rolling.

While Skeeter didn't know Dakota nearly as well as he wanted, he did know enough to realize she'd freeze up, and maybe even run away, if a camera was pointed at her. He wasn't sure what he was going to do, but he'd come up with something. At least it would be on a Saturday night, and he didn't need to chase Dakota as much. He could focus his attention on the maze and the kids surrounding that area while suggesting that Dakota hide out in the maze and stick her arm out as she had wanted earlier in the week.

"Well, I think we should get home and get some sleep. Tomorrow is going to be a big day. We still have chores to do in the morning before coming over here." Skeeter guided Dakota away from everyone and toward the van.

Jerod was already inside, van running and waiting. "It looks like it's just us for the ride home. The rest have already left. How was it tonight?"

They spent the ride back talking animatedly about the evening.

"You should have seen them; the kids went crazy whenever Skeeter went into the maze and chased them around." Dakota laughed. "And he especially loved going after the ones who were near the end. He'd scare them and get them all turned around so they couldn't get out as fast as they thought they could."

Skeeter grinned, blew on his fist, and rubbed it against his chest. "Yeah, I think I singlehandedly tortured the entire senior class."

"Well, at least those who showed up tonight," Dakota added.

Jerod chuckled. "How many people do you think attend the high school?"

She sat back and thought about it. "Oh, they probably were all in attendance, weren't they?"

"In small towns like this, when there's something new, the entire group of local kids will show up and keep coming night after night." Jerod's words hit Skeeter and he realized this was exactly what he had wanted when he was growing up—a small community where everyone knew your name.

"You know, I'd really love to spend the rest of my life here. I think Frenchtown has to be the best place to raise a family and grow old." Without turning his head, Skeeter looked to Dakota out of the side of his eyes and prayed that she'd agree with him.

"I don't know. I mean, it's great here and all, but everyone knows everyone here. Wouldn't that get old?" She scrunched her nose and looked at Jerod in the rearview mirror.

Jerod shrugged. "It hasn't yet, and I've been here several years now."

The next night was electrifying. Dakota couldn't stop laughing and smiling. While Skeeter was busier than usual chasing kids around and getting people turned around inside the maze, she spent an hour hiding and jumping out at unsuspecting teens. She had on a mask, one of those rubber ones from a Halloween store. It was hot and sweaty, but she loved the fact that no one knew who she was.

When Skeeter suggested it to her, she wasn't too keen on the idea at first. But now she wished he'd given it to her sooner. While the weeknights wouldn't allow this level of scary, and Skeeter would probably want to chase her around on those nights, this was actually more fun. She could be as crazy as she wanted, and no one would know.

It was no wonder costume parties were so popular. People could be anyone they wanted to without worrying about what anyone else thought. It was rather freeing.

At least it was until she noticed a camera crew snaking their way through the maze.

Dakota's breathing changed and her chest became tight. Before, there were kids of all ages around her laughing and screaming and just enjoying the carnival atmosphere. She had even enjoyed running through the maze at times finding kids to scare or misdirect. Now, all she wanted to do was find a corner and hide.

Normally, Dakota had a fantastic sense of direction. And with all the time she'd spent in the maze, she knew exactly where the exit was. However, her head started to spin, and her stomach gurgled. If she didn't find a place to sit down, and soon, she'd lose her cookies. While some might think it was part of the show, she'd know the truth and she didn't want anyone to think she had frightened herself so badly she got sick.

With hands out looking for the correct turns, she ended up getting herself turned around. Instead of finding the exit, she found a dead-end with a laughing skeleton hanging from a hook above. She put her hands on her head and tried to keep the recorded maniacal laughter out, but it was no use. Instead of staying there, she turned and tried to head out, only to be swallowed up with a group of girls screaming and pointing to her. They herded her to another dead-end, one with a gory scene on a table.

The bloody head with an axe in it didn't bother her. But the teenaged girls—oh now she needed some Tylenol. Her head was throbbing from the screaming and the laughter. Somehow, she was able to push out of the group and head behind the table where she immediately slumped to the ground.

As soon as the girls ran away, her headache began to lesson, but she couldn't think. Everything around her was covered in a haze. Almost like the festival had brought in a fog machine. But she knew they hadn't, or had they?

Dakota pushed her back further into the hay bales forming the dead-end and she brought her knees up to her chest. When she rested her head on her knees, she felt the world turning upside down. Closing her eyes barely slowed the process. But it did keep her stomach from churning any more.

What was wrong with her? Was she so frightened by the thought of being put on television that it made her this sick? She didn't think it was PTSD since she hadn't had a single issue all week with the crowds and the screaming. In fact, she had enjoyed it all immensely. But something had caused her body to go into a meltdown.

"Skeeter?" She called out but knew her voice wouldn't be heard over the craziness of the maze. "Help, someone help me." She called again when she heard footsteps and kids laughing.

"Look, what a great display. The scene on the table is so scary that woman's on the ground." One kid laughed.

Another snorted. "That's not even scary. Look." The kid must have done something, because the others started to laugh. "It's all so fake."

"Put the ax back in the head, Steve. I don't want to get kicked out of this place. It's the most fun I've had all year." A young woman's voice penetrated the fog surrounding Dakota's head.

Then they must have all left, because Dakota could sense that no one else was near her.

She wasn't sure how long she sat there with her back to the hay and head down, still spinning. After several unsuccessful attempts at getting up, she had decided to stay right where she was, hoping that the spinning would stop soon.

Then, a wetness hit her arms and she wondered if it was raining. But it couldn't be. There wasn't any rain in the forecast. Or was there? Now she wasn't even sure what the weather report was for that weekend.

A sniffling sound at her right caught her attention. Dakota tried to move her head, but it hurt too much, and she sighed. With her head still down, she moved her right hand and felt for what was next to her. At first, she thought someone had dropped a costume or a heavy coat next to her. But then, when that coat moved and lightly chuffed, she knew what it was—a dog.

A dog was at her side. Did Sam send Rogue in to look for her? This time, when she turned her head, it didn't hurt. But her eyes couldn't focus. Her head was still foggy, and her vision was blurry, but it was most definitely a dog. But it wasn't Rogue. He was a rust-colored boxer. The dog next to her was a black lab. Either she had spots in her vision, or the dog had a few white blotches on its coat. If the latter were the case, then it must be Spike who was trying to get her attention. The dog had licked her cheek and was now nuzzling up against her side.

"Spike?" All she could get out was a whisper.

He chuffed and then barked. When he put his head against her side, Dakota could have sworn he was trying to get her to stand. "Sorry, boy, but I'm sick. I think I had some bad food. I can't get up."

Even though her head was still full of fog, the fact that a service dog was right next to her registered. The dogs were trained for this sort of thing, weren't they? While Dakota wasn't exactly sure how to rely on a service dog for help, she did know that they had exceptional senses. If she could get up, then Spike could lead her out of the maze where she could get help.

Dakota had never felt so sick in her life. She'd had inner ear infections as a kid and it'd caused vertigo, but that was nothing compared to how she felt now. If she moved too much, her stomach would churn. This wasn't an inner ear infection, that much she knew for sure. Was it food poisoning? "Ahhh." Her stomach did Olympic-sized summersaults when she tried to lift her head.

Spike leaned his head against her chest and pushed her back against the maze wall. Then he nuzzled her chin so that her head was leaning against the wall.

"Spike?" a distant voice called out.

Dakota couldn't place the female voice. "Help." She tried to call again, but her voice wasn't nearly loud enough to be heard of the excitement of the maze dwellers.

Again, some kids stopped in front of her and laughed. One boy pointed and said, "Look, she's got a dog about ready to bite her head off."

The kids with him laughed and they started to move away. But one of the girls stepped closer and furrowed her brow. "Miss, are you alright?"

Somehow, Dakota had pulled off her mask, but sweat still dripped down her face. She took a breath and let out a small cry for help.

The girl looked at her, then down at the dog next to her and her eyes went wide. "Mike, Steve. Come quick," she called over her shoulder and moved closer to Dakota.

"If you really are hurt, let me know. If this is part of the show, please tell me and I'll leave you alone." The girl stooped down and put a hand to Dakota's face. "You're burning up."

Spike chuffed his agreement.

"There you are." A woman looked from Spike to Dakota. "Dakota? Are you alright?"

"No." Nothing else would come out of Dakota's mouth. But when she realized who stood in front of her, she sighed and closed her eyes. She felt herself leaning to the side, then she was yanked to her feet. But they refused to hold her upright.

"I've got her," one masculine voice said as he wrapped an arm around her side

Then another from her other side did the same. "I can help."

The two male voices pulled her along between them. Behind her, Spike barked, and she knew the dog followed closely on her trail.

"Dakota! What happened?" This voice was familiar and sounded as though he could feel her pain. "Get away from her."

"Skeeter, relax. They're helping to get her out," the somewhat familiar voice said. When the owner of that voice appeared in her line of sight, Dakota remembered who it was—Nelly Wilson. She was the dog trainer. Spike was one of her dogs.

And the scary man holding a chainsaw and looking like he just stepped out of a horror movie was Skeeter. Somehow, seeing them helped her head to clear up enough for her to remember.

Skeeter dropped his chainsaw and moved forward. "I've got her. Thank you both. You can go back to enjoying the festival." He took Dakota and held her close to him.

Then he put one arm behind her back and his other under her knees. When he picked her up, she worried she would be too heavy for him to carry. "I can walk."

"No, you can't. What happened? Did someone attack you?" Worried dark eyes stared down into her confused ones.

"Skeeter." She put a hand up, trying to touch his face, but she had zero energy or strength. Instead, her hand plopped down on her chest, and she closed her eyes.

The next thing she knew, she was on a gurney inside an ambulance. "What? Where?"

"Shh, it's alright. Miss Monahan, we're taking you to the hospital. Do you know what happened to you?" A female paramedic turned warm eyes on her and waited.

"I...I don't know. I think I passed out from food poisoning?" Her head was much clearer, but her mouth was parched. "Thirsty."

Everything was still a bit fuzzy but starting to come back into focus. Maybe laying down was the answer. If she'd known that, she would have laid down in the maze instead of sitting.

Chapter 18

What seemed like days was really only hours. Skeeter paced the waiting room of the hospital in Missoula while waiting for any word on how Dakota was doing. All he knew was that she had been out of it and needed help getting out of the maze. She seemed like she was drugged, or maybe in the process of shutting down from PTSD? He'd seen it before. One of the guys at the ranch had such a horrible reaction to a power outage and the noise caused by the issue that he fell to the ground and curled up into a ball. He couldn't move or speak. Megan had to talk him down.

Even though there were similarities, there were also differences. The fact that the doctors were still running tests on Dakota said a lot. And it wasn't good.

"Skeeter, please take a seat. If you don't stop pacing, you're gonna put a hole in the linoleum." Jerod sat in the waiting room looking almost as frazzled as Skeeter felt.

"That's just a cliché. I won't walk a hole in the ground." Skeeter threw his hands in the air when Jerod gave him the stink eye. "Fine, fine. I'll take a seat." He grumbled as he sat down in a chair that faced the door leading to where Dakota had been taken.

While it was late in the night, it was still dark outside, so they couldn't have been there nearly as long as Skeeter felt. The moment he turned his head to look at the clock above the coffee vending machine, he heard the door swoosh open. He had been contemplating another cup of vile sludge. Instead, he stood and met the doctor before he could get two steps into the room. "Doc, how is she?"

The doctor took two steps back to get Skeeter out of his personal space. "What's your relationship with the patient?"

He knew what was coming, but, before he could argue, Jerod walked up and took over.

"I'm her designated person. She's staying at the Crooked Arrow Ranch, a place I run." Whenever anyone came to the ranch, they signed a waiver giving Jerod and Megan the legal right to talk to any doctor about their situation. It was mostly for instances such as this one, not because they wanted to pry. Someone needed to know what was going on and make decisions if need be.

"Ah, yes." The doctor smiled. "I've heard about you and your ranch. Mighty fine job you're doing there." He put his hand out for Jerod. "I'm Doctor Jenkins."

"Nice to meet you, but can you tell me how Dakota's doing?" Even Jerod was anxious, and it showed in his voice and demeanor.

The doctor looked to Skeeter and noted the costume and black paint on his teeth.

"Oh, yeah. We were working at the Fall Festival. I'm in costume." Skeeter shrugged. What else could he say? He obviously wasn't the psycho he looked to be. But he also didn't want to go into too much detail since that would take time. Time he didn't want to waste.

"Alright. Let's go over here." The doctor led them to a corner in the waiting room. "Does Dakota have any medical issues I should be aware of?"

Jerod rubbed his chin and thought for a moment. "She served in Iraq and survived a car accident, but nothing too serious. And she's being treated for depression." He paused and remembered two weeks ago. "She's also going through some tests to see if her depression isn't something else, but we don't have the results yet. I can get you in touch with her VA doctor, if you like."

"That won't be necessary, I've already spoken with a Dr. Smythe from Fort Harrison. He requested I do an MRI on her tonight while she's having an episode. She's back in radiology now. We should know more shortly." It was obvious the doctor was going to say something else but stopped short.

Skeeter didn't like him. He had no idea if Doctor Jenkins was a good doctor or not, but Skeeter didn't like him strictly because the man was holding back. "What aren't you telling us?"

The older doctor scratched at the stubble on his chin and heaved a sigh. "Generally, I don't like to speculate. But, after speaking with Dr. Smythe and seeing the results of the physical exam so far, I believe that the MRI will come back with proof that Dakota doesn't have depression, but Multiple Sclerosis."

Jerod punched his fist into his palm. "I was afraid of this. Is that why she got so sick? Is she having an episode right now?"

Skeeter's brow furrowed and he looked at Jerod. "You knew this was a possibility?"

He nodded. "Dr. Smythe is an MS specialist. Most doctors misdiagnose MS because they still know so little about the disease. Megan suspected but wasn't sure." He turned to look at the ER doctor. "Was it a lesion on her brain that caused the vertigo in the maze?"

"That's what we think, which is why we are doing an MRI right now. Dr. Smythe sent me a copy of her MRI from a week ago. We can compare the images and see if it's getting worse, or if one or more lesions are active. It would explain everything she went through tonight."

"But, doc, what caused the lesion to become inflamed, or a new one to develop instantly like that?" While Skeeter wasn't with her when it happened, he had seen her not an hour earlier and she was having a great time. The only complaint was the heat inside the mask. And that was to be expected. Who didn't sweat up a storm when wearing a full Halloween mask?

"I'm afraid I won't know more until we get the results. You might as well go home for tonight. I'm going to keep Dakota here. We might send her to the VA hospital tomorrow, depending on the MRI results."

"I want to stay until you have the results. Is that alright?" Jerod wasn't going to back down.

And if Jerod was staying, then so was Skeeter.

Two cups of sludge and three hours passed before the doctor came back out. He walked over to where Skeeter and Jerod sat hunched on the most uncomfortable chairs any waiting room could possibly have.

Skeeter had already complained to anyone who would listen about the hard, plastic chairs. "Who ever heard of using chairs that made a person not want to sit? I mean, you don't want us to be wearing a hole in the ground or standing near you and pestering you all night, do you?"

The night nurse shook her head and rolled her eyes heavenward as though she'd heard the same thing a gazillion times before. "Sir, please take a seat or step outside."

Jerod, who sat in a chair, waved Skeeter over and they both sat until the doctor came out.

"You might as well go home. I'm going to be sending Dakota to the VA hospital tomorrow morning where an MS specialist will examine her again to confirm the diagnosis. But it does look like she has MS." The doctor held a clipboard in his hands as he spoke to the two men.

"Can I see her before we leave?" Skeeter pleaded.

The doctor shook his head. "I'm sorry, but we gave her a sedative and she's already out for the night."

Feeling like a failure for not being there to help Dakota in her time of need, Skeeter hung his head without a word.

"Thanks, doctor. I appreciate you updating us and helping Dakota. We'll follow up with the VA hospital tomorrow afternoon." Jerod shook the doctor's hand and led Skeeter outside to the van.

The moon had already gone behind the mountains when the men arrived back home. The sun hadn't come up yet, but, from the lighting of the sky toward the East, Skeeter knew sunrise would be there soon.

"Why don't you get some shuteye. And don't set your alarm. When you wake up, you can catch the sermon online." Jerod patted Skeeter on the back as they walked inside the quiet house.

It was Sunday morning. A day when everyone would get up after sunrise and go feed the animals before heading off to church. That day was a true day of rest for a rancher. All they did was ensure the animals had what they needed, then spent the day communing with God and family.

"Thanks. I want to be there when you call the VA hospital later today." For the first time, Skeeter had an excuse for not working, but he couldn't enjoy it.

Chapter 19

Even with a sedative, Dakota hadn't slept well. All she could think of was the fact that she was dying. And her death wouldn't be quick, either. She might live to her sixties, but by then she'd wish she had never made it out of Iraq.

Or at least, that's what she thought would happen. While she didn't know much about MS, she knew enough from the celebrities who died of it to know that it was a slow and painful process. One that took years for her vital organs to fail. And they wouldn't do it all at once, either. It would be one at a time. And it would be painful. More than painful, it would be excruciating.

Too bad morphine had zero effect on her.

As they took her to the VA hospital in an ambulance, Dakota wondered how they would manage her pain, and how long she had before she became a vegetable. As far as she knew, there wasn't a cure for MS, and the treatments were so old that they were barely worth it.

If only she'd died in that accident in Iraq and not been rescued. Although, after the crash, she wasn't even close to dead. If she hadn't been rescued when she was, then she would have been taken by ISIS, or one of the other terrorist organizations operating out of Iraq at the time.

Now that she thought of it, that would have been worse. The torture alone would have had her wishing she was dealing with something as simple as MS, which wasn't really simple at all. No, she was glad she made it home.

God, it's me, Dakota. What's going on here? Just a week ago you told me things were going to be alright. All I needed to do was be thankful for what I had. How can a person be thankful to have MS? If she had been sitting in a seat instead of laying on a gurney, she would have put her head in her hands. Instead, she turned her head away from the paramedic as the first tear began its journey down her cheek.

The trip to the VA hospital was faster than she expected. All too soon she was headed inside, a place she hated to be stuck in. "Can I at least sit up as we go in?"

The female paramedic smiled and adjusted the head of her gurney so she was a bit more upright than before.

"Not exactly what I was hoping for. How about a wheelchair?" Dakota looked hopefully at the woman.

"Sorry, it's policy that we keep you on the bed. The VA nurse might let you sit in a chair after you've been examined by the doctor, but I don't know for sure."

"Thanks anyway." Things weren't starting out very well. If lying in bed all day was her only future, she didn't know what she'd do. At least her head was clear, and she no longer had vertigo. That was something.

Once she was settled in a room—all by herself, she noted—the nurse did let her sit in the chair. The room was a sterile off-white with the typical institutional pictures of plants and animals. The only difference was that these pictures looked to be regional ones. There was a buffalo roaming an open field with a snow-capped mountain behind it. Another picture was of pine trees in snow with a few pinecones on the ground surrounding the tree in the middle, as though it was staged.

It could have been worse; it could have been pictures of bumble bees and flowers. She'd seen enough of those in the LA VA hospital.

Her bed was a standard hospital bed, a pole standing next to it with a saline bag dangling. She knew the drill. The VA had a policy that anyone who was admitted to the hospital had to have a needle in their body, just in case they needed something delivered via an IV drip. And they always gave the patient saline to start out. Then she'd spend the next twelve hours or more peeing like a racehorse.

She sighed. At least she knew partially what to expect. Dakota prayed that an experienced nurse would put her IV line in, instead of the usual medical student. It wasn't that Dakota didn't agree with putting medical and nursing students in the hospital for experience, it was that she had bad veins. They always had a tough time getting lines into her.

So, when the nurse said she could sit up in a chair, Dakota immediately pulled a chair to the only window that looked out over the parking lot. When she sat down, she looked into the distance and smiled. "At least there's beautiful mountains to look at." The mountains were quite a ways away, but she could get a good look. The surrounding area was what she expected, flat and desert-like.

Although, she did note a small hill not too far away. The land wasn't all flat like she expected. She'd call it a rolling hills type of typography, with patches of desert landscape mixed in here and there.

All in all, it looked better than the concrete jungle of LA. It hadn't mattered that just a few miles away from the LA VA was the most elegant and historied part of the state, Beverly Hills. She'd never been able to afford to shop or dine on Rodeo Drive, so she'd never bothered with a trip there, even when the community affairs director put together a trip for the veterans in the resident wing of the hospital.

As she sat there, waiting for the doctor to come and check on her, she thought of the Crooked Arrow Ranch and its residents. "What a difference a zip code can make."

Sadly, her quiet moment was interrupted when a nurse came in with a tray. And not a tray of food.

"Hi, Dakota. My name is Ginny. I'll be your head nurse while you're here." The red head walked over to a board and wrote her name at the top. "And here are the names of the rest of my team who will take care of you today. Each day, as we change shifts, the names will change. They'll always be listed here so you don't forget."

Dakota knew the drill. She'd been in enough VA and Army hospitals to know how it worked. "Thanks. Nice to meet you, Ginny." She looked to the tray. "Let me guess. It's vampire time?"

At first, Ginny looked confused, then a slow smile spread across her face. "I'd let Angel take my blood anytime."

"I agree. I'm totally team Angel. Spike was alright, but he just didn't have the angelic face of Angel." Dakota laughed when she realized what she'd said.

"Lucky for you, we're actually showing the entire series of *Buffy* on the on-demand channel we have. But first, time to put in your IV." Ginny motioned for Dakota to come back to bed.

Dakota turned her head and looked out the window as the nurse began to stick her with a needle. Was this her life now? Hospitals and nurses who got her silly humor? The last part was better than expected, but hospitals in general was not where she saw herself spending a lot of time in the future. If she was honest with herself, she pictured herself back on the ranch with everyone. Maybe even sticking with the ranch life when she completed her rehab at the Crooked Arrow. She doubted she'd be going back there now.

"Okay. All done. I'll have Mark bring you lunch shortly. The doctor ordered you on a special diet. Lucky you." Ginny winked and took a step back.

"What? You're done?" Dakota looked down at her arm and shook her head. "I didn't even feel it. Wow, you're good." She may have felt a tiny prick, but it wasn't enough to catch her attention.

"Thanks, I try to do my best. The doctor will be in later today." With that, Ginny left Dakota to her own musings.

While she took advantage of the *Buffy* marathon, a young man came in with a wheeled cart. "Hi, I'm Mark. One of your nursing team."

From the looks of him, and the fact that he was listed at the bottom of the chart of names, Dakota guessed he was a nursing student. He'd do the grunt work, like food and cleaning. He'd also take away the empty saline bags.

But today, Ginny had said she'd only get one bag of saline. It seemed her blood work from Missoula showed she was on the dehydrated side.

"So, what's for lunch? Cream of lunch bag soup?" Dakota smirked. That was one of the things they used to call the chicken soup that was served in LA. It really did taste like they flavored it with those brown lunch bags.

But when Mark pulled the cover off her tray, the scent surprised her. As did what was on the plate. "Today, you'll get vegetable soup and a grilled chicken breast with a whole grain roll. And for a snack later, I've got cut veggies and hummus."

Dakota looked around but couldn't find what she was looking for.

"What? You don't like chicken?" Mark pouted and held the tray of food in his hand.

"No. I mean yes, I do like chicken. But since when does the VA serve good, edible food to their patients?" She continued to scan the room for cameras, or a person who was going to jump out and say, "*Gotcha, you're on candid camera.*" Or something to that effect.

"Since you were put on a special diet. You'll get custom made meals each day. Let me tell you, you're gonna eat much better than most of the people in this hospital, staff included." He grinned.

"Why the special diet?"

"It's part of your treatment. Diet plays a large part in healing the body, especially for people with MS. You'll learn all about nutrition and how to help lower inflammation in your body by eating the right foods."

Dakota didn't know what to say. She'd never heard any of this before. Sure, she knew about inflammation in the body and the havoc it could wreak, but she never knew it could be controlled by food.

What else didn't she know?

Chapter 20

"Jerod, it's been three days. Three whole days without a single word." Skeeter threw his hands in the air and paced the living room. "When are we going to hear how Dakota's doing?"

If it were up to Skeeter, he would have driven to the VA hospital just outside of Helena to see Dakota for himself. But Jerod nixed the idea before Skeeter could even get the whole question out.

"Sit down." With a quick huff, Jerod turned his head.

Skeeter was sure the big man was hiding his laugh, but he didn't care. This was important. "Come on, Dakota is still your responsibility, isn't she?"

"Yup. And when the doctor has something to share, he'll call me." The relaxed posture and uncaring attitude of Jerod was about to send Skeeter over the edge.

"Come on, man. Don't you even care how she's doing? Can't we call her?" If Skeeter could hear her voice, and know that she was alright, he might be able to calm down a little bit.

When Jerod didn't say anything, Skeeter looked toward the man, who was staring at him with a knowing glint in his eyes.

"What?" Skeeter asked.

"You really care for her, don't you." It wasn't a question. Jerod had asked about Skeeter's emotions before, but this time he knew how Skeeter felt. No questions needed.

With a deep inhale, Skeeter let his breath out slowly. He took a seat in the recliner and ran his hand through his messy hair. No one ever said hat hair was attractive. "I do." He held his hand in the air to stop Jerod. "I know, I know. No dating and no flirting with other residents."

Jerod just watched the young cowboy.

"I have followed your rules. Honestly, I've tried to just be friends with Dakota. But that only made me like her more. She's so nice and fun. I swear, that woman can let loose and have a great time. It doesn't happen much, but when it does, she lights up like the sun." Skeeter felt the corners of his mouth turn up and he chuckled. "Shoot, I can't get her smile out of my head."

Jerod snorted. "Fine, how about we call before dinner?"

"Thank you. I mean that." Skeeter stood and made to leave the room.

"Wait. Just remember, no matter how you feel, she's still off-limits as long as the both of you are residents here." The head honcho arched a brow and waited for Skeeter to respond.

Once what Jerod said sunk in, Skeeter's shoulders slumped, and he nodded. "Got it."

"Good, now get back to work," Jerod grumbled.

Good to his word, Jerod brought him inside to his office just before dinner was ready to make the call.

"Dakota?" Skeeter's heart was pitter-pattering at the sound of her voice. Shoot, if he didn't get himself under control, Jerod would see it and probably hang up.

"Yes?" She sounded hesitant, as though she didn't recognize his voice.

But then again, they'd never spoken on the phone before, so how could she know his voice? "Hi, it's Skeeter and Jerod. We called to see how you're doing."

"Hey there. Better now. The doctor said I can probably go back to the ranch soon, if you'll still have me, that is." It sounded as though she wanted to say something else but cut herself off.

Without waiting for Jerod, Skeeter told her of course they wanted her back.

"But, um..." Dakota trailed off.

Jerod cleared his throat. "What is it? You can tell us. It's just the two of us on the phone with you."

"Well, I have a special diet I have to follow. Will that be a problem?"

Skeeter furrowed his brows and looked from the phone to Jerod. He'd never heard of a special diet for someone with MS. But, then again, he'd never met anyone who had MS.

"Of course, I expected as much. We're prepared to make whatever you need. Don't worry about that." Jerod hesitated. "What about beef?"

"Very little, I'm afraid. Mostly fish, chicken, fruits, and vegetables, but not the starchy kind. I mean, I can have some potatoes and corn, but not much. More of the green leafy stuff than anything else." She sounded sad about it.

Skeeter could understand. If he had to give up the fresh beef that they had here, he'd be upset, too. "But fish is good. We can even go fishing for some of our own, right?" He looked at Jerod.

"Of course, we should be eating more fish, too. But there will be times where you'll have to eat something different than the rest of us. We'll still prepare it for you, but we do eat a lot of beef and pork on the ranch." Jerod winced and rubbed his chin.

If Jerod was thinking anything near what Skeeter was, he knew the big man felt bad for Dakota. But the last thing they could do was show anything other than understanding. Pity would set anyone off. And the last thing Skeeter wanted was for Dakota to feel slighted and not come home.

"If you're sure it's no problem, I'll be back on Friday." Dakota paused. "Well, I'll need a ride back. And the doctor wanted to speak with you and go over the dietary requirements if you're sure you can do this?"

"It's not a problem." Skeeter answered for Jerod. Even if he had to take cooking lessons, he'd make sure they accommodated Dakota's needs.

Jerod chuckled. "Dakota, just tell me what time to be there, and I will be." He eyed Skeeter. "Dana and I will both come to hear about your new needs. In fact, this will be good for the ranch. Once we get things going with you, we can also take more vets who have a similar dietary restriction."

When they hung up, Skeeter jumped up and glared at Jerod. "You and Dana? What about me?"

Jerod slitted his eyes. "I thought you and Dakota were only friends?"

"We are." Skeeter slumped back down in a chair. "But I want to help. A friend helps, doesn't he?"

"Yes, but this is ranch business. Dana is the cook, and she needs to fully understand what the doctor requires. And I need to understand any other needs as the ranch owner." Jerod relaxed his posture. "I know you want to help, and trust me, you will when she gets back here. But there are some things you don't need to be involved in. Understand?"

He got it; he really did. Skeeter didn't need to know all the ins and outs of her medical situation, but that didn't mean he wanted to wait even one more day to see her.

The rest of the week was going to be slow going.

Chapter 21

"Are you sure, doctor? Working on a ranch isn't going to kill me?" After a week of testing and talking to the MS specialist, Dakota was excited about her prospects. There had been a difficult two days when she started a new medicine that didn't work well with her, but the new one seemed to be fine so far.

Dr. Smythe's smile worked its magic, and it did what it always did; Dakota calmed down and took a breath.

"Dakota, if you have any problems, call me and we'll switch out the medicine. The next option is to get a twice a year infusion. But you'd have to come here for that. So, let's pray that this pill works." He'd explained the other option, and while it had fewer side effects, the need to travel to the main VA hospital twice a year for the treatment didn't sound good at all.

"Okay. And thank you for all of your time and attention. I don't know if I could have gotten through this without you."

"I'm just glad that we discovered you aren't actually going through depression. And you don't need those other pills anymore. The fewer pills you take, the better you'll do in the long run. But don't skip these pills. You really do need them if you want to stem the progression of your MS." One of the most important things she'd learned this week was that she could have a mostly normal life. As long as the medicine worked, she'd probably die of old age and not complications from MS.

God had been right when He told her the previous week that all would be fine. Boy, that message had really come at the right time. Dakota mused, and not for the first time, how God's timing always seemed perfect.

"Dakota? How ya doing?" Jerod walked into her hospital room and looked around.

She had been ready to leave for over an hour and jumped up out of the chair that she kept by the window. While waiting for her ride, she'd been woolgathering and staring out at the distant mountains that would have snow on them before Christmas arrived. "I'm sooo ready to leave."

Dana stepped inside and hugged her friend. "Did they treat you well here?"

Dakota pulled back and furrowed her brow at first, and then realization dawned. "Oh, yes. They've been great. Much better than the last place. And it's really peaceful here. But it's still a hospital." She shivered and scrunched her nose.

"Ah, yes. The wonderful pungent scents of cleaning products and antiseptics. I remember those." Jerod made a face, agreeing with her assessment. "Is your doctor around? He wanted to speak with Dana and me before leaving."

Just then, Doctor Smythe walked in. "Hello there, I think my ears were burning." He smiled and everyone in the room relaxed. Somehow, the doctor had a way of doing that to anyone he was around.

"Hi, doc. I'm Jerod Stevens, and this is my wife, Dana. She does most of the cooking at the ranch."

The doctor shook Jerod's hand, then greeted Dana. "So nice to meet you both. I've heard a lot about your ranch."

"All good things, I hope?" Jerod asked.

"Of course. In fact, if you don't mind, I'd love to come out sometime and take a tour. See what you all do." The doctor's hand held Dakota's discharge papers.

While she knew her doctor had questions about the ranch, Dakota also wanted to get out of Dodge as quickly as possible. She had missed the ranch this past week, as well as all of its quirky residents.

"When's your next day off? You can come spend the night if you like. Right now, we're mostly working out at the local harvest festival, but we do have our regular meetings still, and the residents are continuing their daily chores. Thankfully we don't run a lot of cattle or anything like that. Our fall schedule is fairly easy right now." Jerod sounded like he was babbling, and Dakota wondered if he was nervous to have the doctor come for a visit.

When the doctor spoke again, it was as though his very words soothed Jerod's soul. The cowboy's shoulders relaxed, and he even smiled.

The doctor put a hand on Jerod's shoulder and smiled. "I don't want to put you out or anything. I just want to see how a ranch can help a wounded veteran heal. That's all."

With his new relaxed posture, Jerod seemed open to the visit. "I'd be honored to show you around whenever you get a chance. We just don't have a lot going on right now. Our crops have been brought in, and we don't plant anything for the winter."

"That's not true." Dana interrupted. "I have a small kitchen garden that's set up in a greenhouse out back. We do plant various things all year round. In fact, just last week I put in some lettuce and cucumbers. Those, in addition to the tomatoes that are still growing, should help to make for some great salads all winter long."

After the group finally made arrangements for the doctor to come visit the next week, they sat down and discussed what Dakota would need. It went faster than she thought it would. The doctor had a clipped group of papers that listed the various foods that she should eat, and those she needed to avoid. Sadly, the doctor didn't forget to exclude sugar from the list of bad foods.

"Doctor," Dana interrupted when they were discussing the bad foods. "What if we used stevia in place of sugar? Could I still make the occasional sweet treat?"

"That would be alright on occasion. But just keep in mind, even sugar substitutes can cause inflammation in the body."

Spoil sport. Dakota pursed her lips but kept her thoughts to herself. She didn't think that an occasional slice of chocolate cake, or even the monthly chocolate chip pancake breakfast that Lottie held at the coffee shop, would be too much. Not that she'd had Lottie's chocolate chip pancake yet. But if her coffee and treats were anything to go by, then she'd love that one Saturday a month treat.

But the funnel cakes at the festival would probably be a no-go.

Which reminded her. "Jerod, will I still be allowed to volunteer at the harvest festival? Or did what happen turn Cody and Sadie off to my help?" She bit her lip and realized she was going to have to apologize to the owners of the farm. That wasn't something she was looking forward to discussing.

An understanding expression crossed Dana's face. "Dakota, of course they want you back. You and Skeeter were one of the biggest draws they've had this year. In fact, Sadie's called me three times week checking in on you. She's worried about you."

"Oh, great." The last thing Dakota wanted was a pity party in her name. "I hope you told her I was just fine."

"Yes, I did. She can't wait to see you again," Dana answered.

After Dakota had said goodbye to everyone at the hospital, she started looking forward to getting back to the ranch—and to a certain someone. She never would have thought she'd end up liking the class clown. But Skeeter had gotten under her skin.

Before she'd had her episode, she wondered if there might be something between them. Then, she pushed that thought aside when she thought she'd not live much of a life. But now, anything was possible for her.

And that meant she was free to fall in love.

Chapter 22

Skeeter was pacing the front room, looking out the window every ten seconds or so. Well, at least that was how it felt.

"Dude, sit down. They'll get here when they get here. Pacing a hole in the carpet won't get them here any sooner." Arthur Landbury chuckled. "I'm just glad that there's nothing keeping me here." He eyed Skeeter knowingly.

"Not everyone wants to leave Frenchtown. I happen to enjoy it here." Skeeter sat on the chair that gave him the best view out the window.

"Sure, you say that now. But about three weeks ago, when you and Jerod were talking about an opportunity out in Wyoming?" Arthur was referring to a job offer Skeeter had from a ranch in Wyoming. The owner was an acquaintance of Jerod's.

While he and Jerod had spoken about it, Skeeter never agreed to accept the job. In fact, he had told Jerod he wasn't interested in leaving Frenchtown, even before he fell for the pretty new veteran. "I never said I'd go."

"Uh-huh. If you say so." Arthur had a sweet job offer with North Western Energy that he had already accepted. The man was leaving the ranch and heading up to Great Falls on December first. The job didn't technically start until January first, but there was a small apartment that had come up and it was exactly what Arthur wanted. He'd be close to the office, even though he'd spend most of his time in the field. But the job was too good to pass up.

Jerod had said Arthur could stay through the new year if he wanted, there was no need to leave before Christmas. But he didn't feel the same pull to the area as Skeeter did, and he was excited to get moved in and settled before he began his new career. The fact that the manager didn't mind him only having one eye came as a shock. Not only to himself, but the rest of the ranch. A job as an electrical engineer seemed like something both eyes would be needed for. But the hiring manager had wanted to hire a veteran. He'd also heard about how Arthur had helped the Christmas Tree Farm in the past, as well as his assistance to Frenchtown when they had any power issues. Even with one eye, Arthur still knew how to do a great job.

While he hadn't said anything, Skeeter wondered if the company hired him just to fill a quota. But when Jerod and Arthur had come back from checking out apartments for Arthur, they talked about all of the veterans who worked in that location. It seemed the weather wasn't very kind, and most civvies didn't do well there. But veterans were used to harsh climates and difficult working conditions, so they tended to do better than most.

While Skeeter envied the fact that Arthur had gotten the job of his dreams, he wouldn't have wanted to go so far from Frenchtown and all of the friends he'd made here. A part of him was sad that the quiet veteran would be leaving.

But Arthur promised to come back for a few days at Christmas. Hopefully he would come and visit once in a while, and a few of the guys from the ranch would go there and visit him, too.

It seemed strange that some of the residents were leaving soon, and new people would be arriving.

As though he could read Skeeter's mind, Arthur asked about new residents. "So, I hear you're going to get a few new inmates before Christmas." The man laughed. He'd thought of the ranch as more of a prison when he first arrived. Now, it was just a joke to them all. They had experienced more freedom here than anyone could remember since joining the military.

"I hear we're gonna get our first Zoomie in December." Each group of the armed services had a different name for the other branches. The Army tended to think of the Air Force as airheads, so the name Zoomie took. There were other nicknames, but none as universally accepted as Zoomies.

Arthur sputtered. "Air Force? Really? I had thought this ranch catered to a higher level of servicemember."

Skeeter laughed. "I know. This should be fun."

"Do you know if it's a man or a woman?"

"Nope, I just overheard that someone from the Air Force would be joining us for Christmas." Skeeter shrugged. He wasn't really concerned about what branch of the military anyone came from. The teasing was more friendly than adversarial. And the Air Force called the Army names, too. G.I. Joe was probably the most common, but, after the movie was made, very few people saw it as a way to tease a soldier.

"I suppose I'll find out if I come back for Christmas dinner." Arthur grinned and waggled his brows. "Wouldn't it be nice if it was another woman? We need more women on the ranch."

"What's that I hear? You want more women around?" a feminine voice called out from the front door.

Skeeter had missed the truck driving up and the group coming inside. He jumped up with excitement. "Dakota. It's great to see you again." He took on step forward with the intention of giving her a hug, but then saw Jerod's face and he stopped.

"If you two are done shootin' the breeze, then I believe Dana could use your help in the kitchen preparing dinner." Jerod arched a brow.

Both men scurried away to the kitchen. Once they were out of sight, Jerod grinned. "I love it when they run away like little mice."

Dana slapped her husband's shoulder lightly. "Jerod, I sure hope you don't tease our kids like that."

Jerod stopped right where he was, mouth agape.

Dakota blinked and then grinned. "Are you pregnant?"

"What?" Dana looked between the two. "Are you kidding me? It's too soon. I was speaking about any *future* kids we might have." With her emphasis on future, Jerod unfroze and pulled his wife in for hug.

"Maybe we should start preparing for kids. You know, for when the time comes." He winked and kissed his wife so deeply that Dakota blushed and ran from the room.

"Get a room." The statement was so soft Dakota didn't think anyone heard her.

"I know, gross. I keep saying the same thing." Skeeter stuck his tongue out and practically gagged. "I mean, I know they're still newlyweds, but come on. Other people live here, too."

"I heard that," Jerod called out.

Both shut their mouths and stared at each other before they ran in opposite directions.

"You know," Dana whispered in her husband's ear. "We could start practicing now. And maybe even every night." She waggled her brows and took two steps toward their bedroom. She blew him a kiss.

Jerod started forward, oblivious of anything else in the world.

Dana giggled and shook her head. "Tonight, lover."

He slapped a fist to his heart. "Oh, that hurt."

"Sorry, I got caught up before I realized that I still had to make dinner."

"We could skip dinner. Let everyone fend for themselves. Most will be at the festival anyway." He glided up next to his wife and wrapped her in his arms. He began kissing her shoulder, then made his way up her neck and nibbled on her ear.

Panting, Dana pulled back. "You know, if you aren't careful, one of these days I'm going to give in and skip dinner."

"I wouldn't mind." Jerod took his wife's lips and kissed her slowly and sweetly.

"Dana?" Arthur, not knowing what was going on, yelled. "I need help."

The married coupled sighed in unison. "Maybe next time?"

"At this rate, we're never going to get in enough practice." Jerod chuckled and lightly patted his wife's bottom. "Go on. I gotta go check on the livestock anyway."

"You know Mike will have it all handled," Dana said over her shoulder as she walked toward the kitchen.

"The cows? Sure. But what about the horses, goats, and the new sheep?"

"Sheep? What sheep?" Dakota asked as she walked into the living room to pick up her bag of things from the hospital. She didn't have a lot, but there were some meds and the pajamas she had purchased from the tiny shop.

"That's right, you've been gone almost a week now. Yesterday, we bought a small flock of sheep from the Huntington's. I was thinking that with more residents coming to stay we might want to try something a little different." Jerod ran a hand through his hair, hoping to hide the fact that he had just been making out with his wife.

"Really? Are you going to butcher them for their meat? I'm not sure I like the idea of eating sheep. Blah." With a shake of her head, Dakota also stuck her tongue out and shivered.

Jerod chuckled. "No. I was thinking we could shear them and try to make our own wool. These are Merino sheep. Next week, I've got some ranchers coming over to show us what we need and how to take good care of them. In the spring, we'll shear them and start processing the wool."

"Huh, it sounds like a lot of work. Will you also buy a loom? Or just process the wool and sell it?" Dakota had seen looms in use when she was in Iraq, but she also knew that the process of making cloth was long and arduous. It wasn't something just anyone could do.

Jerod looked hard at Dakota. Then he scratched his chin. "What do you know about turning wool into yarn?"

She waved her hands. "Oh, no. I don't know anything. I've just seen the women in Iraq carding and weaving after the long process of cleaning the wool. I have zero desire to do any of that." Besides, she thought to herself, now that she wasn't dealing with depression, she'd probably be on her way shortly and wouldn't be here long enough to see spring. She had family she wanted to get back to. And a desire to figure out the rest of her life.

Being off that medicine for almost week now had done something to her. She felt as though she was coming out of a fog and could see a future for herself. The only problem was she didn't know what future she wanted. At least, not yet. Ranching seemed cool, but she'd spent most of her time working at the harvest festival. That was the best part of being here. If she could work the festivals all year long, she'd be one happy camper.

Maybe there were places somewhere in the country that celebrated Halloween all year long? She knew there were Christmas towns, so why not Halloween towns? She could dress up and run around all day long having fun. That wouldn't be work, it would be getting paid to play.

It was Friday night and Dakota was ready to get her *scary* on at the Harvest Festival After Dark. She and Skeeter ate an early dinner, as planned, then headed right over to the Mackinaw farm. She said a silent prayer that no one would make a big deal out of her passing out before and disappearing for a week. She just wanted to forget about that incident and have some fun.

But it seemed God had other plans. *Alright, God. If you don't want me here, just tell me. I don't want to be a burden or a distraction for anyone*. Dakota took a deep breath when both Cody and Sadie walked up.

A huge smile covered Sadie's face. "Dakota, I'm so glad you're back. I missed you." The woman pulled her in for a hug.

"Oh. Thanks." Dakota returned the hug. "I actually missed the festival, too. This place is so much fun."

Cody grinned. "I'm glad to see you looking so healthy. Just be sure you eat and drink enough. I don't want Jerod yelling at me."

That statement caught Dakota off guard. Before she could ask what he meant, a wet nose nudged her hand. "Spike, hey there buddy." She knelt down and gave the dog a good scratch behind the ears before she realized he was working. "Oh, I'm sorry, Nelly. I didn't even look to see if he was wearing his vest."

"Don't worry about it. I think Spike has been excited to see you. Every time we come here, he pulls me around looking for something. And when he spotted you tonight, he literally dragged me over." Nelly chuckled.

"Aw, Spike, I missed you too." Dakota knew that it was Spike who found her in the maze when she was sick. He helped her. And she would forever be grateful to the sweet dog. A tiny part of her wished she could have a service dog. But she also knew that there were other veterans who needed a partner more than she did.

"I think Spike has taken a real liking to you, Dakota." The way Nelly eyed her made Dakota nervous. It was like the woman was looking directly into her soul.

"Ah, thanks. I gotta get to work, so I'll see you all around." Dakota waved and took off before anyone could say anything else about her embarrassing episode.

"Hey, wait up," Skeeter called out and ran to catch up to Dakota.

"We're late. Come on, get a move on, Mister Chainsaw Killer." With a grin over her shoulder, Dakota kept moving.

The atmosphere of the festival was already working on Dakota's nerves. She was smiling and happy to be there. The kids around them were yelling and screaming, but it was all in good fun.

Before they entered the carnival area, Dakota noted that the vendors' booths were swamped with buyers. It wasn't just the kids who were drawn to the festival at night. It seemed the Harvest Festival After Dark had attracted the attention of quite a few people.

If she didn't know any better, Dakota would think she was back home at a night festival in California. The crowds left little room to walk around, but the feeling was electric. As she passed strangers, she noted the smiles and laughter. Walking through this place, she couldn't help but feel the joy and fun all around.

This was exactly what she needed, being surrounded by happy people enjoying the fun, festive atmosphere. Added to it were all the men and women wearing cowboy boots and hats. That was something she'd not see back home. At least, not in such numbers.

She'd miss this when it was time for her to leave. But until then, Dakota Monahan promised herself she'd have fun. Which included a little flirting with a certain cowboy who always had a nice smile for her.

Chapter 23

Skeeter was on top of the world. Every time he chased Dakota, she seemed to get a little flirty with him. While he had promised Jerod he wouldn't flirt with her, it was getting more and more difficult to hold back. Especially when she ran a finger across his cheek, then ran. The little minx was really testing his will.

But, in the end, he didn't get much of a chance to flirt back. The best he could do was rev the chainsaw, scream, then chase her like a little rabbit through the throngs of people. Once, when they were in the maze, he had caught hold of her arm and was about to bring her close, when a kid ran between them, breaking them up.

Dakota ran away laughing, with her hair flying behind her.

His heart was beating overtime, but it wasn't from the running they were doing. If Dakota didn't watch out, she'd have him in love with her before Halloween arrived. And, if all went to plan, by New Year's she would be his girl. But that plan depended on him finding a local job, and soon.

When ten o'clock came and went, Skeeter realized that they hadn't stopped for a break. "Hey, Dakota. I think it's time for a coffee break."

They had just run past a group of teens who screamed and ran for their lives, so it was just the two of them. Well, there were still tons of people around, but no one close enough to hear him.

"Already?" The panting in Dakota's voice worried Skeeter.

"Hey, I think we need to sit down for a bit. Come on. I don't want to run you ragged on your first night back." He grinned and knew he couldn't exactly say anything about her condition. If it came down to it, he'd fake a Charlie horse or something. Anything to get her to take a short break and drink some water. Maybe eat some of those veggie sticks Jerod said she needed.

Thankfully, Dakota didn't need any more reason to stop and rest.

Once they were safely inside the barn where the employee breakroom was located, Dakota eyed him suspiciously. "This isn't because you think I can't keep going, is it?"

He knew he was treading on thin ice there. "No. I know you can run me ragged. But we need to keep in mind that it's only early October. We've got several weeks left of this. I don't intend to tire myself out too soon." He grinned, popped a cherry tomato in his mouth, and about choked on the juice when it squirted down his throat.

His face went red, and he started coughing, hard.

"Whoa, now. Take it easy." Dakota patted his back. "Do you need me to do the Heimlich?"

Skeeter shook his head and a throaty "no" barely escaped his lips. When he finally got the blasted thing down, eyes watering, he grimaced. "Well, that was really manly, wasn't it?"

Dakota had to bite her lip to keep from smiling. "Don't worry about it. If you couldn't clear it, I could have always used your chainsaw to cut it out."

Skeeter snorted. "You'd like that, wouldn't you?" He felt himself moving closer and closer to flirting with her and had to clear his throat to stop himself from saying anything else at that moment.

But when she smiled, all he could see were her sweet lips. Lips he wanted desperately to kiss. NO. He had to remind himself she was off limits until he moved out from the ranch. It didn't matter that she was so obviously flirting with him.

When Dakota did that hair toss thing and smiled demurely at him, Skeeter's heart went into quadruple time. He loved it when a woman did that. It was one of those signs that clearly meant she was into it. The woman was practically begging him to flirt back.

Skeeter took two steps closer to her, with a knowing grin on his lips. "You know, if you aren't careful, I'm gonna get into a lot of trouble."

She batted her eyelashes. "Really? Why's that?"

A deep guttural groan escaped his lips, and he shook his head. "Woman, you're gonna be the death of me."

"How's that?" A familiar voice broke through the hazy fog that had enveloped the two flirty birds.

Skeeter coughed and backed up.

Cute lines formed above Dakota's eyebrows as she looked from Skeeter and Jerod, not sure what was happening.

"Ah, hey boss. We were just taking a break. Needed some water after all that running around." With a nervous laugh, Skeeter nodded to Jerod.

"Good. I just came in to see how things were going." Jerod turned his steely gaze from Skeeter and softened his features when he looked to Dakota. "How ya feeling? Did you want to keep going?"

"I'm fine. And yes, I'm having a great time. I want to keep it up until the event is over." She crossed her arms over her chest and stared at Jerod.

A prickle of unease passed between the two, and Skeeter wondered what it was that he didn't understand. He knew she had MS and needed to take it somewhat easy. And if she got dizzy or nauseous, he had to made sure Dakota sat down and got something to eat or drink. But, other than that, he didn't know anything else.

Jerod opened his mouth, then shut it when he noticed Skeeter staring at him. Instead, he nodded, then added, "Just take it easy. I don't need your doctor giving me a lecture when he comes out next week."

Pink tinged Dakota's cheeks, and Skeeter was momentarily distracted. Then the words hit him. Her doctor was coming to the Crooked Arrow? Why? Was there more to this than initially met the eye? Skeeter prayed that God wouldn't take Dakota from the ranch. Or He at least wouldn't take her from the area.

They all turned around when they heard familiar voices laughing.

"There you are. Did you know that Spike has been all over the place looking for you?" Nelly grinned and held the dog back. He was straining at his collar, trying to get to Dakota.

Dakota leaned down on one knee. "Hey, there, fella. I always love to see you."

Nelly let Spike off the leash, and he ran into Dakota's outstretched arms.

"You know, I never realized how much Spike likes women, until now." Nelly shook her head.

Skeeter leaned over and pet the dog's head. "Hey, Spike. Do you have a happy greeting for me, too?"

Spike licked Skeeter's face and chuffed his greeting.

Everyone laughed.

"So, does this mean he likes me? Or he wants me to move out of his way?" Skeeter arched a brow at the dog while he wiped the dog's saliva from his face.

"I'd say he likes you." Nelly grinned at Spike. "Braver hund."

Dakota stood up straight but kept a hand on Spike's head. "That means 'good dog', right?"

"Yes, well done. Do you speak German?" Again, Nelly looked at her like she knew something that everyone else didn't.

Dakota shook her head. "No, Sam taught me what that phrase meant. But I am trying to pay attention when people speak German to the dogs."

"Well, Spike seems very content." Nelly paused, then looked at Dakota and Skeeter. "How would you feel about keeping Spike with you for a little while tonight?"

Skeeter grinned. "Can we dress him up?"

Nelly laughed. "I was thinking you might want to keep his service vest on and see how he reacts to everything." She arched a brow in Skeeter's direction. "It might be best if Dakota keeps his leash tonight."

"I, for one, think it's a great idea." Jerod nodded. "But it's up to Dakota if she wants to take responsibility for working with Spike tonight. She's not had any training with service dogs yet."

"I'd love to. Is there anything special I need to know?" Without even thinking about it, Dakota ran a hand down Spike's head and then scratched behind his ears. A smile never left her face.

Chapter 24

To say that Dakota was thrilled to have Spike with her was an understatement. The dog was great at keeping people out of her way, but he also served as a very warm companion. He even nudged her out of the way when a group of rowdy college guys pulled out a flask of something they weren't allowed to have at the festival.

When Dakota saw the college guys drinking, she thanked Spike for warning her. Then she headed off to find to Sadie. "I thought alcohol wasn't allowed here?" She found the woman next to the Frenchtown Roasting Company's coffee booth.

"What?" Sadie's furrowed brow and open mouth made it clear Dakota caught the woman off guard.

"Sorry, I should have said hi first. Spike and I almost had a run in with a group of college guys drinking over by the maze." Dakota pointed in the direction she had just come from.

Sadie pursed her lips. "Cody was adamant about not selling any alcohol, or even allowing anyone to bring it in. He doesn't want anyone to drink and drive after being at his ranch. He lost a good friend in high school to a drunk driver, and ever since he's stayed clear of anything that might impair his driving. Plus, the thought of anyone getting in an accident after being at his ranch always makes him uneasy." She shivered at the idea of something happening.

"Hmm, well. Looks like someone didn't get the message." Dakota had seen plenty of signs up stating that alcohol wasn't allowed on the ranch. They had to have snuck their bottle of whatever it was in.

Spike barked, which was unusual for him. The dogs were trained to chuff a little, but rarely bark. The idea of a dog who barked a lot didn't sit well with most people who suffered from PTSD. Any sharp or loud sound could send them into a tailspin.

Dakota looked down and asked what was bothering him. Then she followed Spike's gaze. "Those are the guys." She pointed to the group of five guys in jeans and Montana Grizzlies sweatshirts.

"Figures." Sadie rolled her eyes. "I'll deal with this." She headed to the rowdy men.

Dakota bit the inside of her lip and looked down at Spike. The dog returned her gaze, then looked to Sadie and the college guys. He chuffed and nudged Dakota to follow Sadie.

"Are you sure, boy?" While Dakota wasn't afraid of those guys, she wasn't sure if she should get involved. It wasn't her ranch.

Spike pulled on the leash in an attempt to follow Sadie.

"Alright, I guess she could use backup." Dakota waved at the barista behind the coffee booth. "I'll be back for a latte later."

The woman gave her a worried look and followed them with her gaze until they were no longer in sight.

By the time Dakota and Spike caught up to Sadie, she was glad they decided to follow the woman. She was surrounded by the guys like she was prey, and they were the hunters. She didn't like this one bit.

"Hey, what's going on?" Dakota used her military voice and projected her gruff question.

Spike stood at her side and growled. Dakota knew that service dogs weren't trained to attack, but they could sense when someone had bad intentions, and would growl a warning to not only their handler, but also to the offending human. Or in this case, humans. Plural.

One of the guys, most likely the ringleader, backed up with his hands in the air. "Hey now. We're just making friends with the pretty lady."

"That didn't look like a friendly game of ring around the rosy." Dakota pursed her lips and gripped Spike's leash. "Back off."

"Or what?" Another one of the guys chuckled and took a step closer to Sadie. "What are you gonna do? Sic your dog on me?"

The rest of the guys laughed. The stench of alcohol permeated the air, making Dakota's stomach turn in revulsion.

With a smirk, Dakota looked to Sadie. "I don't think we need a dog to put you guys in your place."

A steely determination glittered in Sadie's green eyes.

If those drunks thought a blond woman didn't know how to take care of herself, they were in for a rude awakening. Dakota may not know Sadie well, but she did know when someone had a look that dared anyone to mess with them. And that blonde looked as though she would chew those boys up and spit them out before they even knew what hit them.

Plus, Dakota would back her up. After dealing with handsy drill sergeants in basic and AIT, she had learned a thing or two. She only hoped Spike wouldn't get hurt in the process. Sensing that something was about to happen, she looked at the dog and put her hand out. "Stay." She didn't remember the German word, but she had seen Nelly do the same hand gesture before.

Spike sat on his haunches and whimpered. He knew what was going on. Dogs were smart that way.

And it appeared that some fair goers were smart, too. A couple of the local cowboys she'd seen in town walked up and glared at the college guys.

"You better be on your best behavior here," a man with a black cowboy hat said before looking to Sadie. "Sadie, you good?"

"Yup, but thanks, Cove."

That was it. Dakota had seen this man before at the coffee shop in town. He was a former rodeo star who married Lottie, the woman who owned Frenchtown Roasting Company.

"Hey, man. We weren't doing anything wrong. Just chatting up these two women. One of them yours?" the guy who seemed to be the leader and was a head taller than the rest in his pack, asked.

"They are both friends of ours. And Sadie here," he pointed to the woman in question, "is married to the owner of this ranch. I highly suggest you not try anything with a married woman. Men around these here parts don't take to kindly to that sort of thing."

Just then, Cody walked up to Sadie and put a possessive hand on her lower back. "What's going on?" He sniffed the air. "Never mind, I think I understand." He pulled out a walkie talkie and asked for help.

It was no time at all before three beefy men wearing bright green jackets over tight black t-shirts joined them.

Cody looked to his security team and pointed to the group of drunks. "These here kids seem to have gotten in with alcohol. They're too drunk to drive. Can you get them home safely?" He looked the boys up and down. "Or call their parents to come get them?"

"Hey, that isn't necessary. We're all over twenty-one and legal." A short, dark-haired guy blinked and swayed on his feet.

"Drinking isn't allowed on my ranch. And driving while intoxicated is illegal. I suggest you let my guys give you a ride home, or I could call the Sheriff to come and get you. But I have a feeling he'd just take you to his office and let you sleep it off there." Cody grinned.

Dakota got the impression that he'd prefer it if they did get thrown in the drunk tank. Shoot, she might like to see them there, too. Drinking and driving was just plain stupid. Maybe it was her military background, or maybe it was all she'd seen, but the idea of men who were supposed to be smart breaking the rules like this really chafed her. It was one thing to drink at home or if you weren't driving, but to sneak booze into a family event and get drunk and cause a scene? Then to think it was fine to drive after that? She shook her head at the stupidity of today's youth.

Even though she was probably only a couple of years older than them, she felt like she was decades more mature. Experiencing war forced a person to grow up. And at that moment, she almost wished that anyone who wanted to attend college had to first serve in the military.

Now that Cody and his guys had it all under control, Dakota was ready to head back to the coffee cart. "Hey, Sadie. Care to join me for a cup of coffee? Something back at that cart smelled heavenly."

Sadie grinned and took Dakota by the arm. "Dakota, my dear. Have you ever tried a toasted caramel almond latte?"

The name of the drink sounded like a mouthful, but it sure did smell like something her tastebuds would love. In fact, the more she thought about it, the more she had to try it. "No, but something tells me I'll be trying it before the night is over."

"Smart girl." Sadie grinned and pulled her friend along for the best drink of the season.

The two of them were sitting at a picnic table and laughing over nothing important. Spike sat there looking at Dakota with love in his eyes. She had given him a special dog treat, a pumpkin pup-pie, that Lottie sold at the coffee cart. They were tiny little pies made from real pumpkin puree, oat flour, egg, and a couple of other ingredients that were all dog safe. Dakota had purchased a three pack since each one was basically two bites. At least, for a dog Spike's size.

If Spike hadn't felt strongly for Dakota before, he sure did now. His tongue lolled out the side of his mouth and he waited for Dakota to give him another piece of the pie.

"Are you ready for another one?" Dakota picked up the mini pie and held it between her thumb and forefinger, basically taunting the dog.

Spike chuffed and stood up, licking his mouth. Then he chomped his teeth together, signaling he wanted to eat.

"What's this?" Skeeter asked when he walked up and saw Spike take the food straight out of Dakota's hand. And all without biting her fingers.

"It's called a pumpkin pup-pie." Dakota beamed and winked at Spike, who happily licked the remnants of the whipped cream topping from his mouth.

"I thought sugar wasn't good for dogs?" Skeeter tilted his head and looked at Spike, who walked over to him and nudged his thigh. "Sorry, buddy, I don't have any treats tonight."

"Well, it depends on the dog, but sugar in small amounts is alright. However, there isn't sugar in this recipe. I think honey and cinnamon are what give it a dog-approved sweetness." Dakota had been very careful about getting the list of ingredients from the barista before agreeing to let Spike have any.

Skeeter looked to Spike. "Is this Spike-approved?"

The dog almost nodded when he chuffed. Then he turned loving eyes to Dakota and waited patiently for the last treat.

"I swear, he can count. I only bought three of them. And he's now had two. How did he know I had another one I was hiding?" Dakota chuckled at how smart the dog was.

The barista walked over and grinned down at the dog. "Dogs can smell much better than we can. I bet he smelled the cinnamon or pumpkin that you were hiding."

"Hey, Sassy. How you liking it here?" Skeeter smiled at the pretty woman.

Anger flashed through Dakota for just a moment before she got it under control. She couldn't believe the pain that shot through her heart. It seemed that Skeeter was flirting with the barista. Something she'd thought she didn't want him to do with her. So why did it bother her that he was attracted to the other woman? She should be happy that someone else was in his sights.

But she wasn't. Dakota wanted Skeeter's full attention. Which was just plain crazy. All sorts of confusing emotions and thoughts began rattling through her. That was, until a wet nose touched her hand. Dakota looked down to see Spike looking at her, full of love. If she didn't know better, she'd swear the dog knew exactly how she felt in that moment, and he was trying to make her feel better.

Almost immediately, the confusion left her, and she felt peace pass through her. Not the same peace she felt whenever she prayed, but it was definitely the sort of peace that only God could give her. Was God trying to show her something here? He had her full attention now.

A sweet-sounding voice interrupted her self-reflection, and she looked up to see Sassy and Skeeter laughing about something that she'd missed.

With a sigh, she turned her gaze to Sadie, but that was even worse. The woman seemed to be looking into her soul. When a glittering smile appeared on Sadie's face, Dakota hoped the woman couldn't read her thoughts.

"I don't know how long I'll be in the area, but I'm enjoying my time here, that's for sure." Sassy grinned at Skeeter, oblivious to the others around her.

Until Cove walked up to them.

"Sadie, I hope those guys didn't hurt you?" Cove's worried expression then turned to Dakota. "What about you? Did they do anything to you?"

She shook her head. "No, they didn't bother me." She almost chuckled as she compared those boys to the life she'd lived in the Army and the experiences she'd made it through. "It takes a lot to intimidate me."

"I bet now even more than before." Skeeter piped in. "There's something about experiencing battle that hardens you." A distant expression crossed his eyes and then left almost as quickly as it arrived.

He got her. It made him even more attractive. "Yeah, something like that."

"What? What guys?" Sassy stared at Cove, waiting for an explanation.

When he finally told her about the commotion, she put a hand over her mouth. "I saw them and wondered what they were doing. But, I mean," she waved a hand, "why would anyone need to bring alcohol in here? There's so much to do here that booze isn't needed."

Cove's face hardened. "They didn't try anything with you, did they?"

Sassy quickly shook her head. "No, they didn't even come close to the cart. But there was a loll and I noticed them laughing and then one looked around quickly before taking a bottle out of his pocket. Before I could think any more on it, a group of tourists stopped by to get coffee." She went into detail about what they all ordered, which of course was all different specialty drinks.

"Even in a small, sleepy place like Frenchtown, we're gonna get some idiots who try to ruin the party for everyone else," Cove snarled when he looked back toward where the guys had been. "I'm just glad you all are alright. We'll have to keep a better eye out. If you see something, report it."

Sassy looked to the ground and moved the dirt around with the tip of her shoe. "I'm sorry. I know I should have said something, but I just got busy."

"Don't worry. What's done is done, but just remember for next time. That's all." Cove smiled, and Sassy's shoulders relaxed.

Dakota's eyes narrowed when she looked between Cove and the barista. She hoped there wasn't anything going on there. Cove was married. Or was Sassy just a flirt? Only a few minutes earlier she had been flirting with Skeeter, and now it looked as though she might have a thing for Cove. She was going to steer clear of the pretty woman as much as she could.

And she prayed that Skeeter would, too.

Chapter 25

W hen Sunday morning came bright and sunny, Dakota moaned and turned over in her bed. The last thing she wanted after a weekend of working late nights at the harvest festival was to get up at the crack of dawn. But pulling the sheet over her head didn't help when her alarm went off only moments later.

"Mm, five more minutes, Mom," she mumbled into her pillow. But the offending sound didn't stop. "Ugh. Really?" Dakota turned over and was about to turn her alarm off when she realized it was past nine in the morning.

Sighing, she slowly sat up, then put her feet on the cold ground. "I'm so going to need a carpet on this side of my bed." The entire bedroom had hardwood flooring, except for the small red and black Pendleton rug that stuck out only a few inches from under the tall dresser. Dakota doubted Jerod would be happy if she rearranged the room just to get the rug. Maybe she could find a cool

Native American one at the festival this week, something she'd want to take with her when she left the ranch.

She stood up and stretched. As she reached upward, a sense of pure exhaustion filled her entire being. All Dakota wanted was to go back to bed and sleep for a week. But she had chores. And one thing the Army instilled in her was the importance of showing up for what you've agreed to do. Once her morning chores were over, she could take a short nap.

Who was she, looking forward to a nap? Wasn't that something old ladies did? She wasn't even twenty-five yet. But she had been pushing herself lately.

Church!

Dakota had almost forgotten all about church. It was Sunday and she always looked forward to learning more about God. The last few sermons she'd listened to had really hit home. Warmth filled her when she thought about church, and she just knew that God had something to tell her again today.

After getting dressed for chores, she slowly made her way down the hall toward the kitchen. Coffee. She needed an IV line of the stuff to help her get going—STAT.

"Good morning, sleepyhead." Dana greeted her with a smile and put a mug in her hands before Dakota had even gotten all the way into the kitchen.

She put the aromatic mug of goodness up to her nose and sniffed long and hard. "Oh, the good stuff. Mmm, you are too good to me."

"I thought you might need a little extra kick this morning. Take a seat, relax." Dana pulled back a chair. "I'll make you an omelet."

Dakota sat and pulled her chair closer to the table. "Thanks, but I have chores to get to." After taking a long, hot sip, Dakota put her mug down.

"Not this morning, you don't. Relax and eat up. Today is a day of rest for you." Dana went to the stove and began mixing in the ingredients she needed to make a ham and cheese omelet.

"But everyone does chores on Sunday before church." Dakota took another sip, then worried at her bottom lip when Dana didn't reply.

She just continued to beat the eggs. When she poured the mixture onto a hot skillet, she turned around and smiled. "Jerod wanted to have a chat this morning. He has a schedule for you and thought now would be a good time to go over it."

"You mean, while the others are out doing all the work?" The coffee had begun to work its magic and Dakota was coming to life. Her brain was starting to fire on all cylinders and she knew what was going on. They were going to treat her differently than the rest of the residents.

"Actually," Jerod walked in and went to give his wife a kiss on her forehead. "You'll have work to do, as well. But Doctor Smythe has a few things he wanted me to convey to you."

That was news to Dakota. She didn't realize her doctor was speaking to Jerod without her present. Sure, she'd given consent, but still. She didn't like this.

Instead of saying anything, she continued to drink her coffee and waited for Jerod to get down to business.

As Jerod worked on pouring himself a cup of coffee, Dakota glared at his back.

He turned around and caught her glare. Instead of being mad or offended, he chuckled. "So, are you extra tired this morning?"

She bristled at the fact he read her situation so well. Was it because she slept in so late? Of course she did, she had been working her butt off the past few nights and staying up until well after two in the morning. "I really didn't sleep in, not when you take into account what time I went to bed."

Jerod nodded. "True, true. But I can see it in your eyes, Dakota. You need more sleep."

Drats, she knew she should have looked at the mirror before coming down. While she could stretch this whole conversation out, she didn't want to. All Dakota wanted was to fit in with the guys at the ranch until it was time for her to leave.

"I don't know how long you're expecting to be here, but I think you don't realize the changes coming to your life." Jerod took a long pause and drank some of his coffee. "This is really the best brew we've had from Lottie in a long time." He turned to look at his wife over his shoulder. "Sweetheart, can you see if Lottie has more of these beans? I'd love to buy in bulk before she switches out to the Christmas blend."

Dakota's ears perked up. "Christmas blend?"

"Yes. Even in small town Montana we love Christmas flavored coffee. Only we have our own roaster who makes it taste better than anything you can get in a store." Jerod grinned over the top of his mug.

Dakota's favorite coffee came at Christmas from one of those huge coffee companies that have stores on every corner. She always bought at least six pounds of beans and ground them as needed. It didn't last all year, but it did last a long time. "Will I still be here when the Christmas blend is ready at Frenchtown Roasting?"

"Yup, you will." Jerod was interrupted when Dana put a plate in front of Dakota with her giant omelet.

"This is too big. Jerod, care to have some?" Dakota pushed her plate toward Jerod.

He put his hands up. "No, thanks. I had my fill earlier. But eat up. It's good for you."

Dakota sighed and looked down at what must have been at least a three-egg omelet. She could rarely even finish a two-egg omelet. There was no way she'd get much more than half of this down, even though her stomach was beginning to growl with anticipation for what was to come.

After taking one bite and swallowing it, Dakota looked to Jerod. "Alright, spill. What do you have to tell me that can't be said in front of anyone else?"

Jerod looked down at the table. "You know that we pride ourselves on helping anyone in the area. And that all of our residents have to do so many hours of community service per month."

Dakota nodded and took another bite.

"Most of our service is for the town as a whole. We help with all of the festivals and events out at the tree farm. And come Christmas we'll do a lot in the town itself for the various seasonal events." Jerod stopped and looked from his wife back to his cup.

Without a word, Dana knew what he wanted. She picked up the pot of coffee and came over to the table. Everyone was quiet while she topped off the mugs. Then she took a clean one from the cupboard and joined them at the table.

Jerod only waited until Dana sat down before he looked back at Dakota. "We also have committed to helping Nelly."

Dakota knew this. That was how Sam and Nelly got together. She'd heard how they fought tooth and nail at first, but, eventually, they'd discovered how well they worked together, and the rest was history.

"Are you a dog person? Nelly has requested that you work with her and Spike. She has several new dogs arriving over the next two weeks. They will need a lot of time and attention. But Spike is basically trained."

"Wait, are you saying that Nelly wants me to have a service dog?" Dakota wasn't opposed to the idea of having a dog. She loved dogs. But she knew how expensive they were, and, when she was at the LA VA hospital, she'd overheard one of the administrators bemoaning the fact that there were never enough trained dogs for veterans who needed them most. She didn't want to take a dog that someone else needed more than she did.

With coffee mug in hand, Jerod nodded. "One of the newest needs for service dogs is veterans living with MS. Nelly is great with training dogs to help veterans suffering from PTSD. But now she wants to train her dogs to also handle MS. The needs are different. And therefore, so is the training."

"But I can get around just fine. I don't need help." In the back of Dakota's mind, she recognized that one day she probably would. But with the advent of new medications and treatments, it should be a long time before she did.

"Maybe so, but your doctor agrees with Nelly. And he thinks it would be great if you had the extra help a partner could give you. Especially while you're learning to live with the changes you're going to have to make."

"What changes?" Dakota understood the need for medicine. And she also knew that exercise would help keep her healthier, longer. But there wasn't anything else she could remember the doctor telling her.

"The vertigo isn't going to go away now that you have medicine. It may not be as bad as that one day in the maze, but you will still suffer from bouts of dizziness. A partner dog will recognize when your equilibrium is off and know how to guide you to a seat. And memory is going to be an issue, no matter how well the meds work for you." It wasn't pity in Jerod's eyes, but he did look sad.

Dakota didn't remember having a conversation about those issues continuing. The doctor didn't tell her any of that, did he? "When did you speak with Doctor Smythe about all of this? And why wasn't I there?"

Dana and Jerod both turned worried eyes to each other. Dana coughed.

Jerod cleared his throat. "Dakota, you were there with us. It was when we picked you up from the hospital."

"Do you remember that the doctor is coming this week for a visit?" Dana asked.

"Yes, I remember that. He'll be here on Wednesday, right?" Boy did she hope her memory wasn't so bad that she had it all wrong.

Jerod nodded. "Yes, and he's going to want to talk to you more about the service dog program. He also wanted to visit Nelly at her ranch and see the dogs in action."

Dana put a hand on her husband's arm. "Dakota, it would mean a lot if you could spend this week working with Nelly and her dogs. If Doctor Smythe likes what he sees, then Nelly could end up getting more funding and expanding her program. Then more of our local veterans could get the help they need from service dogs."

Dakota felt a stinging sensation in her nose and her eyes clouded up. If she agreed to this, she could help a lot of veterans. And if there were more and more veterans in Montana who developed MS thanks to the chemical exposure during their time serving in the Middle East, then she really could make a difference. All she ever wanted was to help others. That was part of why she joined up in the first place, to help those who couldn't help themselves.

"Do you actually think I need a dog? I mean, the doctor said it would be years before my body started really breaking down and experiencing the worst symptoms. And by then the treatments will be better. Shoot, there's even a cure being tested right now."

Jerod looked her directly in the eyes. "I know, and I truly hope that cure works and is given to you the second it's available. Until then, I do believe a dog would be beneficial."

It was a lot to take in. On the one hand, she really should do what she could to give back. But, on the other, she wasn't sure she was the best candidate to work with Nelly. Although, she was the only one at the ranch with MS. The rest of the guys were dealing with PTSD and learning how to live with their physical injuries.

When Dakota had originally been diagnosed with depression, she thought they'd give her meds and then she'd be fine. Once she learned she would need regular counseling to go with those meds, she wasn't happy. Not too many people enjoyed sitting around telling a stranger their deepest, darkest fears or desires.

And the meds only caused other issues.

Then, she'd learned she really didn't have depression. Well, she probably did have some form of temporary depression, but it wasn't something that medication could treat. Coming to Montana and learning about the ranch and the local festivals perked her up. All she'd really needed was a change of scenery and to be with people who understood her and didn't want to overmedicate her.

However, all the changes at once were a bit overwhelming. The anti-depressants would be out of her system soon, but that didn't guarantee she would be her old, overactive self. The medication she'd been on for the last few months had taken away a lot of her energy. But, since she arrived in Montana, some of it had come back. And that was before she stopped taking the meds.

So many thoughts were bouncing around in her head, it was enough to give her a headache. "Um, what about my role at the Harvest Festival? I really enjoyed that. Will I have to stop?"

Dakota waited with bated breath for what Jerod had to say. It was that job that had helped her get back some of her energy and clear her head.

Giving up working with Skeeter wasn't an appealing prospect, either.

Jerod scratched his head. "I'm not really sure. I think for the first few days you'll need to just give Nelly your time. But once she's ready for you to go out with Spike, I think she'd probably be happy to see you at the festival. It will be a good chance for Spike to show what he can do."

"He's already proven that he can handle the crowds. Not to mention how much he helped me when I had that episode." Thoughts of that day flitted through Dakota's memory, and a lot of it was hazy. But Spike? He was clear in her mind.

"Why don't we finish up breakfast, then you can get ready for church. We've got to leave soon if we don't want to be late." Jerod's gaze briefly shifted to the back of the house. "And I think the guys are coming in now."

"Right." Dakota ate as much as she could stomach, which was a lot more than she realized she could. Probably because the taste was out of this world. She didn't' know what Dana used for flavoring, but it had to be real butter along with those fresh eggs. The omelet was fluffy, flavorful, and really hit the spot.

Chapter 26

Skeeter held his tongue the entire ride to church. He, as well as the rest of the guys, had noticed that Dakota didn't come out that morning to help with chores. Not that he was upset or jealous. He was worried about her.

Every time he looked her way, she looked so sad. He couldn't help but wonder if she wasn't feeling well. So, when they all walked inside the church, he finagled a spot next to her on the pew. "Hey, there. How's it going?"

Dakota startled. "Oh, sorry." She put a hand on her chest. "Guess I was off in another galaxy or something."

"What's going on?" Skeeter whispered.

"I'll tell you after service. Shh." Dakota put a finger over her mouth.

Then the choir began singing "Our God is an Awesome God".

The opening chords hit Skeeter right in his chest.

And when they began singing, he felt it all throughout his entire body.

"Our God is an awesome God, he reigns from heaven above with wisdom, power, and love, our God is an awesome God." The entire choir continued to sing as the congregation joined in.

With everyone in the building, almost one hundred people, raising their voices for God's enjoyment, the Spirit was flowing and filling everyone with power and love.

Once the song was over, Skeeter looked to his right. He could see pure joy on Dakota's face. It was such a change from when she walked inside that he knew God's hand was on her and on today's praise music.

As the songs continued, Skeeter focused on the music and the words. He let Dakota enjoy her praise time while he did the same. He let God take all of his worries and decided he wasn't going to take them back like he sometimes did. Today, he was just going to listen and learn.

When the pastor got up and read the verse for the day, Skeeter smiled.

A merry heart doeth good like a medicine. But a broken spirit drieth the bones.

-Proverbs 17:22

It seemed today's message was for Skeeter, and probably for a lot of others in the building. As the pastor gave the message, Skeeter prayed and asked God to help him to always have a merry heart. His joy was in God, and the

Lord would continue to remind him of that fact when he needed it.

"Wow, that was exactly what I needed today." A bright smile greeted him when Dakota turned to look his way. "How does the pastor always know what I need?"

Skeeter chuckled. "I think a lot of us needed this today. Look around."

They both watched as many people smiled and wiped tears of joy from their eyes. Others hugged each other. And Skeeter could hear many voices agreeing with him about the sermon. "You know, I think God is the one who tells the pastor what to say."

"I think you're right." Dakota nodded and looked around at all the joyous faces in the room.

"So, what's for lunch?" Skeeter looked to Dana and grinned.

"After a message like that all you think of is food?" Dana shook her head and tsk'd. But, from her smile, it was obvious that she knew Skeeter was teasing her.

Jerod put a hand on Skeeter's shoulder. "I thought today we'd grill up some chicken breasts and corn on the cob. How does that sound?"

If the ranch residents' grins and laughter that greeted the question were any indication, Skeeter knew everyone felt as he did. Jerod was a master of the grill. The man knew exactly how to flavor the food, and nothing ever came off his grill burnt or undercooked.

As the day came to an end, Skeeter enjoyed his night off from scaring people at the harvest festival. He took Sundays and Mondays off. The festival was closed on

Mondays, so he really only missed Sundays. But he needed the rest and enjoyed the time at the ranch with everyone. It was the only time everyone was all together.

It felt more like a family gathering each week than a Sunday dinner that a group of veterans shared together. It was at that moment that he recalled something one of his Sergeants said on the battlefield— "You can't choose your family, but you do choose who you let into your family." At the time, he didn't get it. None of them chose to be in that platoon, they all received orders from some general at the Pentagon.

Now, he finally understood it. While he wasn't ordered to move to the ranch, he was assigned there by his VA hospital. But, somewhere along the way, he had chosen to make this group of misfits his family. Not by blood or marriage, but by choice.

These were the people he thought of when he thought about home lately. It was Jerod who acted more like his big brother than anyone he was related to by blood. And it made him want to be a better brother to his little brother who was still in high school.

Before bed that night, he called his brother. "Joshua. Hey there, little bro. How goes it?"

"Skeeter? Is everything alright?" The shock in Joshua's voice was like a dagger to Skeeter's heart.

They were never close, and Skeeter felt like a heel for not keeping in touch with his brother. "Hey, man. Everything is good. I just wanted to see how you were doing. How's school?"

When the conversation was over, Skeeter got down on his knees and asked God to forgive him for not being a better brother and to help him keep in touch with Joshua. The kid was going to need his brother after graduating. They didn't have the best parents. Skeeter thought that, maybe, Joshua could come and work with him on a ranch in Montana.

When Monday arrived and everyone was in the barn getting their assignments for the day, Skeeter looked around for Dakota.

Jerod noticed Skeeter's roving eyes, and, once everyone was off doing their jobs for the morning, he pulled Skeeter to the side. "She's got a different assignment this week."

"What's she doing?" Agitation filled him and he couldn't stand still. He started pacing in front of the horse stalls.

"She's working with Nelly. In fact, she won't be at the festival until later in the week." A half smile curved up the side of Jerod's face.

"Oh. Is everything alright?"

"Come on." Jerod slapped a hand on Skeeter's shoulder. "Let's get to work. And yes, Dakota is just fine. She just has a different assignment right now. But don't worry, she'll be back at the festival when Nelly gives her the all clear to take Spike with her."

Skeeter took a step back. "Wait, what? She's getting a service dog?" He hadn't realized she was that bad off. In fact, since the diagnosis of MS, Dakota seemed more full of life and energy.

"Skeeter, don't look so worried. Like I said, she's fine. This is just part of her MS treatment."

The sound of brakes squealing interrupted their conversation, and Skeeter furrowed his brows. Both men walked out of the barn and headed toward the house to see who had come. They didn't see many visitors at the ranch.

When they saw the forest green Ford truck in the driveway, they knew who they would find on their front porch. It was no surprise to see the tall brown-haired man with a brown Stetson and dark boots grinning at them.

"Mr. Henderson, so good to see you." Jerod shook hands with the man who lost his entire ranch the past summer to wildfires.

"Jerod, please call me Mason." He shook the ranch owner's hand and then reached out to Skeeter. "Just the men I came to see today."

Skeeter's eyes widened, but he smiled at the man. They had known the Henderson family for a while, and the entire Crooked Arrow Ranch had mourned the loss of the stock and land with all of Frenchtown this past summer. "How can we help you?"

"Well, as you know, our farm was a complete loss. Fortunately, Missy had made sure we kept up on our insurance payments all these years. Thanks to her, we were fully covered for everything." Mason took his hat off when the front door opened, and Dana walked out.

"Mason, it's so good to see you. Please, come inside and I'll get y'all some iced tea." She held the door open for everyone to enter.

"Thank you, kindly, ma'am. That sounds great." Mason walked inside, followed by Skeeter and Jerod.

Once everyone was seated inside with their tea, Mason laid out his plans for their new farm. "You see, if we start off with cattle right now, come spring I can plant new crops and get everything up to speed within a year."

"That seems like a lot of work. Will you be hiring a crew?" Skeeter didn't want to get his hopes up, but if Mr. Henderson was here to hire people, then he'd be staying close by. Which was exactly what he wanted.

"Yes, and that's why I'm here. Do you know of anyone who is looking for a job on a farm? It would be long-term if all worked out. I don't have a bunk house, obviously. But I can bring in a trailer for a foreman." Mason looked expectantly at Skeeter.

Chapter 27

Dakota must have died and gone to heaven. The dogs were all so much fun, especially Spike. He rarely left her side from the moment she walked up to the barn. He had come running out with his tongue hanging out the side of his mouth.

The dog seemed very happy to see her and even nudged her hand when she didn't immediately reach down and pet him.

When Nelly walked out with a basket in her hand, Dakota wasn't sure what to expect.

"Hiya. I see Spike has already made his presence known." Nelly laughed and clicked her tongue.

After a light chuckle and a good scratch behind Spike's ears, Dakota let the dog go. "He sure is friendly. Does he greet all of your guests like this?"

Nelly shook her head. "Not even close. He seems to have taken a real shinning to ya. I think he even understood when I told him this morning that you were coming. He kept looking at the front of the ranch any time there was the slightest noise as though he expected it to be you."

While she knew dogs were smart, Dakota didn't think they were that smart. But what did she know? These dogs were smarter than humans at times. They could sense what a patient needed and help them get it or bring it to them. All without a command. "Well, I'm glad to be here. But I don't really understand what you want my help with. What can I do?"

"You can start by playing with the dogs. They need their daily exercise." Nelly handed Dakota the basket she held. "There's lots of different toys in here. Some of the dogs have their favorites, and I'm sure they'll let you know once they realize you have the basket."

"That's it? Play with the dogs?" Dakota chuckled. "That's not work, it's play."

"Okay, let's have a chat in an hour and see if you still feel the same way." Nelly whistled and called out, "*Hier.*"

At her command, five more dogs ran outside all excited. Two barked, but the rest ran to Nelly's side and stopped.

"You have more dogs? I thought you weren't getting more for a couple of weeks?" Did Dakota remember that wrong? She wasn't sure, now. Which bothered her more than the idea that she might have forgotten. Her memory had been playing some very unfair games on her lately and she really wasn't sure what was up and what down anymore.

"I'm getting two more next month. These are the new dogs I received once Sam moved in. Now that I have help, I can take on more. Although, just between you and me, it's a lot more than I expected." Nelly laughed and looked around. "Sam is great with the dogs, but he loves to play more than work."

Three dogs were sniffing at the basket Dakota held. One barked, and another chuffed. The rest circled Dakota. It wasn't that she was afraid of the big dogs, she knew they wouldn't hurt her. But she didn't really know what to do.

"I see those deer in the headlight eyes." Nelly reached into the basket and pulled out two balls. "Start with these."

Dakota took the balls and threw them toward the side of the barn causing Pebbles and Bam Bam to run after them. The rest sat on their haunches looking up at Dakota with excitement. "Alright, let's see what we got here." She rummaged through the pile of toys, taking out one at a time and looking at the dogs' reactions.

They each sniffed the items, and as one discovered his favorite toy, he nudged her thigh.

The first item of interest was a rubber chicken that squeaked when she squeezed it. "Oh, who likes this one?" A brown boxer with a black face barked and tried to take it from Dakota. She pulled her hand up and the dog practically jumped up.

With a loud laugh, she had to raise her hand even higher to keep the dog from getting the toy.

"That's Nemo. He loves the chicken. If you throw it, he'll run after it. After he's had his fun he'll bring it back to you, which means he's ready for you to hang it up." Sam walked out with a huge smile on his face. When he got close to Nemo, the dog looked back and forth between the toy and the man, almost like he couldn't make up his mind which he wanted more.

"Hang it up?" Dakota wasn't sure what that meant. Did Nemo like jumping up and trying to get something that was out of his reach? That didn't seem like a fun game for a dog.

"Why don't you give the rest of the toys out, and when Nemo comes back, I'll show you," Sam offered.

She did as commanded. "Who's the white lab?" Dakota pointed to the beautiful dog with a glistening coat that looked almost like snow when the sun shone on it.

"That's Curly."

Dakota looked to Nelly. "No, the white dog with the straight hair."

Sam and Nelly both laughed.

"His name is Curly. It's a bit facetious, I know. But when he was a tiny puppy, he would curl up next to a doll that looks just like the one he has in his mouth now. The family who fostered him named him Curly because of the blonde curly hair on the doll." Nelly shrugged. "I didn't see a need to change his name."

"I love it. How adorable." Dakota sighed and patted the dog's head. But Curly didn't want her touching his baby, so he ducked away and ran off.

She watched until the last dog nudged her leg.

Dakota looked down at the cutest German Shep-hard-Labrador mix she'd ever seen. "Oh, you're so adorable. What's your name?" she cooed, then reached for his name tag. "Bison. Well, that's a big name for a big dog. I take it you're the king of pack?"

Sam chuckled. "Anything but. He's more of a lover than a fighter. Which is why he waited until you were done to get your attention."

"Oh, I see. I just thought you were the smartest and knew that once the other dogs were away, I'd give you more loving." Dakota winked at the dog and reached down to scratch behind his ears. Then she ran her hand down the back of his neck and along his back. "What's your favorite toy?"

Bison stuck his nose in the basket and pushed out a tug of war rope with a ball at one end and a loop at the other.

Dakota grinned in triumph. "See, I told you he was the smartest. He knew that if he wanted me to play with him, I had to send the others off on their own first."

"Huh. I hadn't thought of it that way." Sam looked at Bison. "You really are the smart one, aren't you?"

Bison looked at Sam, then back to Dakota and chuffed.

They all laughed and agreed Bison was the smartest dog.

An hour later, Dakota wondered how Sam and Nelly did it. She was exhausted. Not five seconds after playing tug of war with Bison, Spike came over and wanted her attention. Then the rest of the dogs started coming back to her. She had to throw balls, chase dogs, and find a way to hang a rubber chicken up for Nemo to get him to stop nudging her toward the barn. Eventually, she realized that there was a string in the barn just for this very thing.

Nemo was busy for at least thirty minutes jumping up and down as the chicken wobbled on the bouncing cord.

When Nelly joined her, Dakota sat down with a thunk and shook her head. "No wonder you wanted help. They really are a lot of work, aren't they?"

Nelly laughed. "You get used to it. I started with two, then had four. And I didn't get more than four until Sam was here regularly. And now that he lives in the barn, it made sense to get more dogs. He's a huge help."

"And I bet all of this activity is good for him, too. Right?" Dakota knew a little bit about Sam and his history. Not much, but enough to know that as long as he stayed in good shape, he'd do well on the ranch with Nelly.

Nelly tilted her head and looked Dakota up and down. "It's exercise for anybody, regardless of their physical or mental issues. Staying active and doing something that gives you a real sense of accomplishment is healthy for everyone."

"Yeah, I can see that. So, tell me, Nelly. How many dogs do you think you can train at once?" Dakota knew that the dog whisperer wanted more, but how many could one trainer take on?

"I think I'm at my max right now. Spike will be choosing his partner any day now, I think." She looked from Spike to Dakota. "And with Rogue already paired up with Sam, and Buffy with Tony, I only need to place Angel. Then the original four will all be gone."

"So, you really think I'm a candidate for a service dog? Why?"

"Come on, let's get some tea. We can sit and talk while the dogs take turns with Sam and Rogue."

Dakota expected Spike to go with the rest of the dogs, but he followed closely on her heels. "Is it alright if Spike goes with us?"

Nelly smiled and patted Spike's head. "Braver hund. And yes. He can go with us."

When Dakota took her seat, Spike sat at her feet. She felt as though he was already her dog, even though it wasn't a done deal. Not yet anyway.

As Nelly explained how Spike could help her when she had an episode, Dakota pulled back into herself. She didn't like the idea of these issues coming out so soon. Shouldn't she have years, if not decades, before she needed any help?

"I can see the fear in your eyes, Dakota." Nelly bit the inside of her lip. "I doubt you'll have any of these problems any time soon. But it's important to be prepared."

"If you weren't here, in Frenchtown, do you think any doctor would be considering a service dog for me at this time?"

Nelly thought about it while she took a drink from her iced tea. As the condensation dripped from the glass into her hand, and then in her lap, she came to realize something. "You know, I think this is more for me and my business than it is for you right now. You may never need a service dog. But, if you plan on leaving the ranch soon and living on your own, having the dog will go a long way in helping you. And it will give peace of mind to those who care about you and worry about you living all alone."

The thought of her family worrying over her living alone had never crossed her mind. When she had called her mom, of course the woman had asked her to come home and live with her. And Dakota was going to do that, but only until she found a place of her own. She was a grown woman now, one who had experienced things most people can't even imagine. She should be on her own.

But a niggling feeling in the back of her mind wouldn't leave her alone. "You're saying that if I have another episode like the one that sent me to the hospital, Spike could bring help. Or assist me in getting somewhere safe?"

"Exactly." Nelly agreed.

That changed things.

Chapter 28

As the week progressed, and Skeeter worked the festival alone, without Dakota, he realized she was the one who had made it so much fun. He still scared people, dressed up, and went around the festival. But he really was just "phoning" it in this week. He missed Dakota, and it showed in his performance, even though no one said anything to him.

However, just that morning, Dakota said she might be able to start coming back to the harvest festival. If Nelly felt she and Spike were ready, she'd be there Friday night, with bells on. Her words, not his.

"I do miss the festival. But I'm learning so much about service dogs, and the process is very helpful for Nelly. Plus, Doctor Smythe said he was impressed with Nelly's set up and would recommend her dogs." Dakota had said she enjoyed having the doctor visit.

While Skeeter understood the importance of this visit, and the time Dakota was spending with Nelly, he still missed her. However, he had some big news of his own to share with everyone at breakfast. "I hope you and Spike do join us tonight, that would make it so much more fun. Do you think we could get a costume for Spike?"

The dog, who had taken to following Nelly around since he moved to the ranch with her only two days earlier, chuffed and nodded.

"Did he?" Skeeter pointed to Spike, then shook his head. "No, he couldn't have."

Dakota giggled. "Yes, I think he did. We'll have to find something for him to try on when we head back to Nelly's after breakfast."

"Now, that's something I'd love to see." Jerod grinned at the dog.

All of the service dogs who had moved to the ranch seemed to recognize that Jerod was the alpha male. And each one accepted him. Except for Spike. For whatever reason, Spike didn't want to have anyone else over him. He was the alpha, especially when it came to the other dogs in the house.

Skeeter had laughed the night before when Spike pushed his way in front of Rogue and Buffy as they all went for their nightly walk. "I think you're gonna have a handful with that one, Dakota."

"Don't I know it." She called out over her shoulder as Spike led her on a walk, instead of the other way around.

But now, it was Skeeter's turn to share some news. He cleared his throat. "So, um. I have something I'd like to share with the group."

Most everyone was at the breakfast table. Only Mike was missing. He had eaten earlier and was outside preparing for a new calf to arrive.

All eyes turned to the cowboy who had asked for their attention. Now, he squirmed in his seat. Normally, he loved being the center of attention. But now? He was nervous. "I was offered a great position with the Henderson's on their ranch." He paused as all eyes rounded, along with a few mouths. "He's offered me the position of ranch foreman, and I accepted. I'll be moving into a trailer on his property next month."

"That's fantastic," Tony called out.

"Great job. I knew you'd be the one who got it," Jerod said.

Everyone congratulated him and a few even patted him on the back. When he looked at Dakota, she was sitting there quietly watching him.

"So, what do you think?" Skeeter asked her.

"Me?" Dakota put a hand to her chest. "Actually, I thought you'd find a way to get hired full-time at the Big Sky Christmas Tree Farm and Ranch. With all the events they put on, and how well you're doing, I thought for sure Cody would want to keep you around." She rubbed one eye, and when her hand pulled back, the whites of her eye was all red.

Skeeter wondered if she was trying to keep from crying. It was good news, wasn't it? His staying in the area?

"Well, they don't have the budget right now for anyone else. Cody did say he'd love to hire me when he could, but he didn't think it would happen for at least another year, maybe more."

"Too bad. I know how much you love playing the role there." Dakota blinked and then stood up. Spike was right at her side, and he guided her to the front door, already knowing where they were headed.

Once Dakota and Spike were gone, Skeeter sat there staring after her. "I thought she'd be happy I was gonna be so close."

Dana pursed her lips, then stood up. When she came back to the table, she topped off Skeeter's coffee as well as her own. "Give her time. She's had a lot of change to deal with lately. I'm sure she's happy for you. Maybe she had just hoped to be able to work with you at the tree farm this Christmas?"

After a long sip of his hot coffee, Skeeter looked around the room to make sure no one else was nearby. "Do you think Jerod would mind if I tried to ask Dakota out now? You know, since I'll only be here for a couple more weeks?"

Dana sat back and looked as though she was seriously considering the question. Lines began to form on her forehead and she focused her eyes on Skeeter for a few heartbeats. "You know, I think he'd be fine with that. But just be careful. I don't know if Dakota is ready for dating."

"You mean you don't know if she'll say yes to me?" Skeeter had wondered if she was interested in him. They got along so well and had so much fun together. He couldn't imagine her not wanting to spend more time with him. But that didn't mean she wanted to date him. It was very possible the vibe he'd picked up on was one of friendship and comradery, nothing more.

"That's not what I said. Not everything is about you, Skeeter. Sometimes when a woman says no it has nothing to do with you, and everything to do with what's going on in her life." Dana arched a brow, then stood to clear the table. "I've got to get going. Today is my day to work at the Frenchtown Roasting Company. I'll probably not see you until tomorrow morning. Enjoy your night." She winked and went off to do the last of dishes before heading out to work.

He sat at the table, cup in hand, as he thought about what Dana had said. For the past few days, he'd heard snippets of conversations with Dakota and her doctor. Even one that included Jerod and Megan, the counselor. Although, he didn't understand why Megan was involved now that they all knew Dakota wasn't suffering from clinical depression. But everyone did have to do weekly meetings with the counselor, so maybe that qualified as her required session?

Anyway, she had heard Dakota say she was overwhelmed with everything. But that Spike was a great companion. He had somehow already begun to help Dakota relax and let her stress go. Maybe he should get a dog? Not that he needed a service dog, but he had seen how having dogs around worked well at calming people. If Sam could turn into a nice guy, then anyone would benefit from having a dog, even if it was only as a pet.

He snickered as he remembered what a grump Sam had been only a few short months ago.

He'd have to ask Mr. Henderson about getting some working dogs for the ranch. That would probably work well for him. Now, however, all he wanted to do was take Dakota out for dinner Monday night when the carnival was dark.

A huge grin spread across his face when he remembered that Dakota was going to be at the carnival that night, working with him. "Maybe that's when I'll ask her."

It wasn't.

Friday night was utter chaos. It seemed word got out about the man who chased teens around with a chain saw. The kids were running him ragged. Even when he had only a second to catch his breath, a new kid would walk by taunting him. It wasn't a real taunt; they did that to catch his attention and get him to chase after them.

Normally it was a lot of fun.

Now, Skeeter just wanted a break, and maybe a drink of cold water.

"You don't scare me." A kid with pimples all over his nose, who barely even made it over the forty-eight-inch height requirement for most rides, stuck his tongue out at Skeeter.

The dark-haired kid couldn't have been more than thirteen, but the other kids who were with him, were laughing and looked to be a few years older than him. Skeeter knew what was up. The younger kid was trying to prove himself to the older boys.

Skeeter couldn't let the kid down. "Grrr," he revved his fake chainsaw and glared at the kid. When the boy yelled and took off, Skeeter knew he had to make the chase look good for those watching.

And that was when a ratty old dog stepped in his path and chuffed.

Skeeter stopped just short of stepping on the dog. "Spike. You look fantastic." The dog had a grubby old denim hat on. His ears poked through holes on the hat in just the right spot for him.

"He better, it took hours to get him to sit still long enough to paint on the spots of blood. And that hat." Dakota rolled her eyes. "Spike thinks he looks really great now. But an hour ago, he practically refused to keep it on. That was until Nelly showed him how great he looked in the mirror." She chuckled. "You'd think he was a model preparing to walk down a Milan runway, or something."

Skeeter had to hold back his laugh. He was still in costume, and those kids were watching. "Grrr," he revved the chainsaw again and glared at Spike.

The dog took a que well. He barked and turned to run. When he looked back over his shoulder for Skeeter, Dakota couldn't help but laugh. Spike took a few steps forward and Skeeter followed. Not wanting to be left behind, Dakota ran after them pretending to fear for her dog's life.

The new schtick worked so well, that they were all over social media within thirty minutes. And more local area kids and young adults showed up.

When the festival finally closed down, all three practically fell down in the barn to rest before heading back to the Crooked Arrow.

"You three were awesome. I can't thank you enough for all of your hard work." Cody had come in carrying take-away cups of hot tea. "Here, I think you might need this." He handed the tea to both humans and then pulled a piece of beef jerky out of his back pocket.

Spike's head perked up from the ground and his ears twitched, but he made no effort to move towards the special treat. But his eyes never left Cody.

"Can he have this?" Cody asked Dakota, who nodded.

"Sure, just as long as he doesn't get too much. He worked hard, and so well tonight, that he deserves a special treat." Dakota sighed when she tasted the peppermint tea. It had cooled off enough that she was able to take a larger drink. It was already helping her to feel better. She needed to get back to her ranch and then she'd fall right to sleep.

Cody handed the treat to Spike, then scratched his head. "You were fantastic, boy. You're welcome any time you want to come for a visit."

Spike took the offered dried meat and ignored everyone else as he ate it.

Chapter 29

The next morning at a late breakfast, Dakota was smiling. "I think last night was the most fun I've had in…" she shook her head. "I don't know. Maybe ever." Then she took a piece of bacon off her plate and handed it to Spike. "You had a lot of fun, too, didn't you, boy?"

Spike chuffed before he took the offered bacon and then laid down and went to town on his special treat.

"Now, don't get used to this. I'm not supposed to be feeding you from the table. But you earned it." Before Dakota took Spike home with her for the first time a few days ago, Nelly had been adamant about not feeding Spike from the table. It was one thing to add some leftovers to his food dish, but if she handed him table scraps, he would eventually start to beg from people at the table. And no one wanted that.

"Say, Dakota." Skeeter sounded a bit nervous, which caused Dakota to look up at him.

It was then that she realized they were all alone, except for Spike. "Yes?"

His hesitant voice worried Dakota. She had hoped she'd not done something wrong, or that he wasn't about to get after her for giving one piece of bacon to Spike while still at the table. Surely, Skeeter didn't know what Nelly had said, right? Or did he?

"I was wondering..." Skeeter cleared the frog from his throat. "Do you have plans, uh... I mean." He paused and took a deep breath. "Would you like to go to dinner with me Monday night?"

That wasn't at all what Dakota expected him to say. She almost blurted out no. But then she stopped herself. Maybe she should go out with him. What would it hurt? He was moving out soon, so if it didn't work out, then there wouldn't be any awkward moments at the ranch.

The attraction was there. Skeeter was a handsome man, and he was a lot of fun. If nothing else, she was sure they would have a good time.

She realized Skeeter's smile had diminished while she had her little mental discussion. "Oh, yes. Sorry." She giggled. "I think that would be nice. Where did you want to go?"

While the town had a couple of decent places, she wasn't sure the local diner was really first date material, and neither was the pub.

"Really?" Skeeter's wide eyes and open mouth almost had Dakota second-guessing her decision. He seemed as though he couldn't believe she wanted to go out with him. But then he seemed to catch himself and his look of surprise turned to a smile and a little bit of his usual cockiness shone through. "I mean, great. I was thinking we could drive over to Missoula and eat dinner at a steakhouse. How does that sound?"

"Steak?" A slow smile spread over Dakota's face. While she loved a good steak as much as the next person, she also had to keep her red meat to a minimum. But, if she remembered correctly, they also served up some local fresh fish. "I think that sounds perfect. What time should I be ready to leave?"

For the rest of the day, Dakota, and even Skeeter, seemed to have a little extra pep in their step. And when it came time to head out to the festival again, she was full of energy. It seemed making a date with the cowboy had energized her somehow. She had something real to look forward to and it did wonders for her mental wellbeing.

Even Spike picked up on her good mood. The dog's tongue lolled to one side and his eyes were bright as they set out for work. Well, work might not have been the correct term for what they were doing. Playtime was a better description of what she did that night.

Spike loved the attention everyone was giving him, and he didn't even give Dakota a hard time when she got him ready for the night. It was as though he knew what they were up to, and he was totally, one hundred percent onboard with the plan.

Since there hadn't been time to tell Dana anything without the rest of the house hearing them, it wasn't until Sunday afternoon, when they were cleaning up from Sunday supper, that Dakota was able to tell her friend about the date.

"Get out of here. You really said yes?" Dana stopped with her hands still in the sink full of soapy water and dirty pots and pans.

"Hey, what's that supposed to mean?" Dakota glared at her supposed friend and waited for a response.

"I mean, I thought you said you weren't interested in dating for a while? You told me only a couple of weeks ago that you had too much on your plate to even think about men." In an effort to ease the tension, Dana threw a handful of bubbles at Dakota.

With a little squeal, Dakota blocked the soap and zapped her friend on the thigh with the towel she was using to dry the pans. "Hey, now. You don't want to go there."

Dana laughed and put her wet, soapy hands in the air. "You're right. Because if we did, you and I would be left cleaning up a very large mess."

Dakota rolled her eyes. "I know. What is it about guys that they never help in the kitchen?"

"I don't know. I think the guys will sometimes help." Dana tilted her head and squinted her eyes. "Are you trying to change the subject?"

Wide eyes blinked and Dakota put a hand her to her chest. "Who? Me? Never."

"Uh-huh. So, where is lover boy taking you?"

Dakota got back to drying the large pot she had been working on. "A steakhouse in Missoula."

"Oh, that sounds romantic. I bet he takes you to the kind where they have the red-checkered tablecloths, candles, and low lighting. Perfect for you know." Dana waggled her brows and grinned.

"Stop that. It's a first date." Dakota felt her cheeks warm and she turned her head away from Dana.

"I saw those pink cheeks. No need to be shy about a kiss."

Dakota had thought about what it might be like to kiss Skeeter, once. Okay, fine, maybe more than once. But since it was a first date, she knew she had to keep it sweet.

The dinner was wonderful, and the ambiance had Dakota practically praying that Skeeter would kiss her. And not just a peck on the cheek, but one of those deep kisses that didn't leave a woman in doubt of the man's feelings.

So, when they said goodnight, and Skeeter moved in to kiss her cheek, she turned her head and surprised not only herself, but also the man whose lips met hers. For one second his eyes widened, but then he closed them and pulled her tight to his body.

Dakota wrapped her arms around his neck and returned the passion in his kiss. But when he took his lips off of hers and began to move them slowly, lightly, along her skin and headed toward her neck, she moaned deeply.

BEEP, BEEP, BEEP. The grating sound pulled the couple apart and when Dakota opened her eyes, it was only to close them again and pray she could go back. Then, when she looked again, her heart sank.

Instead of her arms wrapped around the handsome cowboy, they were wrapped around her second pillow. With a spot on the purple case that let her know she had been busy kissing alright, but not Skeeter.

She pounded her fist against the pillow and laid on her back staring at the ceiling. "I can't believe it was only a dream."

The noise was still going, and she threw her arm over the off button. "Thank goodness." Dakota sighed when the grating sound ended abruptly and sat up. After she blinked a few times, she realized the sun had already begun to make its long journey over the tops of the mountains in the southeast. She needed to get up and get going or she'd be late for her chores.

That day, she was assigned to get the eggs from the henhouse. Not exactly something she enjoyed, but it was a good time to woolgather. And when she caught herself reliving the kiss from her dream, she would have slapped her face it the chicken wasn't already doing it for her. "Ow, you know Betsy that I have to take the eggs, right? We do this every day."

Dakota pulled her hand back from the onery chicken's nest and frowned when she saw a tiny egg. "Betsy, you're killing me here. Dana," she said to the air, "it's all your fault." If they hadn't been talking about kisses and first dates the previous day, she would never have had that heated of a dream. Still, an hour later and her heart was beating in overdrive when she thought of the warmth from Skeeter's lips in the dream. Then she wondered if it would be like that, or like kissing a fish.

Her last date had kissed her like a fish, and she promised herself to never let a man near her lips who couldn't kiss well. The only problem? Unless she knew the guy's smooching partners, she wouldn't know if he was a good kisser. Which meant, the only way to know was if she let him kiss her. Thinking of fish lips gave her the chills.

Not wanting to have to deal with a poor kisser, she prayed that Skeeter would be a better kisser than her last date.

The day passed without incident, with only a few interactions with Skeeter. And all of those were in front of others. As time got closer and closer to when they were to leave for their dinner date, she felt her nerves begin to fray.

When she heard a knock at her door, she jumped.

"Dakota? It's just me. Can I come in?" Dana's welcome voice sounded through the wood door.

"Yes, please do." With a sigh, she turned in her chair and watched as her friend entered. "I need help."

"Oh!" Dana put a hand over her heart and Dakota noticed her friend's eyes began to shine as though she was about to cry.

"Don't you dare." Dakota pointed a finger at the woman's face. "I just did my make-up."

"You look beautiful. Why do you need help?" Dana looked her up and down and frowned. "I think you are wonderful just as you are."

"I'm so nervous. What if he doesn't like what he sees?" Dakota was about to bite her lower lip, then remembered she had just applied her pink rose lipstick. She didn't want to get it all over her teeth - or have to reapply so soon.

With a chuckle and a shake of her head, Dana let Dakota know just what she thought about that. "There's no need to be insecure. You look beautiful. Skeeter is going to go crazy when he sees you. Trust me."

Ten minutes later, and a whole bevy of breathing exercises, Dakota took one last look at herself. What she saw staring back at her in the mirror surprised her. She had worn a pretty, frilly, summer dress with a floral print that fit her bodice nicely, and flowed down past her knees, over the tops of her brown cowboy boots. Her long brown hair had been curled at the ends and shimmered from the hair spray that had hints of glitter. Her make-up really did look as though she'd come from the department store make-up counter after a great make-over.

Although, it should look good considering the fact that she'd spent over an hour watching YouTube videos on how best to apply it for her hair and eye coloring. Dakota had wondered why she'd put so much effort into her looks. Especially since she'd worn almost no make-up since her arrival at the ranch. Of course, every morning and night she moisturized, but other than that, it was just a bit of eyeliner and a jab of mascara. She didn't even use the eyelash curler like she had back in California before joining the Army. Actually, since joining the service, she'd not worn much make-up anyway.

As she continued to stare at the woman looking back at her, she wondered why she hadn't bothered with much make-up until now. For the first time in a long time, she actually felt pretty. Dakota moved to the door, and with her hand on the handle, she took a deep breath, let it out, then opened the door to a new possibility.

Chapter 30

He was about to have a heart attack. There was no way other than that to explain the pounding in his chest as he watched the most beautiful woman he'd ever seen walk down the hallway. How'd he get so lucky? Skeeter knew he could never deserve the love of a woman as sweet as Dakota, and as beautiful. Did she even know the power she now held over him?

"Hi." The sweet voice that greeted him, actually stopped his heart.

Skeeter couldn't get a word out. His mouth went dry, and his eyes widened. After he licked his dry lips, he tried to swallow past the lump in his throat, but found he couldn't.

Jerod walked up and smiled at Dakota. "You look beautiful. I hope you have a great time tonight." Then he slapped the back of Skeeter's head. "Dude, say something. It's rude to stare at a woman."

"Sorry." Skeeter cleared his throat. "Whoa. I, uh, you look amazing." He looked down at his black jeans, scuffed dark boots, and was grateful that he'd at least pressed his red and black checked shirt before getting dressed. Normally, Skeeter didn't feel as though he was underdressed for a date.

But tonight? He knew that anything short of slacks, dress shirt, and tie wouldn't be enough to be worthy of this beautiful goddess. *Thank you, Lord. I can't believe she said yes. Now, please help me to be on my best behavior.*

When Dakota's cheeks turned that perfect shade of pink, and she tilted her head down at just the right angle that he could only see her eyes through her eyelashes, Skeeter prayed that heaven would be this wonderful.

The two stood there looking at each other, without saying anything else. Neither could. They were both mesmerized by the other.

At least, until Jerod chuckled. "All right, you two. You better skedaddle, or you'll miss your reservation."

That got Skeeter out of his fog. "Right. Yes." He cleared his throat and offered Dakota his arm. "My lady?"

"Why, thank you kind, sir." Dakota put her arm through his and smiled sweetly as they walked to the front door.

Skeeter had to let go of her arm in order to help her into her jacket, and hold the door open for her, which he hated to do. Not helping her, but letting her go. The moment they had walked out, before he even closed the door behind him, Skeeter reached for her hand.

When Dakota easily slid her hand in his, he instinctively smiled and knew she was the one. The sun was still shining in the sky, but it was getting close to the tops of the mountains to the West. They'd get to the restaurant before the sun set, but then they'd have the light from the full moon to guide them home, just as he had hoped.

For the entire night, Skeeter was on his best behavior. He opened all the doors for her, pulled her chair back, asked her to order first, and did his very best to keep the conversation focused on her.

But she was on her best behavior as well and would always try to get the focus back on him. Whenever he asked her a question about herself, she'd give a polite answer, then ask him one. As with most men, Skeeter did enjoy talking about himself, but tonight all he wanted to do was stare into her beautiful brown eyes and count the green sparkles.

Later, if anyone asked him to describe how the food tasted, he'd not even be able to remember what he ate. But when they asked about Dakota, he could answer any and all questions from what she wore, to what she ate, and how many times her eyes sparkled when she laughed. That dinner would forever be etched in his memory.

"You know, I don't think I've had such a wonderful dinner before." With her hand in his, Dakota looked up into his eyes.

In the past, on any other date, this would be the time he'd lean in and go for the kiss. But tonight? He knew he wanted everything to be perfect with Dakota. He was going to wait until they got home before he tried to kiss her. He wanted their first kiss to be under the full moon, with no city lights to interfere. Maybe he'd even pick out a few constellations to show her before leaning in for her sweet lips.

"Tonight should be a great night for viewing the stars, once we're out of the city." Dakota leaned forward in her seat and looked out the front window as they headed away from the restaurant and toward the Crooked Arrow Ranch.

"Do you know many of the constellations?" Skeeter hoped she liked them, but wasn't as up to speed as he was. The fun part of looking at the night sky with a beautiful woman, was getting behind her and aiming her head toward the right stars. The feel of a woman in his arms had made the hours he'd studied the stars so worth it.

While some might call him cheesy, he knew most women loved it just as much as he did. If Dakota didn't seem to be into it, he'd back off. The one thing he never wanted to do was make her feel uncomfortable with him.

"I know a few, like the Big Dipper. But then, I think most people can find that one." She turned and smiled at him.

"Did you know that you can see Andromeda within Cassiopeia right here?" Skeeter had specifically looked up what constellations they'd be able to see in October and the past few nights he'd paid close attention to their location. Just so he could show her.

"Really? Andromeda is inside of Cassiopeia? I didn't know that." She looked back through the windshield and smiled. "I can't see it."

He looked up when they stopped at a light. "I don't think we are in the right place to see it. But I did see it back at the ranch the past few nights. I can show when we get home, if you like."

There, he'd given her a chance to accept his offer, or politely reject him. He prayed she'd do the former. The drive was peaceful with the moon rising behind them, and very few cars on the road. He had the local country music channel playing on the radio and since it was Monday night, it was mostly music. The weekend DJ talked a lot about the different things to do in the area, but the weeknight ones stayed kinda quiet, unless something major was happening.

Skeeter had to keep himself from snorting when the next song played- Jesus take the wheel by Carrie Underwood. What a difference his life was from the song. It was one of those that he'd always liked. But tonight, it was a dry, warm night, instead of a cold snowy one. And while he had a baby in the truck, she was nothing like what Carrie sang about. This one was more of a babe, than a baby. And they were doing quite well, even with their medical issues.

In fact, his were healing quite nicely. He'd always have a bit of a limp from the shrapnel he took in the legs, but the army docs had saved them both. There was a time not too long ago that they weren't sure if they could. And the rehab that he had to endure in order to get his muscles working again? Well, it was worth it. But at the time he almost wished he'd had one amputated.

He couldn't believe he was already pulling into the ranch. When he turned to look at the woman sitting in the cab next to him, he saw something in her eyes. Was it sadness? Did she not enjoy their date? Skeeter thought they had hit it off so well.

"I'm kinda sad the night is just about over. But I know, we have a long day tomorrow that's going to start very early." Dakota sighed and looked up at the night sky.

His heart soared. He'd been right, she was having a great time. "How about we take a little walk and do some stargazing?" If he got his way, he'd be doing some Dakota gazing.

"I'd like that." The soft smile she gave him, warmed his heart and sent shivers down his spine. If he wasn't mistaken, she was looking forward to this just as much as he was. Did that mean she was open to a goodnight kiss under the stars?

After he parked, and helped her out of the truck, they headed away from the house, and the barn, toward the side of ranch. Where there were no lights to interfere with the stars shining down on them.

Feeling a bit bold, Skeeter took her hand and entwined his fingers with hers. When she squeezed his hand, he knew he'd done the right thing. It was amazing how the little things a person did said so much. So much more than words could ever say.

"Wow, this is so beautiful here. You know, we see the sky every night when we work the festival, but I'm so busy, and with those lights, it just isn't the same." Dakota's words sang a melody to his heart.

He couldn't help but nod his agreement. When Dakota spoke, she whispered her words, as though they were on sacred grounds, and she didn't want to disturb any-one. He felt it too, the grandeur of the skies, and the vastness of Montana. God really was alive here, wasn't he? Skeeter had heard so many arguments over the years about how this was all just some cosmic mistake. But he knew better.

"Just look up, and you can see God's creation." He hadn't meant to voice his thoughts, but he did.

"I know what you mean. If you really looked at what was right in front of us, you'd see God's hand at work. The complicated beauty of the universe could only have come about through divine intervention." She leaned her head on Skeeter's shoulder when they stopped to look up.

"Do you see it?" He asked.

"See what? God?"

"No," he chuckled. "The giant "W" in the sky."

When she didn't answer him, he pulled her body in front of his and took her hand in his and pointed to the spot in the sky. "There, that's Cassiopeia. The big W. Look at the bottom, it points to a cluster of stars. That's the Andromeda Galaxy. Do you see it?"

Dakota moved her body only a few millimeters to get a better angle at where his hand was pointing, but it felt natural. As though they had been together forever and the closeness they currently shared didn't bother her in the least bit.

Her scent enveloped him and all he could do was close his eyes and picture her smile as she would look when he leaned in later for a kiss.

"I see it!" Dakota's voice broke through his thoughts, and he opened his eyes to see she had moved their hands to point to the Big Dipper. "That's the Big Dipper. And if you follow the bucket, you'll see a long line with four bright stars. It's not a straight line, but it's a line nonetheless."

"Mm hm." He couldn't get the words out. Her excitement hit him hard, and he prayed this moment would never end.

"That line is Andromeda. But I can't really make out the galaxy. I do see a cluster of stars between Andromeda and Cassiopeia, but there are several clusters. At least from what I can see." She chuckled and pulled away, smiling at him as she did so.

The look of utter amazement on her face warmed his heart and he didn't even think. He put his hands on her cheeks and pulled her face to his, but before his lips touched hers, he pulled back and looked into her eyes. Without words, he asked her if this was alright.

Chapter 31

No, no, no.

Yes, yes, yes.

Dakota's heart was going round and round. This was better than her dream, but she had come to the conclusion earlier in the day that she should wait for at least date number two or three before she kissed him. It was old fashioned, but by waiting, she'd spend more effort on getting to know him better.

Her fear was that if she kissed him right away, that would be all she could think of moving forward. And before she knew it, they'd end up in bed. Not a mistake she wanted to make again. Three years ago, she'd promised not only herself that she'd wait for marriage, but she also promised God. It was one thing to lie to herself, but to go back on her word to God? She wasn't going to do that.

Oh, but the warmth of his breath on her lips and the look in his eyes. He wanted this as much as she did, but his hesitation told her that he'd wait, if that was what she wanted. Who was she kidding? She wanted this, oh so badly. Her entire being hummed with the electricity that passed between them.

One little kiss wouldn't hurt.

One kiss wouldn't get her into his bed.

All she had to do was remember her promise and she'd be fine.

Without even thinking, she closed her eyes and moved closer to him. She could feel his warmth coming closer and closer. He took his time, and she was about to just pull him to her like in her dream, when she felt the lightest touch on her lips. A sigh escaped and she tilted her head so their lips would meet perfectly.

The way his mouth moved on hers was perfection. When Dakota wrapped her arms around him, he groaned and deepened the kiss. She could feel herself falling, and falling, and falling.

No one had ever kissed her so tenderly, and yet so intimately before. If this was what true love felt like, she could understand how the poets responded to heartbreak. Without a shadow of a doubt, she'd die if he pulled back now.

"There you two..." A deep voice called out but stopped and then chuckled. "Alright, lovebirds. It's time to come up for air now."

Jerod's voice had done its job. She felt as though he'd thrown a bucket of ice-cold water on her body that felt as though it was on fire. A fire that would never die out. At least until Jerod's voice interrupted them.

Maybe she wasn't truly feeling love if one voice could stop her cold as a heart attack.

"Oh, Jerod. It's not what you think." Skeeter pulled back so suddenly, that Dakota almost fell forward. He put his hands in the air and diverted his eyes to the ground.

"Really? You weren't just making out with Dakota?" Jerod arched a brow and crossed his beefy arms over his chest.

If the heat radiating through her face was any indication, Dakota knew she was redder than a tomato at that moment. She turned her face and put a hand up to her cheek and felt the warmth on her hand. "Oh, boy."

With a shake of his head, Jerod chuckled. "Come on you two. I think it's time to come in and cool off."

All Dakota could think about was how badly she'd be razzed by the guys when she got inside. Images of them watching them out the window using binoculars flashed through her mind. She'd heard the stories about their habit of playing practical jokes on each other. She couldn't even imagine what they were going to do to her. Poor Skeeter. He didn't deserve their pranks.

"Hey, who else knows?" Skeeter practically whispered before they entered the house.

"I doubt anyone besides Dana knows anything. They went to bed before I saw the headlights from the truck coming up the drive. I gave you two a little bit of time, but then thought I should come get you." Jerod looked between the two lovebirds. "And I'm glad I didn't wait any longer."

"It wouldn't have been like *that*." Dakota was mortified. Sure, she'd thought about it, but it was just a fleeting thought. She never would have acted on the idea on the first date. Even before her promise, she was the sort who waited until she was in a committed relationship. In fact, she'd only been *that* way with two other men. And how badly she felt when they broke up? It was enough to keep her from doing anything too much with another man for quite a while.

"I'm just teasing you. But you two did seem to be pretty hot and heavy there for a moment. Just remember, keep it clean."

"Oh, like you and Dana?" Skeeter had recovered faster than she had and was totally giving it back to Jerod.

But Skeeter was right, Jerod and Dana had been a bit too kissy face around everyone lately. Although, she had to give them a bit of slack. They were recently married. And with everyone living in their house, it was probably difficult to get some alone time. If she were being honest with herself, they were really cute together. Exactly what she hoped it would be like if she ever married. But she'd never admit that to anyone else.

Dakota decided to let the two men tease each other and she was heading straight for her room, before any of the other guys could see her red face.

Instead of hiding out in her room, like she had planned, she walked in to find Dana sitting on the bed with a huge cheesy grin.

"So, tell me all about it. Is he a good kisser?" She clapped her hands together and practically squealed like a cheerleader talking about her new boyfriend.

Dakota rolled her eyes. "Please, don't get up and start doing the 'Go, Fight, Kiss' cheer or I swear I'll puke all over you."

"What?" Dana stood up and her brows furrowed so strongly, she had a unibrow. "What are you talking about?"

Dakota waved her hand in front Dana. "That whole...giddy cheerleader thing you did when I entered."

"I wasn't a cheerleader." Dana pursed her lips. "You better not be trying to get out of telling me all about it. This is exactly what girlfriends are for."

"Pft," Dakota chuffed. "Maybe when we were in high school. But now that we're adults, we don't share that sort of thing."

Dana shook her head. "Oh, yes, we do. Now spill the beans."

"Really?" Dakota arched a brow. "Are you going to tell me all about your honeymoon with Jerod?"

She blinked. Then Dana opened her mouth and shut it. "Okay, you may be right. Back when we were kids, and kissing was a big deal, it was alright to share details." She put a hand on one of her hips. "But at least tell me if he's a good kisser."

A chuckle escaped Dakota and she shook her head. "Of course, he is."

"So, no fish face there?"

It was exactly what Dakota needed. She giggled her way to her bed and plunked down. Then she patted the spot next to her and Dana sat down. Against her better judgement, Dakota did spill the beans and the two women laughed and giggled until their sides hurt.

Chapter 32

Breakfast the next day was a bit awkward. But it wasn't because the other guys knew what she and Skeeter had done, it was because he didn't sit next to her like she had wanted. Instead, he sat down the table where she could barely see him. Let alone speak with him.

Even after they ate, he jumped up so quickly, she thought he might have eaten a whole can of Mexican jumping beans just so he could make his escape.

When Dakota's eyes blurred, she thought it was just the tears that began to form. She'd done something wrong last night, but what was it? Did she come on too strongly? She'd heard that some guys didn't like a woman who was forward. But was she really forward? Or just too into him?

That must have been it, he just wasn't that into her.

It was time for her to cowgirl up and get to work. Dakota wiped her eyes and began clearing the table. Dana must have sensed her need to think because she didn't say anything while they washed the dishes and cleaned the kitchen together.

"I'm not feeling so hot. I think I'm gonna go and lay down for a few. I'll be back to help with lunch." Dakota didn't wait for a response, she left and headed to her room. A power nap was exactly what she needed. Her limps felt too heavy as did her eyes. Thanks to staying up late with Dana she didn't get nearly enough sleep.

Thirty minutes later, when her alarm went off, Dakota tried to rub the sleep from her eyes. Then she tried to blink away the fuzzy. Her body felt so heavy, she knew she must be coming down with something. There was no way she could feel that bad after a short nap. In fact, she should have been full of energy, not feeling depleted.

Instead of getting up, she turned on her side and went back to sleep.

A loud pounding in her head woke her up.

"Dakota, if you don't answer, I'm coming in." The feminine voice yelled through the door.

"Dana?" Her voice sounded weird, and she tried to lift her head, but it felt like a fifty-pound bowling ball was attached to her shoulders instead.

"Dakota?" The door opened just an inch and one eyeball looked through. "Are you alright?"

"No." She mumbled.

The door flew open, and Dana rushed in. "Dakota? What's wrong? You're so pale." She put a hand to the prone woman's head. "You don't feel like you're running a fever."

"Tired. Can't see." Was all Dakota could get out before closing her eyes and falling back to sleep.

"Jerod!" Dana yelled and ran to the door. "Jerod, get in here!"

While Dakota wasn't quite asleep, she wasn't fully awake either. She felt as though she was floating in space and the sounds around her were distorted radio signals. Her entire body ached and all she wanted was to go back to sleep.

"Dakota? Can you tell me what's going on with you?" Jerod's deep voice penetrated her haze, and she blinked her eyes open.

"Jerod? Is that you?"

"Yes, now tell me what's happening," he demanded.

"I don't feel so good. A lot of pain. Blurry eyes."

"I was afraid of this. But didn't think it would happen so soon." A large lump sat on the edge of Dakota's bed. "We need to get her to the hospital."

"What? Why? What's going on?" The worry in Dana's voice penetrated the fog around Dakota's brain just a bit more than the man's voice had.

Dakota opened her eyes, but everything was blurry. "What's going on?" She was too tired to ask anything else.

"Dakota, you're having an MS episode. The fatigue and the fact you can't see well tells me you need a hospital. You might need that solumedrol treatment the doctor told us about."

She felt hands under her and then she felt herself being lifted into the air. "No, no hospital." She'd just come home from a stay at the VA hospital. The last place she wanted to be was that sterile environment. She wanted to stay at the ranch.

"Dana, get the doors. And call Doctor Smythe. I'm going to take her to the Missoula hospital, it's the closest. Maybe he can call in to them and tell them what she needs." Jerod rushed her out to the truck.

"Hey, what's going on?" That voice, it sent a chill through her entire being.

"Skeeter?"

"Baby, I'm here. What happened?" Skeeter was next to her head.

"Skeeter, get in the back. I need you to hold her and keep her safe while I drive to the Missoula ER." Jerod ordered.

Once they were all inside, and heading down the dirt driveway, Skeeter kissed her forehead. "Shh, it's all going to be alright."

"So tired. And thirsty." Her mouth was parched and all she wanted was a giant, cold bottle of Fiji water. And she wasn't even a frou-frou water type of gal. But something inside her said she needed it. She probably needed the electrolytes from the spring water.

A moment later Skeeter sat her up a little bit and put a bottle of water to her lips. "Here, try this."

It felt so good going down her throat.

Time seemed to go in and out for Dakota. One moment she was in Skeeter's lap drinking water, the next she was in the hospital. And not even the ER, but in an actual hospital room all by herself. "Hello?"

Dakota looked around. She knew it was a hospital from the bed to the heart monitor and the IV line in her arm. But it wasn't one she recognized. All she could remember was a sense of fatigue and blurriness. Things were still not totally in focus, and she was tired, but not so much that she couldn't move her head.

"You're awake. Good. The doctor will be happy." A woman in a nurse's uniform smiled and entered. She checked the monitors that Dakota was hooked up to. "How do you feel?"

"Where am I?" Dakota didn't care about how she felt, what she cared about was knowing where she was. And what happened.

"You've been admitted to Missoula General Hospital. Your MS Doctor called in a prescription of a solumedrol drip. You'll be here for a total of three days. How about I go get the doctor on duty and he can explain everything. He's been waiting for you to wake up." The nurse patted her arm and left.

"Steroids? I had to have a steroid treatment? But that means..." Dakota felt tears prick her eyes and everything went blurry again. The MS had progressed.

"I see Sleeping Beauty has awoken from her slumber." A big, bald man walked in. He was relatively handsome for an older man, but not what she expected to see in a Montana hospital. He looked like someone on one of those hospital soap operas her grandmother used to watch. "I'm Doctor Aldrich. How do you feel?"

"Confused. What's going on?"

"You have what's called Optic Neuritis. It's common for people with MS, especially when you're first diagnosed. In time, you most likely won't have to deal with this. If you're put on the correct treatment regimen." The doctor's words went right over her head.

"Uh, what does that mean?"

"Your eyes are experiencing an inflammatory reaction to your MS. But there is a simple treatment." He pointed to her IV. "Right before you woke up, you finished a two-hour drip of steroids. You should start feeling pretty good soon. It will also help with your overwhelming fatigue."

Things were beginning to fit like puzzle pieces in her mind. "Yes, I was totally exhausted this morning. Wait? You said a two-hour drip? What time is it?"

"You've been out of it for several hours now. Almost from the moment you arrived, you've been in this room receiving treatment. I'd say you've been here for about four hours now. It's a good think your doctor called me right away. I was able to get everything set up for you by the time you arrived. I just had to wait for the pharmacy to get the meds together."

"Wow, that's a lot. How long am I going to be here?" The nurse had said three days, but surely she could go home soon, right? Dakota knew she was starting to feel better.

"I'm sorry, but you have to stay here for the three-day IV treatment. After that, we'll examine you and see how you're doing. I think your doctor is going to come for a visit as well." Doctor Aldrich shook his head. "I've never seen a VA or military doctor who cared so much for his patient."

"Spike!" All of a sudden, she remembered her dog. "Who's taking care of my dog?"

The doctor furrowed his brows and looked down at the chart in his hands. "I'm not sure. I can have the nurse call your ranch if you like."

"Wait, how'd I get here? Wasn't it Jerod and Skeeter? Are they still here?" Surely, they wouldn't have left her there all alone and passed out, would they?

"Yes, the two men who brought you here had to go home. But they said to call when you woke up. I told them you'd be out of it most of the day. I'm actually surprised you're awake so soon." He put the chart under his arm. "I'll send the nurse in to help you call home."

"Thanks, doctor." As she waited, she realized she wasn't going to be alright. She'd never be alright again. The MS would flare up whenever she was happy, and it would ruin anything good she had. How could anyone love her.

No one would love a woman who was always sick. If she couldn't even go a week without some episode hitting her, then how could she even have kids? She'd never have a normal life. And with her luck, they'd never find a cure while she was still young enough to have kids.

All of a sudden, she wished she'd never come to Montana. She'd never know what she was missing out on with Skeeter if she had stayed in California. Even if it meant she'd never be diagnosed properly.

Tears pooled in her eyes before he even left the room. The moment the door closed behind the doctor, they fell in rivulets down her cheeks. All the ideas that had come to her the past week were rubbish. Skeeter was a physically fit man, who was still very young. He'd even mentioned wanting a family. There was no way he'd want her now. How could he? Dakota knew she'd never be able to give any man what they wanted – a family.

"Why, Lord? Why did you bring me all the way here and tease me with the promises of a good life? It's not fair." Dakota wasn't sure how long she lay there crying and grumbling to God, but eventually the door opened, and she heard a woman trying to get her attention.

"Dakota? Are you alright? Are you in pain?" The nurse came immediately to Dakota's bedside and looked at the equipment she was hooked up to.

"No, I'm upset." Dakota sighed and wiped the tears from her face. "My life is over now, isn't it?"

"Oh, sweetie. It's not over. This is just a hiccup in your treatment. It's very normal for someone who's just been diagnosed."

"I'm sorry, what was your name again? I forgot." Dakota realized that she was still having memory issues and it was just one more problem to deal with.

"I don't think I told you my name." The nurse smiled and walked over to the whiteboard across from Dakota's bed. She pointed to the top name. "I'm nurse Monahan. I'll be your head nurse today and tomorrow."

Dakota took a closer look at the woman who'd be taking care of her. She couldn't have been more than five feet five inches tall. Her blonde hair was pulled back into a bun and helped her blue eyes to stand out.

"Dakota, why do you think your life is over?" The nurse walked back to the side of Dakota's bed and looked at her with soft, tender eyes.

"Because I'm already starting to deteriorate from the MS. It's going to kill me, isn't' it?" Dakota sniffed and rubbed her nose with the back of her hand.

"No, that's not what's happening to you. Trust me when I say you are going to live a long life. This is just one little instance. If you do everything the doctor says, you should be feeling normal very soon and not have any more issues for a long time, if ever." Nurse Monahan patted Dakota's arm. "How about I get you a sugar-free popsicle?"

Dakota's stomach growled and she put a hand over it. "Uh, I think that might be nice. And what about lunch?"

Nurse Monahan laughed. "That's what I like to see. An appetite is a good sign. I'll see if your special lunch is ready." She winked. "Your lucky that Dr. Smythe sent in orders for special food. Today's lunch for the rest of the patients is a mushy stew." She scrunched her nose.

"Yeah, I'm supposed to eat only certain foods." Dakota wouldn't go so far as to say that she was lucky, but in this case, there was a silver lining, of sorts.

Chapter 33

Today was the day that Dakota was due back at the ranch. Skeeter couldn't help but be excited. He wasn't allowed to visit her, which hurt his feelings, but he could understand. When he had been in the hospital after the explosion, he didn't want anyone to visit him.

However, this was different. Dakota wasn't put back together with tape and glue like Humpty Dumpty was, or him for that matter. So, Skeeter wondered why she didn't want to see anyone from the ranch. All she had to deal with was an IV.

No surgeries.

No casts.

No patches.

So, what was so wrong with her that she refused a visit from friends? Skeeter had asked himself that over and over for the past two days. The first day, it was the doctor who said no visitors, which Skeeter could understand. Rest was very important for anyone with medical issues.

Then the next day when Jerod told him Dakota didn't want any visitors, he tried not to take it personally. But how else was he to react? They had gone on a date, and it was fantastic. He still thought about that kiss and prayed he'd get another chance.

"Tony, why do you think Dakota didn't want anyone to visit her?" Skeeter and Tony were working in the barn, putting away their supplies from checking the fence lines. Apparently, that was one of those chores that ranchers, and their hired hands, had to take care of on a regular basis.

That day, they did find a fence post down and they had to replace it with a new one. When Jerod first instructed them on this chore, he said there were many reasons a fence could break. One of the biggest reasons was cattle trying to get away, or people trying to steal cattle, or other animals. They didn't have much in the way of cattle, or supplies, so Skeeter figured it was their ornery bull, Custard.

Tony looked up from the stack of fence posts he had just organized. "Maybe she wasn't feeling well. Or," he shrugged, "maybe she just didn't want to see your ugly mug."

Normally, Skeeter would have laughed at Tony's joke. But today, he was feeling a little sensitive. Just that morning he figured Dakota had already lost interest in him. He couldn't blame her; she was the sort of woman who could attract attention from anyone she wanted. He was a flirt who was lucky enough to get her attention for one date.

One part of him wanted to run to the truck when he heard it coming up the drive. Another part told him to play it cool. Women liked it when they had to work for a man. Maybe that was his problem? He'd made it too easy for her. He had done the chasing, hadn't he?

This time, he'd let her stew a little before he showed up. Maybe if he showed her he wasn't going to always be right there, she might want him and go after him.

"Hey, Loverboy. Aren't you going to go chasing her down? I believe that's Jerod's truck I heard coming up the drive right now." Tony grinned and nodded to the front of the ranch.

Skeeter frowned. "She can wait. I'm finishing up my chores."

Tony arched a brow. "Oh, really? Trouble in paradise already?"

"I don't know what you're talking about, man." Skeeter looked away from the barn entrance and focused on putting the tools back where they belonged. There was no way he was going to rush this job. If she was dying to see him, she could come back here and look for him. Otherwise, Dakota could wait until supper to see him.

When Skeeter put the hammer back on it's peg on the board, his foot began moving as though it wanted to head out. Instead of heading the call of his stomping foot, he took the mallet and hung it up. Then when all the tools were back in place, he looked around for something else to do.

Tony chuckled. "It's all done. We've put everything back and cleaned up the work area."

When Skeeter looked to his work buddy, he noticed the smirk on the man's face. "I see what you're trying to do. It won't work." He looked around for something else to occupy his time. When he noticed a length of rope had been pulled from the shelf, he took the entire thing and began recoiling it.

"Alright, I'm heading inside to clean up for dinner. Should I save you a seat?" Tony chuckled and waved before leaving the barn without a response from Skeeter.

Grumbling under his breath about how Tony should mind his own business, Skeeter put the coil of rope away and prayed there was more work to find. When he realized that the supply room was cleaner than he'd ever seen it, he knew it was time to leave the barn behind and get inside. He'd need to clean up if he wanted to eat at the dinner table.

Skeeter's desire to be clean had absolutely nothing to do with the fact that Dakota would be at the dinner table. She'd probably sit down at the other end of the table and ignore him all night. Well, two could pay at that game.

However, his resolve to stay away from Dakota withered the moment he saw her smile.

Dakota was sitting next to Dana at the table and talking to Mike. The cowboy was telling her all about how the new bull calf was doing. Dakota seemed to be enjoying the tale of how Don Juan was already trying to grab the attention of the cows... and succeeding.

Skeeter had spent most of the previous day laughing and watching the little bull try to live up to his name, even though he was way too young for any of that. The kid had moxy, and he knew he was cute.

But that didn't mean that Skeeter was going to ignore her. He may not have been the most grown up of all the men at the ranch, but he did know a thing or two. So, when he took his seat down the table from Dakota, he looked at her and caught her attention.

"Hi, Dakota, it's good to have you home. How ya doing?" Skeeter's mother would be proud of him.

"Much better, thank you." Dakota's cheeks turned pink, and she turned her gaze down to her plate.

Skeeter loved it when she blushed. It made her eyes sparkle. But he wished she had kept her gaze on him so he could see the shine her eyes.

Dinner moved along as usual, the entire table talking. Well, with the exception of Mike. The only time he spoke was when the topic of cows came up. His whole life was about the cattle. And churning butter.

So, when Mike cleared his throat and got everyone's attention before desert had been served, Skeeter was shocked.

Mike stood up and looked at Jerod. "I have an announcement." He waited for everyone to look his way before continuing. "I've decided it's time to move on."

You could have heard a pin drop; it was so quiet at the table. Which was a huge feat.

"What?" Skeeter heard his voice and realized he'd said what he was thinking. "I thought you were staying here to work?" Nothing had ever been finalized, but most of the guys just assumed that Mike would stay there and work with the cattle.

Mike shook his head. "I was never offered an official job here. And Megan thinks I'm good enough to get a job and move on."

"Where are you going?" Dixon asked.

A slow grin crossed Mike's face and he stood a little taller. "Actually, not far. Mr. Mason hired me to work at his dairy farm."

Jerod and Dana shared smiles.

It was Skeeter who spoke first, "Wait, you got a job with the ginormous dairy farm two hours away?"

For the first time Skeeter could remember, Mike looked as though he was both happy and proud of himself. He should be, since that farm is one of the biggest in the state. They supply dairy products to most of the region, going as far south as Northern Utah. He let a long, low whistle out and clapped his hands. "Great job, Mike. I knew you could get a fantastic job wherever you set your mind to."

The man of the hour looked down and Skeeter picked up a hint of pink on the big man's cheeks. "Jerod helped."

"I'd bet all he did was get you the interview. It was your own skills that got you the job, Mike." Dakota grinned from ear to ear.

Even though she didn't know Mike well, it was obvious she cared about the quiet guy. Shoot, the entire ranch liked Mike. They might have teased him, but no one could anything bad about the man.

"Wait, does this mean no more homemade cheeses?" Skeeter's eyes widened and all of a sudden, he wished Mike was staying. Which was crazy since Skeeter was leaving. But man, could the guy make some great Swiss cheese.

Mike chuckled, "you could always buy the cheese we're gonna sell in the little gift shop at the dairy farm."

"Wait a minute. The Mason Dairy doesn't have a gift shop." Dana arched a brow.

"They will by Christmas." Mike waggled his brows in a very unlike Mike way.

"Are you going to manage their new store?" Dakota asked.

"Will you still make cheese?" Tony asked.

Mike put his hands in the air. "Hold up. Yes, I'll make cheese, and manage the store. But I'm also going to hire a few people to help me."

Dinner didn't go as Skeeter thought it would. The focus went off of Dakota and right onto Mike. It seemed the ranch was losing several of its founding residents all at once – the first of November.

Skeeter sat there listening to everything, and then he wondered what Jerod was going to do. When there was a lull in the conversation he asked, "Jerod, does this mean the ranch is going to be empty for a while? Or are you getting more new residents next month?"

The question got everyone else's attention as well. With everyone leaving, only Dakota, Tony, and Dixon would be there for Thanksgiving. Although, Skeeter had already been invited to join them. But the rest might not come back until Christmas.

"Actually," Jerod wiped his mouth with his napkin. "With all of the openings, I've called my contacts at the VA. As you know, we have a woman from the Air Force coming next month. And it seems that there are a few more injured veterans looking for a place. I don't know yet who will be coming, but my contact assures me we will be full by Thanksgiving."

With the winter storms, ranch work was light. But the Christmas festivities did take a lot of time. Not only had the ranch promised to help the tree farm every year, but they had also offered to help the town with their events. And since the new residents would be coming from a VA hospital with untold injuries, Skeeter wasn't sure how much help the ranch would be able to offer this year.

While he had some ideas, he couldn't say anything until he spoke to his new boss, Mr. Henderson.

However, at the moment, his main concern was finding a chance to speak with Dakota. She hadn't said much to him since she arrived home. And to be fair, there wasn't really a chance for them to speak. Not until everyone left the dining room and headed off to their own rooms.

"Dakota? Got a minute?" Skeeter caught her right before she ducked out of the dining room.

Chapter 34

This was exactly what Dakota had wanted to avoid, time alone with Skeeter. She looked around for some back-up but didn't see anyone else. *Great*, she thought, *the entire house must have conspired to get her and Skeeter alone.*

"Ah, I think Dana needs my help in the kitchen." She was a chicken, and she knew it. But Dakota wasn't ready to have this talk with Skeeter. Not yet.

"I only need a minute. Please?" Skeeter's eyes bored into her, and she gave in.

"Alright, how about we stay here in the dining room? We can talk while I begin gathering the dishes." At least this way, she could make a mad dash when Dana came back in to start cleaning the dishes away.

Dakota started picking up the dinner plates and stacking them. "What's up?"

Skeeter cleared his throat. "I wanted to see how you were doing. I wasn't allowed to visit you in the hospital, I had hoped you would have wanted to see me."

After stacking the sixth dish, Dakota sighed. "I'm sorry. I wasn't feeling good and in a really bad place."

"The hospital was horrible? Why didn't you tell us? We would have come and picked you up and taken you somewhere better." Skeeter took a few steps closer to her and put a comforting hand on her back.

Dakota pulled back, but it wasn't what she wanted. What she wanted to do was turn into him and have him hold her and comfort her. But that would only send him mixed messages. "No, of course not. The hospital itself was fine. It was me." She sighed. "This is a lot worse than I thought it would be. I don't think I can be in a relationship with anyone, other than friendship right now."

Skeeter stood there, blinking. After a few moments he spoke, "Are you saying you don't want to date me anymore?"

His words sent a sharp pain through her chest. She wanted nothing more than to say no, that wasn't what she wanted. But she knew it was what had to happen. If she dragged this on, then one, or both of them, would end up with a broken heart. They had no future together.

She had no future. At least not a good one. Not one she could offer a man who wanted a family.

"What I'm saying is, I think we should just be friends." There, she'd said it. It was the phrase every man hated to hear. Even with her limited experience, she knew enough to know that.

Skeeter exhaled and sunk down into one of the dining room chairs. "Ouch. Why?"

This was the part that Dakota hated, explaining why she had to say no to him. One part of her wanted to come clean, but another knew that if she told him the real reason, he'd still want to date her – at first. But eventually, when he really thought about his future, he would then break her heart. Dakota didn't think she could handle that.

"I had a lot of time to think about this." She motioned between them. "And I don't see a future for us. I really do like you as a friend, and I don't want to lose that. If we keep dating, then it's going to end badly, and I'll lose your friendship."

"No, you won't. And we won't end. Dakota, don't you understand?"

"Understand what? That you're already in love with me?" Dakota scoffed. "Please, it's way too soon for those feelings. You don't really know me enough to be in love with me."

The pain in his eyes was almost enough to have her apologizing and asking for a second chance. But she had to do this, she had to let him loose. It was what he needed, and the only way to protect her fragile heart.

Skeeter took a shaky breath, then reached for her hand. "Dakota, how do you know how I feel? I don't even know for sure yet."

"Exactly, it's too soon. And I don't plan on staying here in Montana. I'm going back to California as soon as I can. There's no future for us, Skeeter." Before her last episode, Dakota had thought it might be fun to stay in Montana. Stay with Skeeter. But now that she knew her quality of life was shot, she couldn't do that to him. Even if he wanted to take care of her, it wasn't fair to him.

"I thought you liked it here. Are you sure you don't want to stay in Montana? I bet we could find you a job somewhere around here once you're ready to leave the ranch." Skeeter stood up and tried to take her in his arms, but she backed up and put a hand between them.

"I can't, Skeeter. This isn't for me." Dakota whirled around and ran from the room just as Dana entered.

"What's going on?" Dana turned worried eyes from Dakota to Skeeter.

As Dakota ran from the room, she could hear Skeeter telling Dana what had just happened.

When Dakota made it back to her room without anyone stopping her, she was glad she didn't have to explain why she was crying. Now would have been a great time to have Spike with her. Jerod had explained that Spike was spending the night with Nelly back at her ranch, and Sam would bring him over in the morning. She hadn't complained, but now she wished she would have asked they stop off at Nelly's at get her dog.

Even though the paperwork wasn't finalized yet, Dakota knew that Spike was her partner. Especially after the past few days, she knew she needed a service dog.

When a knock sounded on her door before she even had a chance to dry her eyes, Dakota almost screamed. "Go away. I don't want to talk."

"Dakota, it's me, Dana. Can I come in?"

Technically, Dakota could say no, but it was Dana's ranch and Dakota was only a guest. "Sure, come on in." She sat on the edge of the bed facing the door.

"Dakota, is this what you really want?" Dana didn't have to explain, Dakota knew exactly what she was talking about.

She nodded. Then shook her head. "I don't know. I want to get to know him better, I do. But then I think about the future and know I can't do that to him."

Dana closed the door and sat on the chair next to the dresser. "What can't you do?"

Dakota threw her hands in the air. "What do you mean? You've seen what happened this week. It's only the beginning. I'm going to get worse and worse." She put her head in her hands and wept.

Dana stood and walked over to her friend. She put a comforting hand on Dakota's shoulder. "Dakota, you don't know that."

She sniffed and rubbed the back of her hand under her nose. "Yes, I do. I've read all about how Annette Funicello died. And it was awful. I wouldn't want to put any loved one through that." She didn't say it out loud, but she also prayed she wouldn't have to suffer as Annette did. Having her organs shut down one at a time had to be so excruciating. Knowing you were dying a slow death, and not being able to do anything about it, was one of the worst ways Dakota could think to go.

"Honey, who said you were going to get that bad? Aren't there all sorts of new treatments now? And what about the cure they're working on? I hear there's a really great chance it will work." Dana pulled her friend into a hug and let Dakota cry on her shoulder.

"I'm sorry. I should be much stronger than this. I'm a soldier, for Pete's sake!" Dakota wiped the signs of her crying from her face and sniffed. "I don't know if anything will happen in my lifetime, but I'm not going to subject someone I care about to this." She motioned all over her body in an effort to show what a mess she was.

"Dakota Monahan, you listen to me. You are a strong woman. And so much younger than Annette was when she was diagnosed. Did the doctor say you were headed to a wheelchair and an imminent death?" Dana put her hands on her hips and glared at Dakota.

For a moment, Dakota thought she was back in basic training and Drill Sergeant Dana was chewing her out for wanting to quit the twenty-five-mile hike with a full ruck sack on her back. She shook her head and sat back down. "No, no one said anything like that. But I don't see how I can be in a relationship with anyone. He'd have to care for me, and probably end up having to carry me around. Not to mention the fact that having kids probably isn't even a possibility for me."

Dana shook her head. "That's not true, and you know it. I was there when Dr. Smythe said you could have children. And the type of MS you have isn't hereditary. So, no need to worry you'll pass it down to your kids."

"But how am I going to take care of children and a husband if I'm in a wheelchair?" Dakota knew what she said was stupid. Many women in wheelchairs had kids and families that they took care of. While her head knew it, her heart didn't quite grasp it. Not yet.

"Why don't we pray and ask God to give you peace? And don't push Skeeter away. Give it some time. If you decide that he's not the man for you, then fine. But if you're pushing him away because you think he can't handle your MS, then you need to take another look at the man. He's strong. And he cares a great deal about you." Dana sat next to Dakota on the bed. She took her friend's hands in her and they prayed.

When they were done, a sense of peace stole over Dakota. "Thank you. I needed that."

"You must be tired. Why don't you go to bed early? I'll get one of the guys to help me clean up."

"Are you sure?" Dakota kinda felt like a heal for not helping. But she was tired. Why was it that crying always took so much out of a person?

Chapter 35

"What just happened?" Skeeter asked the empty room. He took a seat and put his head in his hands.

A few minutes later, Jerod popped in. "Hey, what's up?" He took a seat next to Skeeter.

"I think Dakota just broke up with me." Skeeter lifted his head and tried to focus on the man sitting next to him. His eyes burned with unshed tears.

Jerod scratched his head. "I thought you only had one date?"

Skeeter pursed his lips. "Semantics. But she said she didn't want to date me anymore."

The sound of a man scratching the stubble on his chin distracted Skeeter for a moment.

"Did she say why? Was it because of her MS?" Jerod had wondered if this might happen. It wouldn't be the first time someone thought they should stop dating the person they really cared for because of a medical issue. He'd almost missed out on the greatest thing to happen to him since he got saved. If he had stayed single, he wouldn't have Dana as his wife. She was truly a gift from God. One he thanked God for daily.

"She said she was moving back to California once she was released. And since I just got the job of my dreams right here in Frenchtown, she didn't see a future with me." There were a few other things, but Skeeter didn't want to say any more.

"I see." Jerod pursed his lips. "Why don't you give her a few days to adjust to things. I'm betting she's scared right now. Let her see that life isn't always going to be about her MS, and that she can have a normal life. Then maybe talk to her again."

Skeeter scoffed. "I've not been dumped much, I'm usually the one doing it, but I know a brush off when I see it. And she's just given it to me."

Jerod knocked on Skeeter's head. "Hello? Anyone home? Did you just hear what I said? She's scared. Give her time and space. Then see what she wants." He stood. "I swear, youth is wasted on the young."

When Jerod left the room, Skeeter rubbed the spot on his head where Jerod had knocked. "He's not much older than I am. What does he mean youth is wasted on the young?"

The rest of October went as planned. Skeeter helped out on the ranch, but he spent most of his time at the Harvest Festival. It was fun, but without Dakota, it just wasn't the same. She did help out, but she refused to dress up and play the part of the scared co-ed being chased by a chainsaw carrying murderer.

Instead, Dakota spent the rest of the month helping in various places. She took tickets, helped sell drinks, worked on crowd control, and even walked the festival with Sadie and identified areas where they could improve for next year.

When Dakota was working with Sadie, Skeeter noticed her eyes were brighter, and she seemed to have more bounce in her step. She liked the management part. And that realization helped Skeeter to accept their new roles. All he wanted was for Dakota to be happy and healthy. If learning about the management of the festival did that, then he was content.

So, it came as a huge surprise to him to see both Dakota and Spike all dressed up in their old costumes on Halloween night.

"Does this mean you want me to chase you around all night?" Skeeter grinned, but it didn't have the effect he was hoping for. Since he was already dressed up, he forgot his teeth had been blackened out.

Dakota laughed and pointed at his mouth. "Great job, Axe Murderer."

Skeeter growled and put his chainsaw up. "I'm a chainsaw killer, not an axe murderer. Do you need me to show you the difference?"

Spike chuffed and pushed Dakota away from Skeeter. It seemed, he figured out the game was a foot.

Dakota screamed and ran away with Spike at her heals. And Skeeter not too far behind them.

His heart swelled and he couldn't believe it when the night was over.

"Did you see that young teen who really thought you might hurt me?" Dakota bent over laughing and Spike jumped in place to get her attention. "You know who I mean, don't you, boy?"

Spike nodded and licked Dakota's hand.

This was exactly what Skeeter had prayed for.

Chapter 36

November first was declared a day of rest at the ranch. That didn't mean no work was done, they still had to take care of the animals. But other than that, it was a day for everyone to relax and recharge.

The very next day was move-out day. Skeeter, Mike, and Arthur were all leaving for their new jobs. Well, Arthur wasn't going to start for a little bit, but he wanted to get settled in his new apartment before the weather got really bad, so he decided to move a little bit earlier.

"Arthur, you're always welcome to come back and visit. And every holiday we'll have a spot for you at the table, if you want." Dana tried hard to keep the tears at bay.

Arthur gave the woman a big hug. "Thank you. I think if the weather isn't too bad, I'll be back for Thanksgiving and Christmas." He looked around at everyone gathered and gulped back the tears that wanted to form in his one eye.

"Let's all keep in touch. We're family now." Mike swiped at an errant tear on his cheek. Then he hugged Dana, Megan, and even Dakota.

"You know, we aren't that far away. I think we could even manage regular coffee meetups. You do get days off, right?" Dakota grinned and slapped the man's shoulder.

"I think I'd like that." Mike nodded. "You'll still be here for Thanksgiving and Christmas, right?"

Dakota opened her mouth, then closed it. She wasn't sure where she'd be for Christmas. "Sure, I'll be here for Thanksgiving. I'm actually looking forward to this giant town gathering. I can't imagine everyone eating a turkey dinner together." She shook her head.

Skeeter picked up on the lack of Christmas plans. But he kept that to himself. The past two days had been great. Almost like they were before her last stay in the hospital. He didn't want to cause any problems right before he left. With his job only a mile away, he'd be back here often enough that he wanted to ensure Dakota stayed his friend.

Everyone waved as both Mike and Arthur pulled away in their vehicles.

Once they were no longer in sight, Jerod turned to Skeeter. "So, when do you have to report to the Henderson farm?"

"After lunch. Mrs. Henderson wants to show me my new home. But it's a trailer, so I doubt it will take much time. I don't actually start work until tomorrow morning. Today is more about getting settled, which should only take five minutes." Skeeter chuckled. "Then I want to take a look around and see what supplied have arrived since last I looked and get a feel for what we're gonna do tomorrow."

"Mason told me that he plans to raise the new barn this week, once you're ready." Jerod led the way back inside the house and toward the living room.

Dana brought out coffee and muffins for those who were still there.

Those left chatted about the Henderson farm and the plans for its rebuilding. Then, about thirty minutes before lunch would be served, Dana and Dakota stood up and went into the kitchen.

Jerod noticed how Skeeter watched Dakota leave the room and the look of pain in the man's eyes. "You still care for her, don't you?"

Skeeter sighed and looked around the room. Tony was still there, as was Megan. But they had turned their heads for a little chat of their own once Skeeter looked their way. He knew they'd be listening, but he also didn't care. The entire ranch knew how Skeeter felt about Dakota. "I don't know what to do. How do I show her that I care and am happy to take her just as she is?"

Megan sighed.

Tony snorted.

Jerod glared at the two. Then he looked back at Skeeter. "I think you tell her just that. I probably shouldn't get involved, but I've seen how she looks at you when you aren't looking her way." He stood up. "I think you need to ask her out again."

Tony and Megan followed Jerod out of the room while Skeeter sat there thinking about what Jerod had said.

It was time for Skeeter to cowboy up.

Chapter 37

The one thing that had crept up on Dakota was the fact that she couldn't remember the last time she had a scratching fit. It wasn't something that she looked for. But when a bug landed on her arm and she flicked it away, she realized her skin was clearer than it had been in a long time. And for the life of her, she couldn't remember the last time she scratched the heck out of herself.

While one good thing wasn't enough to counteract all of the bad she now had to deal with, it was something. The next time she spoke with Jacinta, she'd have to tell her what she'd just discovered.

She and Dana worked quietly as they prepared lunch. Since the morning hadn't been full of work, they had decided that a lunch of soup and sandwiches would be great with the cold weather. Dana finished the chicken noodle soup, which she had started earlier in the morning, while Dakota fixed up grilled ham and cheese sandwiches.

It was one of Skeeter's favorite cold weather lunches, and Dakota was happy to make it for him for his last official meal with the ranch. A week ago, Dakota thought she'd be happy to see this day come and go. But now? She was starting to think she'd made a mistake in pushing him away.

On Halloween night they'd had so much fun together. Even Spike had a great time. The dog really liked Skeeter, and that meant the world to Dakota. Especially since Skeeter seemed to return the dog's affection.

"Dana?"

"Hm?" Without looking up from the pot of soup she was seasoning, Dana waited for Dakota to ask her question.

"Do you think I'm crazy for turning down Skeeter?" What she really wanted to know was if Dana thought she should ask Skeeter out on a date. While it was the twenty-first century and woman took the lead all the time, Dakota wasn't the sort to ask a man out. At least not until they were seriously dating.

Dana tasted the soup base and added a dash more salt. "I think you needed the time apart so you could realize what a catch he is. And so you could get past your fears. If you're ready, then you should let him know."

"But, what if he's moved on?" Dakota bit her lower lip, fearing that was exactly what the handsome cowboy had done. He was a catch. Especially now that he had the foreman job at the Henderson farm.

Ladle in hand, Dana stirred the pot some more. "I think the question is really are you ready to date him? You know he hasn't moved on yet." She turned to look at Dakota. "Or are you afraid that now he won't be living here, some other woman will catch his eye?"

That was something she had worried about. Dakota had even asked herself just last night if she wanted to get Skeeter to ask her out now only so that he didn't ask anyone else out. Or was she really ready to date him? Since she came home from the hospital, she'd had several private counseling sessions with Megan. And the one thing that got her thinking about a real future, was the detailed information about MS and life expectancy today.

Megan had come to each session with an armload of data. More than Dakota could even imagine possible. And everything pointed to the fact that since her disease was so new, she would most likely have a good life. Sure, there were no guarantees in life, but with all of the different therapies they had now, Dakota had a real shot at a family. The sort of life that Annette Funicello couldn't have had a decade ago.

There were even some very good indicators coming from the clinical trials for the cure. If all went well, she could be cured within the next ten years.

Prayer also played a huge role in her turnaround. God had been working on her heart ever since that night she and Dana prayed for peace. And her daily Bible studies had been spot on. If Dakota really and truly trusted God, then she could move forward with Skeeter. All that she wanted at the moment was a date. They hadn't discussed marriage or anything else yet, all that was on the table was dating.

God would be the one to guide their relationship. If God wanted them to marry, then it would happen. If He didn't, then Dakota would have to accept that and move on. Even if it meant she'd have a broken heart in the end. The verse that kept coming to her all week was:

Trust in the Lord with all thine heart: and lean not unto thine own understanding. In all thy ways acknowledge Him, and He shall direct thy paths.

• Proverbs 3:5-6 KJV

She was going to do it. Well, she wasn't going to ask him out, but she was going to let him know that she was ready.

"Why don't you go tell everyone lunch is served and I'll bring the pot out." Dana motioned for Dakota to head to the living room.

When she got there, it was empty, save for Skeeter. "Skeeter? Where is everyone? Lunch is ready."

He looked up and a tiny smile curved up on his lips. "I thought they had made their way to the dining room already."

"Not that I saw." Dakota worried at her lower lip with her teeth and looked around. "But, um...do you have a minute?"

His face brightened. "For you? I have a few minutes."

His little joke broke the ice, and she entered the room with a grin.

"Here, have a seat." Skeeter motioned to the seat next to him.

"Thanks." Dakota sat down and put her hands in her lap. This wasn't as easy as she thought it would be. "I'm going to miss you when you leave."

"Really?"

She nodded. "I...ah..." Dakota sighed and slouched. "I don't know how to say this."

"Do you want to go out to dinner with me this weekend?" Skeeter jumped right in with both feet.

To say Dakota was surprised would have been an understatement. She was shocked. But a warming sensation began to make its way up her body and settle into her heart. She couldn't speak, so she nodded. Dakota was afraid if she spoke, she might cry.

"Is that a yes?" The hopeful expression on Skeeter's face was enough to get Dakota's voice working.

"Yes, I'd love to go out with you."

Epilogue

Skeeter took Dakota out for dinner Friday night. Then he took her out again Saturday night. And Sunday, after church, they had a picnic. It was freezing cold, but they still enjoyed the sandwiches and chips that Skeeter had packed that morning while sitting in his truck, with the heater running.

"You know, I was foolish to push you away." Dakota felt strange admitting this to Skeeter, but they had just both agreed to be honest with one another.

If Skeeter felt her medical situation was too much for him to handle, he promised to let her know. And Dakota promised not to push him away out of fear again. She might need help with keeping that promise, but it was what she wanted.

"I think it might have been a good thing." While Skeeter hated the time away from her, he had recognized the importance of that time for Dakota.

"What do you mean?" Now Dakota wasn't too sure if she'd made the right decision in going out with him again.

"Don't, Dakota. Don't start second-guessing us now." Skeeter put his sandwich down on the dashboard. "What I meant was that I think we both needed the time to discover how we really felt, and to make sure we both were willing to make sacrifices to be together."

It was only the night before that Skeeter had offered to follow her to California when she was ready to leave. He was willing to give up his dream job to be with her, if that was what it took.

Dakota had shaken her head and said he didn't have to leave. She would stay there. But on one condition, they had to take a yearly trip to see her mom.

Even though they were both willing to sacrifice what they wanted, in the end, it wouldn't be a sacrifice to stay in Montana. Dakota had fallen in love with the quaint town of Frenchtown, and its people.

Skeeter would gladly go off to La La Land each year. Especially if he was able to see the beach once in a while or meet Mickey Mouse.

So, in the end, neither had to give anything up in order to be together. Instead, they decided to date until they knew for sure that God wanted them together.

It wasn't until after the new year that Dakota figured out what she could do in order to stay in Frenchtown.

"Dakota, man am I happy to see you. Both of my baristas called out sick today. Can you help me out?" Lottie begged Dakota to help out.

"Lottie, I'm happy to help. But I don't really know how to make the fancy drinks." Dakota shrugged and looked at the intimidating espresso machine.

"Don't worry about that. If you can work the register, I'll take care of the drinks. It's not going to be a crazy busy day, but I can't do it all by myself."

"What about Cove?" Dakota had seen her husband helping in the shop once in a while when they were crazy busy.

"He took Quinn to Missoula for the day." Lottie put her hands together and continued begging for help.

Dakota laughed and put her hands up. "Alright, alright. But don't say I didn't warn you." The only reason Dakota hadn't suggested she call Dana was because Dana was one of those who had called out sick. It seemed a flu bug was making its way around town. It was nothing that a few days of rest and chicken noodle soup couldn't cure, but it was the beginning of Dakota's new career.

And come summer, she had even come up with a new type of puppy-pop that Spike and the rest of the service dogs had given their full support for.

In the spring, Dakota and Skeeter sat together on the porch swing watching the sun set.

"You know, I never would have thought life after the Army would be so wonderful." Dakota snuggled close to Skeeter. While the sun had shone all day, when it went down that night, it took the warmth with it.

Skeeter pulled her tighter to him. "I know what you mean."

They sat there watching the final rays of the sun set and the sky turn different shades of orange, then purple and black.

He took in a ragged breath. "Do you really love it here? Is this where you want to settle?"

"Yes, it is. I'm so excited about the tiny apartment over the Sheriff's garage that I'm moving into next month. Spike has even given his approval of the place." Dakota chuckled when she imagined her and Spike living in the six hundred square foot apartment together. It was going to be a tight fit, but they wouldn't be there long. Any day now she expected a ring that would signal she and Spike would be moving to the Henderson farm once she relinquished her name and took the last name of Murphy.

Skeeter coughed and pulled away from Dakota. "I'm so glad you feel that way. You know how much I love you."

Spike chuffed from the spot next to their feet.

Skeeter chuckled. "And I love you too, Spike."

The dog lowered his head back onto the cowboy boots of the man he had chosen for Dakota.

"I love you, too Skeeter." Dakota leaned up and placed a sweet kiss on his cheek.

Shaking hands pulled something out of his vest pocket. Then Skeeter stood and knelt on one knee. "Dakota Monahan," he looked down to Spike. "And Spike." He looked back into the sparkling eyes he could never get enough of. "I have loved you almost since the first time I saw you. It didn't take me long to recognize that I couldn't see a life without you in it. While it's going to be sometime before I have an actual house, would you do the honor of spending the rest of our nights with me, as my wife?"

Dakota couldn't believe what she saw and heard. When he finished with his proposal, she about jumped up. But she couldn't move.

Spike chuffed and nudged her leg.

Somehow, she managed to get out of her stupor long enough to say yes. Dakota couldn't believe it. She thought she had to be in a dream. It was all so perfect.

After a toe-curling kiss, and a few more long, sensual kisses, Skeeter pulled back. "If you want to wait until I have an actual house, and not a trailer, I'll understand. But I must warn you, it's going to be tough to wait. Especially after kisses like those."

Instead of answering with words, Dakota pulled his mouth to hers and kissed him until they both had to come up for air. "Skeeter, I want to marry you as soon as we can arrange it. I don't care if we live in a tiny trailer, or a tiny apartment above a garage. As long as we're together, any place will be home for me."

Author's Notes

So? What did you think about the end? Do you agree with Dakota? That as long as you are with the one you love, anyplace is home? Be sure to leave a review on Amazon, BookBub, or Goodreads. But please, don't do any spoilers. LOL

If you want to tell me what you thought about the end, feel free to reach out to me via my various points of contact below.

You might be asking what's up next for the Crooked Arrow Ranch? Just about all of the characters are either gone, or paired up with someone now. But no fear, there are new characters coming just in time for Christmas! So, keep an eye out for the announcement. If you join my newsletter, you'll be one of the first ones to find out when the next book is coming, as well as any future sales I have.

This book took longer than expected to write. In fact, it took longer than any other book I've written so far. A lot was going on in my life while writing this one. Things I hope to one day tell you about. But suffice it say, life was super stressful. So, the next book I write is going to be full of fun! Then I'm going to get started on writing Christmas books! I also have a huge announcement, but can't say anything just yet.

If you follow me on social media or join my newsletter you will hear about what is coming soon for me and my writing career! So many wonderful changes are coming, but one thing will stay the same – I will keep writing stories that honor God.

One of my favorite things to do is write about flawed people who may have made some mistakes in their lives, but they come back to God, or in some cases, meet God for the first time, and everything changes. I'm far from perfect. I have made a lot of mistakes in my life, but God always forgives me. Healing comes when I go to my Heavenly Father and ask for His forgiveness. And my characters learn that along the way, too. Forgiveness is probably the biggest theme in my stories.

If this is the first book of mine you've ready, welcome! And if it's not, I'm so glad you are still with me. I hope you've picked up all of my books and enjoyed them!

The kindest thing you can do for an author is to leave a review or tell your friends about the book.

Thank you for spending your time with my fictional characters! See you again soon, I hope!

Contact Me

For those of you who love social media, here are the various ways to follow or contact me:

BookBub: https://www.bookbub.com/authors/jenna-hendricks
TikTok: https://www.tiktok.com/@jennacleanauthor
Instagram: https://www.instagram.com/j.l.hendricks/
Twitter: https://twitter.com/TinkFan25
Facebook: https://www.facebook.com/JLHendricksAuthor
Website: https://jennahendricks.com

Newsletter Sign-up

Do you love clean & wholesome contemporary cowboy romance? Want more? Then check out Finding Love in Montana today!

By signing up for my newsletter, you'll not only receive this book, but a couple more free stories as well!

If you want to make sure you hear about the latest and greatest, sign up for my newsletter at: Subscribe to Jenna Hendricks newsletter. I will only send out a few e-mails a month. I'll do cover reveals, snippets of new books, and giveaways or promos in the newsletter, some of which will only be available to newsletter subscribers. (https://jennahendricks.com/newsletter/)